Archipelago of the Sun

By Yoko Tawada
AVAILABLE FROM GRANTA

The Bridegroom Was a Dog
The Last Children of Tokyo
Facing the Bridge
Memoirs of a Polar Bear
The Naked Eye
Scattered All Over the Earth, Suggested in the Stars
& Archipelago of the Sun (a trilogy)
Where Europe Begins

Yoko Tawada

Archipelago of the Sun

the third volume
of the *Scattered All Over the Earth* trilogy

*translated from the Japanese
by Margaret Mitsutani*

GRANTA

Granta Publications, 12 Addison Avenue, London W11 4QR

First published in Great Britain by Granta Books in 2025
First published in the United States in 2025 by
New Directions Books, New York

Originally published in Japanese as *Taiyo Shoto*
in 2022 by Kodansha Ltd., Tokyo.

Copyright © 2022 by Yoko Tawada
Translation copyright © 2025 by Margaret Mitsutani

Yoko Tawada and Margaret Mitsutani have asserted their moral rights under the Copyright, Designs and Patents Act, 1988, to be identified as the author and translator respectively of this work.

All rights reserved. This book is copyright material and must not be copied, reproduced, transferred, distributed, leased, licensed or publicly performed or used in any way except as specifically permitted in writing by the publisher, as allowed under the terms and conditions under which it was purchased or as strictly permitted by applicable copyright law. Any unauthorized distribution or use of this text may be a direct infringement of the author's and publisher's rights, and those responsible may be liable in law accordingly. Please note that no part of this book may be used or reproduced in any manner for the purpose of training artificial intelligence technologies or systems.

A CIP catalogue record for this book is available from the British Library.

1 3 5 7 9 10 8 6 4 2

ISBN 978 1 80351 320 1
eISBN 978 1 80351 321 8

Offset by Patty Rennie

Printed and bound by CPI Group (UK) Ltd, Croydon, CR0 4YY

www.granta.com

The manufacturer's authorised representative in the EU for product safety is Authorised Rep Compliance Ltd, 71 Lower Baggot Street, Dublin D02 P593, Ireland. www.arccompliance.com

Scattered All Over the Earth & *Suggested in the Stars*
SUMMARY AND CHARACTERS

Hiruko, whose country sank into the sea while she was studying in Scandinavia, sets out on a trip across Europe to find someone who speaks her mother tongue. Her new friend Knut, who happened to see her on a TV program, joins her, and their first destination is an Umami festival in Trier. Here they make two friends: an Indian student named Akash and Nora, a German woman. Nora tells them about Tenzo, a young man from the land of sushi, who is supposed to be participating in a culinary competition in Oslo. When they arrive, they discover that Tenzo is actually a Greenlander named Nanook. He tells them about Susanoo, a countryman of Hiruko's who may be working as a sushi chef in Arles. Although they eventually manage to find Susanoo in Arles, he does not speak at all. Knut suggests taking him to be examined by an older friend of his, a doctor of speech loss in Copenhagen.

Seeking to minimize their carbon footprint, Hiruko and her friends hitchhike, hop the train (learning about railway strikes and "packed-train yoga"), and bum late-night motorcycle rides to Copenhagen. There they find Susanoo in a strange hospital, working with the scary speech-loss doctor. In the half basement of this weird medical center, they also find magic radios, personality swaps, ship tickets, and two special kids washing dishes. But friendship—lending one another the heart to keep going—is their greatest discovery. The intrepid band decide to travel on together, heading toward the lost land of sushi, and so starts *Archipelago of the Sun*, the concluding book of Yoko Tawada's rollicking, touching, cheerfully dystopian trilogy.

HIRUKO   A woman from the land of sushi, an archipelago somewhere between China and Polynesia, who traveled to Scandinavia as a foreign student. Just as she was about to go home, her country vanished. While living in various parts of Scandinavia, she invented a language, Panska (Pan-Scandinavian), that is generally comprehensible to all Scandinavians. She misses her native language, though, and is looking for someone who can speak it.

KNUT   A budding Danish linguist, living in Copenhagen. Fascinated by Hiruko and Panska, he joins her in her search.

AKASH   An Indian studying in Germany, in the process of transitioning. He dresses in saris in various shades of red. He meets Hiruko and Knut in Trier.

NANOOK   An Eskimo (not an "Inuit," as explained in *Scattered All Over the Earth*) from Greenland. With financial aid from Knut's mother, Mrs. Nielsen, he comes to study in Denmark, but finding his language classes boring, sets out on a trip during summer vacation. Frequently mistaken for Japanese, he develops, with the help of his considerable linguistic talents, a second identity as a sushi chef called Tenzo. He arrives penniless in Trier, where he is helped by Nora but later runs away from her.

NORA   A German woman working in a museum in Trier. To help Nanook, who is pretending to be from the land of sushi, she planned an Umami festival. She meets Hiruko, Knut, and Akash when they come to Trier for the event.

MRS. NIELSEN   Knut's mother. As part of her charitable activities for foreign students, she pays for Nanook's tuition and living expenses.

SUSANOO   A native of the land of sushi, born in a place called Fukui. At an undetermined time, he stopped aging. After he came to Germany to study shipbuilding, his life went through various twists and turns, and he finally ended up in France, working as a sushi chef.

DR. VELMER   A very peculiar doctor. A speech-loss specialist with control issues, he is also in love with Mrs. Nielsen.

MUNUN and VITA   Two children with unusual gifts and a special language. They wash dishes in the basement of the strange hospital where Susanoo is being treated for aphasia by Dr. Velmer.

Archipelago of the Sun

CHAPTER 1   *Hiruko Speaks*

Our boat left the port of Copenhagen and slipped into the calm waters of the Baltic Sea. Knut looked over at me.

"What you've lost—" he said as the sea breeze ruffled his hair, "what you're looking for—is in the East. That much is certain."

Was this my journey? If so, then Knut and the others were here to keep me company. Were I by myself, I would've been lonely enough to feel the wind whipping through my bones. Gratitude warmed me inside, but seconds later I was nauseous and dizzy as a vague anxiety started closing in on me, tighter and tighter. Pushing my hair off my forehead, I took a deep breath.

"What's wrong?" asked Akash, "are you seasick?" That might be it, I thought. Except that in English it's a sickness, while I was feeling drunk, like after too many glasses of wine, or when I'm carried away by music—intoxicated, drunk on the sea. Realizing I wasn't sick made me feel a little better.

Akash's red sari waved wildly around him. It was made of silk, with various colors woven into an elegant swirling pattern, with only the gold threads standing out, gleaming in the sunlight. He noticed I was watching him. "Men's clothing might have been better," he said, his nostrils flaring slightly, "in a strong wind like this. But I'd rather wear my sari, despite the inconvenience."

"A guy I've known since we were kids," Knut chimed in, "married a Scottish girl who wanted a traditional wedding, with the groom in a kilt. He told her he couldn't handle that, so she gave up on the idea."

3

"They got married anyway, though, didn't they?"

"Sure. But everyone wore jeans at the wedding, including the bride and groom. Those two always swing from one extreme to the other."

I saw a ship near the horizon, loaded with green containers. Though it looked as if it wasn't moving at all, it must have been, or it wouldn't have suddenly loomed into view.

"Even in Europe men used to get arrested for dressing like women in public," Akash said. "And not so long ago, either."

I took stock of my own clothes. Designed for women, but without any lace or frills, my shirt hung straight down so you couldn't see where my curves were. Yet it wasn't a sack that completely covered the body like medieval nuns used to wear, to prevent sexual stimulation. In clothes like mine, the sex of the wearer disappeared, all on its own. Her eyes taking me in, from my neck to my ankles, Nora asked cheerfully, "That outfit's from Muji, isn't it? I really like it."

Ever since Muji was exported overseas it's been a popular brand, even though its country of origin may no longer exist. Companies can apparently survive even after nations disappear. But as that wasn't where I'd bought these clothes, I shook my head.

"Oh, then you got it at Uniqlo?" she asked, still eager to know. "It took me a while to get used to the name, but I like their clothes. Somebody told me once that the *u* is pronounced like 'you,' not 'oo'—is that true? In German, it comes out 'ooniklo.' *Ooni* means university, and *klo* is toilet."

The words *university* and *toilet* rolled around in my head like dice, and out came "Toilet University."

"A famous man once said, 'The toilet is a university,' meaning that the toilet is where you learn about life," I announced confidently, but then couldn't remember who'd said that. The president of a once well-known electronics company, maybe, or a politician who was arrested for corruption.

"The toilet is a place to learn about life?" Nora repeated, savoring each word. "That sounds like Zen."

I remembered hearing that cleaning the outhouse was an important part of Zen training. So maybe it wasn't a CEO or a politician, but the meister of a Zen temple who'd said that.

Knut, lost in his own thoughts, tried to join our conversation by half-heartedly asking, "There's a brand called Toilet University?" No one answered, though, so he gave up, and went back to what he'd been thinking about before. "We planned to cross the Mediterranean, then go through the Suez Canal, didn't we? So what are we doing on the Baltic? I know people call it the East Sea, and since we can't wait to get to the East you could say it fits our purpose, but can you really get to the East by traveling east?"

"To go east, head south," said Akash, looking over at Knut.

"Anyway, let's have a toast," said Knut, lifting up his thermos of water. "To Hiruko!" Upset to see him looking only at me, Akash slipped between us.

"This boat isn't headed east," he explained seriously. "It's actually going south. The Baltic will take us eastward, but first we have to go south."

"Yes, we're going south for now," Knut teased, "but at this rate, we'll never get to India."

"That's true," Akash replied, fluttering his thick, dark eyelashes, "if we went straight south, we'd cross Germany and end up in Italy."

"If," Nora joked, "our boat could travel through the forest, you mean."

"Italy was the heart of the ancient Roman Empire," he said, ignoring her. "More than once we've found the ruins of this vanished empire so fascinating that we couldn't move forward and leave them behind. But there are problems that can't be solved even by returning to Rome. So, this time, let's go straight East. Keeping in mind, of course, that on an ocean voyage you can't really go straight."

When he was calm, Akash's voice was as soothing as a spring breeze, but now he was excited, talking so fast he was a little hard to understand. Getting no reaction, he turned to Knut.

"Are you homesick?" he asked, staring at him. "Copenhagen is getting farther and farther away."

"Not at all," Knut replied with a smile. "I've always dreamed of leaving home. Whenever I try to be independent, some inevitable force always drags me back to my mother. It's tough being a Danish prince. I can only be the hero of my own story by looking down on my mother." For some reason, he then looked over at me.

Just then, a huge wave splashed *JAPON* against the side of our boat. Staggering from the impact, I thought how much I envied Knut's self-irony. I was always longing for my homeland, attracting everyone's sympathy, which seemed embarrassing until I realized something odd. I wasn't actually homesick at all. Just as "seasickness" was a disease of the sea, homesickness was also an illness. But I wasn't sick—I didn't want to return to my home country. I simply wanted to know what had happened to it.

"I don't feel homesick. I have no home to be sick for."

A wild pitch, but Akash caught it neatly and tossed it back to me. "For that very reason you might be homesick for the phantom of it, the way some patients feel pain in an amputated limb."

As I watched his slender fingers hold down his sari, which billowed out like a sail with every breeze, my thoughts listed off to the side, and "country" turned into "sex," while "travel" became "transition."

"You were a man," I said. "Now, you change into a woman. Relocating to a different sex. Do you feel homesick for the male sex?"

Akash laughed, showing his white teeth. "Homesick for being a man? Never."

"No return, no risk," I fired back, and he grinned.

Though I talked to Scandinavians in Panska, my homemade language, I always spoke English with Akash. I was afraid that Panska would be hard for an Indian studying in Germany to understand, yet recently, my English was sounding more and more like Panska.

A language like Panska sometimes leaves meaning floating in the air. I'll probably never know why Akash laughed at my homemade proverb "No return, no risk," or how he understood it. I've heard that the saying, "No risk, no return" means that you need to take a risk in order to gain something; by turning it around, I intended to say that as long as you never look back, there's no danger. But hearing myself say it out loud, I had the strange feeling that it might actually mean that you should look back, even if it's dangerous.

Unlike mine, Akash's English was like a suit of old clothes, worn until the soft folds followed his every move.

"By return, do you mean going back to infancy?" he asked. "Babies never think about whether they're boys or girls. There are people who want to go back to that time, but in my case, it's a little different. Until I started primary school, I was all boy, from the top of my head down to my fingertips. But then I started feeling that something wasn't quite right. Puberty was the worst—I was always so utterly alone—but toward the end of it, I got friendly with my girl cousins. We'd go to the movies together, and have lively discussions about what makes a woman a perfect lady. My transition progressed rapidly at first. I got much better than the girls at using makeup and choosing fashionable clothes. After I started university, though, I never seemed to get any closer to my goal no matter how hard I tried. I may end up stuck in this 'moving' stage for the rest of my life."

"No one is a more perfect lady than you."

"Thanks, but now I've realized that becoming the perfect lady wasn't my aim after all."

"What do you mean?"

"Well, being a perfect lady is like the idea of completely belonging to a different ethnic group—it's just an illusion. For instance, an Indian woman I know decided she was going to be

Swedish, and for more than a decade she worked really hard at it. She stopped wearing saris, and dyed her hair blonde. Then one day, for no particular reason, she suddenly went back to wearing saris. Not because she was homesick. If a journey goes on long enough, traveling itself becomes the destination. And when that happens, you don't need to be in a hurry anymore, so anything goes, and you start to enjoy having your past mixed in with the present. The past stops being something you have to cut off, throw away. What I'm feeling now is something like that."

"In German," Nora said casually, "homesick is *Heimweh*, or 'homeland pain.' An intense desire to see faraway places, on the other hand, is called *Fernweh*, or 'distance sickness.' Perhaps you're longing for a distant country that may not even exist, and you've given it the name 'woman.'"

"That's it!" cried Akash, clapping like an enthusiastic student in a lecture hall. "What I've been feeling all this time is sexual *Fernweh*. I've been calling the gender that's far away from me 'woman.' Which may not be the same as a real woman."

I myself wasn't either homesick or longing to see faraway places. But it had been so long since I'd heard anything from the country where I'd lived in the past that it had disappeared from what we call "the present," which might have been why my life now was so unsettled. Waves pushed against the boat, making it list slowly to one side. My belly pressed against the handrail, I hung my head and stared down at the water.

"You're seasick," said Knut. "You'll feel better with a cold towel on the back of your neck. Wait a minute—I'll get one." He broke into a run, but just then the boat swayed again, nearly knocking him off his feet. He must have given up hurrying, because he then strode slowly back to his cabin. The sky was perfectly clear, so much so that it seemed almost lonely.

"They say you're more prone to get seasick if you're worried," said Nora, putting her hand on my shoulder. "Is something troubling you?"

"Guilt. Because everyone has to travel with me." I really wanted to say that I was "a burden" or "a nuisance," but I couldn't think how to express that in English, and ended up using "guilt," which was way too heavy.

"But none of us is here out of duty," Nora said, her eyes widening. "This trip's such a wonderful experience, we're all grateful to you. We're fed up with tourism. I'd like to go exploring if I could, like Schliemann. Of course I can't, though. Discovering vanished civilizations is no longer possible now, but thanks to you, we're on our own exciting journey to the unknown."

"You make it sound as if we're using Hiruko's sad fate as an excuse to enjoy ourselves," Akash protested. That brightened my mood, and I felt like joking.

"Go ahead—use me!" I said, "In my native language, we call that 'taking dashi from someone'—using a person to make your life more enjoyable."

Lots of Germans are interested in Asian cooking terms like umami and dashi, and Nora, who'd once planned a dashi workshop at an Umami Festival, was definitely one of them. Just as I'd expected, she broke into a wide smile.

"That's right—it's the dashi that's important. We're the soup, and Hiruko's the dashi—she gives you a better flavor than kombu or bonito flakes." The smile suddenly faded. "The idea that prosperity lies in the East," she said, now very serious, "has been around for a long time. Back in the Middle Ages, lots of peasants went to Eastern Europe, thinking they'd find land there where they could start their own farms. In Germany, we call that the Ostsiedlung—the East Settlement."

Sensing someone behind me, I turned around to see Nanook.

"So, you're saying we're like those German peasants from the old days, heading east. I was hoping this trip would be more interesting—too bad I came."

He was speaking Danish, so I doubt Nora understood, but she must have heard the disgust in his tone, because her shoulders stiffened, and she frowned. Was their relationship like a smashed plate that no amount of glue could mend? Or, if he went back to being his old self, was there still a chance that he and Nora could get together again?

Nanook was basically a lovable guy, but for some reason, back at that hospital in Copenhagen, he'd let Dr. Velmer—an arrogant man everyone hated—talk him into an experiment where they'd switch personalities. Although Nanook should have returned to normal when the experiment ended, now and then he showed signs of lingering aftereffects, or perhaps side effects.

"Ever since I quit my job at the hospital I've been unemployed, and it's all because of you, Hiruko," he groused in Danish. Then suddenly looking as sweet and innocent as a snow hare, he switched to English and said, "If it wasn't for you I'd never have gotten to see the Baltic. Thanks, Hiruko. I've also wanted to take a trip like this. The Baltic is like a magic circle, a gathering place for so many different souls. There's no place like it. How many countries border on the Baltic? Let's see, there's Denmark, Germany, Poland, Lithuania, Latvia, Estonia, Russia, Finland, Sweden..." He went on, counting them on his fingers. Looking relieved, Nora smiled over at him.

"You'll circle around it once," she said, "and come back the way you used to be—I'm sure of it."

But this seemed to worry Akash. "No—you've got it all wrong," he blurted out. "We can't just go around the Baltic. We'll never get to the East that way. The Baltic is just the gateway to the East."

Knut, who'd just come back with the wet towel for me, agreed.

"He's right. We can't go back to where we started from. We're not going home—we're going east."

"Why east?" snorted Nanook.

"Because we're not on vacation. If we were, we'd go south for a visit and then come home again. But we're dreaming of going far, far away, to the east."

Though Knut started off facing Nanook, his head gradually swiveled in my direction until he seemed to be pouring those last few words right into my eyes. Meanwhile, I was having a hard time finding the right spot on the back of my neck for the towel, which had turned into an unknown body of water between the back of my head and my spine.

As long as I was looking at Knut, the hand searching for the hollow in my neck meandered around, lost, but the moment I closed my eyes, the towel settled in nicely, so I stood there that way for a while, enjoying the cold.

"Will I ever go back to being my old self?"

I couldn't tell who'd said that, Knut or Nanook, so I quickly opened my eyes again. Judging from the content, I figured it must be Nanook, but their voices were so similar I was genuinely confused.

Nanook was staring out at the sea, so I followed his gaze to a ship loaded down with three layers of dark green containers. The lettering on the side was in hangul, the Korean alphabet. This ship was probably delivering Korean household appliances to the Baltic countries. Placing her hand gently on Nanook's shoulder, Nora said something to him in German. Shaking off the kindness she was trying to foist on him, Nanook snapped back in English, "Are you saying that when I boarded this boat, I turned back into the guy you met that day in the Roman baths in Trier? That this is the real me? To tell you the truth, I was happy while I had that doctor's personality. I was finally free to openly express the nastiness that had been trapped inside me all my life. And now that I've learned how to let the evil out, I'm never going to forget it."

Nora bit her lip. I was wondering if Nanook really believed that people should intentionally let their inner evil out when a seagull flying by turned its head so that our eyes met. It seemed to have something to say. Translated into Panska, it might have been, "you bread have? to me throw!" but even if I'd got that right, the worlds the bird and I saw were so completely different that the gap between them was as wide as the Baltic Sea—no, the Pacific Ocean.

Nanook threw his bottle at the bird, which, catching the wind under its white wings, flew up into the sky. Far below, the bottle made an arc and disappeared into the waves.

"Throwing bottles at animals shows bad personality," I said in English.

"Better than the Nazis who loved their dogs," he snorted bitterly, "but killed lots of people," completely missing my point. Akash, who hated seeing ominous clouds on the horizon, took the helm and steered the conversation in a brighter direction.

"Do you know the chain store in Germany called *Go East!*?" he asked. "You can buy food from all over Asia there, including Indian spices and pickles of course. The westernmost food they sell is *kumru*, or the Izmir sandwich. It's Turkish street food, and Turkey's on the western edge of Asia, or the eastern edge of Europe, maybe—take your pick. So, what's their easternmost food? Probably either Kaminari-okoshi or Bay Bridge Sablé. Hiruko, which is further east, the temple with the Kaminari Gate or the Bay Bridge?"

My mind was suddenly tossed out into space, floating somewhere between Asakusa and Yokohama. Before my eyes place names from my past, like Tokyo Station, Haneda Airport, and Kawasaki blinked on and off, but I couldn't place them on a map that showed north, south, east and west. Nanook, who'd sullenly ignored everything Akash had said up to then, made a complete 180 when he heard the word *kaminari*.

"Does the *kami* of Kaminari mean god," he asked eagerly, "or paper?" People are fundamentally trusting and kind while they're learning a foreign language. Having picked up my native tongue naturally, I respected the effort Nanook had put into studying it all on his own. As a language learner, he was humble, friendly, patient, sensitive.

"god big temple bell strikes, so *kami* (god) *nari* (sounds)," I answered in Panska.

Without sounding exactly frigid, he observed coolly, "Your language has no articles."

He was right, and I was embarrassed. Nanook, who had gone to Denmark from Greenland as a foreign student, had no trouble understanding Panska, but as an autodidact interested in speaking properly, perhaps he dismissed it as the sort of broken Danish foreigners tend to speak.

"sorry—in my brain, no article."

"It doesn't really matter," he said. "What I want to know is whether it's one god among many, like in ancient Greece, or the one God you find in monotheistic religions."

"One is all, and all is one," Knut said excitedly. "Maybe we'd all be freer without articles. And a world where there's no difference between singular and plural might be just right for people with multiple personalities like you, Nanook."

"You may be right about that. I have plenty of reasons for rejecting the singular, but what about Hiruko—why would she want to?"

Knut answered for me, in Danish. "Hiruko created Panska while she was moved around Scandinavia. As you yourself know, most non-Europeans can get permission to live in Europe, but it's hard for them to stay in one country. So, Hiruko mixed several different languages together to make this delicious cocktail she calls Panska. It seems like one single language, but it isn't really. It keeps changing every day, aiming for comprehensibility rather than grammatical correctness."

"She could have just studied Esperanto."

"But what if she got lost? If she'd had to wait for someone who knows Esperanto to come along so she could ask them the way, she'd probably have frozen to death. And any Scandinavian can understand Panska. When you need to survive now, you can't spend thirty years holed up in a research laboratory until you've come up with the perfect language. The words coming out of her mouth now are her solution."

"Why not just use English?"

"English speakers are sometimes forced to move to the United States. Hiruko has a condition that makes it impossible for her to live in a country with such an underdeveloped healthcare system."

I thanked Knut for explaining Panska for me, then turned to Nanook and honestly told him about my fears for its future.

"you kayak oars use, elegantly linguistic sea navigate. you in cold water drown not. books studied, my native tongue by yourself learned. english and danish freely speak. boat of panska, in baltic sea may sink?"

"If it starts to go under, I'll be there to help," Nanook replied automatically. The good side of his personality had reappeared, naturally. Knut looked surprised.

Having given up trying to understand our conversation, Nora and Akash were looking down at the sea. On a boat, the scenery doesn't fly by like on a train, nor are there movies to watch, like on airplanes. So people gather on deck to look out over the sea, then talk a while, then turn back to the sea again. The cold towel on the back of my neck made me feel better, but now a chill was spreading through my body.

"cold. anorak in my cabin."

When I was about to start down the narrow flight of stairs, I saw a tall woman climbing up. There wasn't enough room for both of us, so I waited on deck. She was wearing high heels, and a dress trimmed with black lace. Behind her, I heard a man's voice, speaking what sounded like Russian. Dressed in a white suit, he hurried after her, gasping for breath. They glanced at me, silently greeting me with their eyes, although their faces looked grim. They were dressed for ballroom dancing; next to them, I looked ready to put in my shift at a factory.

Our boat, the Baltic Light, was not a typical passenger liner.

Owned by a private shipping company that made money by transporting goods between Scandinavia and Eastern Europe, it also offered a small number of tourists the chance to experience the atmosphere of the old mail boats that used to ply the Baltic. It made lots of stops to load and unload cargo, at small ports without many sights to see. Boxes were stacked on deck, labeled with the names of companies that sold things over the Internet. Sailing directly, we could have reached Rügen Island in a few hours, but on this boat, it took a night and a day. The fare was cheaper than most passenger ships, but the mattresses in the cabins were so thin you could feel the wood beneath your back. Still, I liked my small, dimly lit cabin.

Once inside, I felt that a space like this was all I needed to feel safe, whatever country I was in, whether I was on land or at sea. Both my bedroom at home and this cabin far away from it were small rooms that held me close. Before we're born, we never wonder about the location of the womb we happen to be in. Greenland or Guatemala—it's all the same to us. In the future there may be pregnant women on the moon, but to their unborn children, it won't be any different than being on earth. The womb is where your time in this world begins, where you are most protected. The fetus floats in amniotic fluid. Where else, other than a tiny ship's cabin, can you feel so close to that complete serenity?

On deck, I was immediately thrown out into a much larger space. The dome called the sky sends out light, but is far too deep for the human eye to penetrate. The waves reflect that light all the way to the horizon and beyond. The colors of the water are so heavy we can't help thinking of the unimaginable depths beneath the surface. Words like *deep green* don't capture that heaviness, that weight that makes us feel so powerless. The minute I left my cabin, I found myself in a vast, endless, turbulent space.

The deck has to rise and fall along with the much bigger sea, to keep it happy, but why should even the horizon seem to be tilting, first left, then right? Knut, beside a red life preserver attached to the hand rail, was the same height as Nanook, standing near him. Akash, by Knut's side, was lithe and slender, while Nora, leaning toward Nanook from behind, was not fat but sturdily built. I was probably shorter than any of them. But I'd never seen the whole group, myself included, from the outside. We hadn't taken any group photos, either. As we weren't tourists, or at a class reunion, no one had ever suggested it.

"Are you warmer," asked Akash, noticing me standing there, "now that you've got your anorak?"

"What about you—aren't you cold, in just your sari?"

"Saris have talent—they know how to keep you cool on hot days, and warm when it's cold. The same can be said of kimonos, too, I believe. Be that as it may, is Susanoo still in his cabin?"

"I don't know. He said he'd come to dinner."

Because Susanoo and I come from the same country, people assume that I understand him better than they do, when actually he's more foreign to me than to anyone. Knut and I were on the same wavelength the moment we met, and Nora is like an older sister to me. Akash's words slip nimbly into narrow spaces, where they meet up with mine, and talking with Nanook about language is always fun. Susanoo, on the other hand, was as far away as a mythical character. He can be silent one minute, then suddenly explode in anger. Yet I have to treat him like an older brother—I can't abandon him now that we're in the same boat. That's what I kept telling myself as I knocked on the door of his cabin. He opened the door, looking sleepy, wearing pajamas, striped like a prison uniform. The drowsiness made his face seem gentler than usual, so I relaxed and asked how he was feeling. Afraid he'd cast a spell on me if I spoke to him in our native language, I wanted to use English, but that wouldn't do either, so I decided that since he was from Fukui, the Niigata dialect I'd spoken as a child could keep some distance between us. The first word I thought of was *najirane*.

"*Najirane.* That's what we say in my part of the country. It means something like 'How are you?'" Trying not to think too much about how ridiculous that English bit at the end sounded, I waited for an answer.

"My feeling is serpent," he said, looking down at me with glassy, expressionless eyes, "but if I stay in my cabin maybe I can shuffle off the snake, and go back to being a normal citizen. A citizen of the sea. I'll come to dinner. Leave me alone until then. Don't knock again." This sounded vaguely familiar, yet strangely awkward, like a bad script.

I was afraid of Susanoo. Because he was suffering from aphasia when I first met him, I'd opened the door to my heart and showered him with all the words I could think of in our mother tongue, to get him to talk. He repaid me by stomping through that open door with his shoes on. I couldn't remember exactly what he'd said to me—it was all like a bad dream now—but I was still wary of him.

Back in my own cabin, I wondered what he'd meant by "shuffle off." Was he pregnant with a huge, unruly snake that he had to get rid of somehow in order to settle down and be quiet? And once he'd aborted the serpent, was he going to slice the meat up and serve it to us? I knew he'd once been a sushi chef, but I didn't want to see him with a cleaver in his hand.

It was now late afternoon, but rather than sinking, the sun was in its element, shining brightly on the waves. Yet it must have lowered a little, because the shadows between the waves were growing deeper, moving toward the gravity of evening.

In the ship's dining room there were six big round tables attached to the floor, like you see in Chinese restaurants, with a "reserved" sign in the center of each, along with the table's name plate. Each table had six chairs, which was perfect for the six of us, but meant that the other passengers, most of whom were either solo travelers or married couples, had to sit with people they didn't know. The tables were named "Earth," "Mars," "Mercury," "Venus," "Jupiter," and "Saturn." Ours was Earth.

The napkins were faded, the silver knives and forks were much too light so they were probably aluminum, and the cloudy water and wine glasses were covered with tiny scratches, but everything was neatly arranged. Nanook sat down first, with Nora quickly taking the chair next to him, and when Knut sat next to her, Akash moved in beside him, leaving me the chair to his right. I'd wanted to sit next to Knut, but Akash got there first. The empty chair between Nanook and me was waiting for Susanoo.

Looking around me, I saw three couples dressed like the Romanovs at the Venus table—

One couple I thought seemed familiar. Although the people at Saturn seemed to have come from different places, they all had the same tanned faces, sun-bleached hair, bright eyes, and slender bodies, giving them the appearance of a troupe of street performers. Turning my head, I heard Spanish coming from Mars, and British English from Jupiter, though I couldn't see the speakers from where I was sitting. Language had apparently been a factor in deciding the seating arrangements, but perhaps the people at Mercury all spoke different ones, because that table was silent. We were also multilingual, but never quiet.

"I wonder if Susanoo has decided not to come after all," said Akash, who always told us what was worrying him. He was looking straight at me, so I had to respond.

"Susanoo said he'd be here, so he'll come. Susanoo may not come, even though he said he would."

"How did he seem? Did he look depressed?"

"No, he looked like the star of an action movie."

That made everyone at our table laugh. Just as the waiter started serving cabbage soup, the door opened, and Susanoo came striding into the room. We felt a little guilty, but said nothing. Except for Akash, who raised his hand and cheerfully called out, "Hi! Welcome to dinner."

Seeing Susanoo glower back at him, we waited for poison to spew out of those thin lips of his, but he surprised us.

"Where, exactly, is this boat going?" he asked innocently. Akash was the only one resilient enough to chuckle in response.

"We're heading east," Nora answered gently. "After all, we're making this trip to see if the island where Hiruko was born has really vanished. That island's your home, too, isn't it?"

"And when you find out it's not there anymore," Susanoo snorted, "what then?" He obviously wasn't waiting for an answer.

"The main dish is vegetarian," the waiter said, "but if you'd like meat, you can order sausages." There'd be no extra cost, as meals were included in the price of the ticket. Nanook quickly raised his hand and asked for two sausages.

"Vegetarians usually have to order separately, but here it's just the opposite," said Akash, looking relieved.

"I'm not a vegetarian," Nora declared, "but I'm not going to eat sausages—they have chemical additives."

Dessert was strawberry ice cream, the color and flavor of children's tooth paste.

After one mouthful, Susanoo growled, "What kind of idiot would eat crap like this?" in our native tongue. His tone startled everyone, but I was the only one who understood him.

"What did he say?" asked Akash.

"This dessert is not delicious. Who can eat this sort of thing?" I translated Susanoo's complaint into awkward English for him. The sting of the original was softer in broken English.

"People living in countries where the food isn't so good are happier overall," Knut said with a mischievous look in his eyes. "Denmark and the Netherlands always top those 'happiest country' surveys, way above Italy or France."

"That's why there are so many miserable people in India," murmured Akash. "The food's too good."

I suddenly felt sadness well up inside me, and ended up saying something I hadn't meant to: "Poison poured into the sea. So frightening. Everyone asked what they should do. This was the answer they got: Find a restaurant that serves delicious fish, and you'll forget your fear. Some people believed that. And what happened to them after that? I have no idea." While I was speaking tears clouded my eyes, and I couldn't see the food on my plate.

I left the others and had just gone to bed in my cabin when the ship docked. I heard voices. The ship stayed at the port for quite a while. Then it set sail again, rocked by the waves. The bed in my cabin felt more like a spaceship than a cradle. It made no sense for me to feel that way—I'd never been on a spaceship. I lay awake, thinking about spaceships for about an hour until the ship docked at the next port. There were so many stops it was like being on a cross-country bus. The ship stayed in port much longer this time. About as long as time feels when you can't get to sleep.

When I woke up the next morning and went up on deck, I was surprised to see everyone gathered in one spot, looking out to sea. After exchanging good mornings, I leaned against the handrail and stared at the ocean until suddenly something huge and white came into view. I got so excited I blurted out, "Look! Moby Dick's swimming over there!"

CHAPTER 2   *Knut Speaks*

Hearing Hiruko shout, "Moby Dick!" I looked in that direction and saw something huge and white floating in the sea. "There're no whales in the Baltic," I said, and immediately regretted sounding like I was flat-out denying what she'd said, but the words were already spoken.

"Why are there no whales in the Baltic?" The question came not from Hiruko, but Akash, whose thick eyelashes were like a brush that polished his brown eyes, making them brighter every time he blinked.

"Why? Well, the Baltic isn't the Pacific Ocean, you know—it's much too small for whales. It would be like keeping carp in a bathtub."

"So, not a single person has ever seen a whale in the Baltic?"

"Maybe small ones, but I don't think you'd see the giants here, like sperm whales."

This talk of whales reminded me of Herman Melville's novel *Moby-Dick*, which I read in high school. I'd curl up with it on the sofa every day from morning to night until I felt like I was turning into a whale washed up half dead on the shore, my belly heavy with lard, my eyes bleary, my legs long gone.

Ahab, the one-legged captain of the *Pequod*, is obsessed with finding the sperm whale Moby Dick, and get his revenge on him. The last time Moby Dick appears is near the Pacific shore of the island of Honshu, where Hiruko's from. Did she believe that if only she could find that white whale and chase him in this boat, she'd find her way back to her homeland? Perhaps that dream had appeared to her in the form of a phantom white whale.

"How big are the smaller whale species?" asked Akash innocently, standing beside me. "About the size of a porpoise?"

"Porpoises are whales, too," I said, hoping to shrink that ghostly whale that was expanding in Hiruko's mind down to size. "Harbor porpoises, for instance, are about the size of a human being, so pretty small. Whales aren't necessarily huge. But in any case, you can't find the really big ones in the Baltic."

"That's not a miniwhale—it's Moby Dick!" Hiruko protested, still pointing at the big white mass floating in the sea.

"That white you see isn't a whale," said Nora, gently placing a hand on Hiruko's shoulder to calm her down. "It's the chalk cliffs of Rügen Island."

Nora was a realist whose eyes were never clouded by imaginary whales. Hiruko's shoulders slumped in disappointment, while Akash, his curiosity piqued, rattled his questions off at top speed.

"You mean those cliffs are what we used for writing on the blackboard at school? Whole cliffs made of chalk? That's really something. I've seen white sandy beaches, but how can cliffs be that white? Is this phenomenon peculiar to that island? Did they scrape off bits of chalk for kids to use in school?"

Nora managed to answer only the last question. "That's right," she said, "the chalk kids used in school came from those cliffs. Now that they're a tourist attraction, they're not scraping it off anymore, though. Walking along the top, you can look straight down at the bluish-green sea, and that vertical rock wall is pristine white. You're so high up it makes you dizzy."

"Are there many suicides?" asked Hiruko. I wondered if she immediately associated the word "cliff" with suicide. Did she have relatives or classmates who'd ended their lives that way?

"A tourist falls into the sea once in a while," Nora replied, apparently unfazed, "but I've never heard of anyone jumping off on purpose. Before Germany was reunified—when this area was still East Germany, in the socialist bloc—the number of suicides wasn't made public. After reunification they said the data had been lost, but a certain sociologist—determined to dig up the truth—claims there were about two hundred thousand suicides during East Germany's forty or so years of history."

"Two hundred thousand in forty years," said Hiruko. "Only about five thousand a year. A very small number."

"Small?" Nora sounded shocked. "I'd say it's a lot—about twice as many as in West Germany over the same period, according to that same sociologist. Of course, he may have exaggerated, but I've done some research, too, since it's a topic I'm interested in, and on the whole I think you can trust his data." I was surprised to hear that Nora was interested in suicide. If life and death were on the opposite sides of a river, staring each other down, I'd picture Nora with both feet firmly planted on the side of life, never even glancing over at the other side.

"In my country, the number of people who kill themselves in a year is twenty or thirty thousand," said Hiruko. Her lips parted slightly as if she was going to say something more, but she must have changed her mind, because she pressed them together again. It occurred to me that all those suicides, plus the early deaths of their grieving loved ones, might have caused Hiruko's country to vanish, but I'd never heard of anything like that.

Akash, who didn't care for dark subjects like suicide, shifted course toward something lighter.

"I doubt that anyone came to Rügen Island from East Germany to commit suicide. It was a tourist spot, a bright, happy place. I remember doing some research on it once, for a presentation on Leisure Under Socialism I did for a sociology seminar."

Hiruko, too, steered her thoughts out of the shadows and into the light.

"In my native language, Rügen can be written as 'dragon's origin.' That's the name of a Zen temple, too."

"So this is a Zen island," said Nora, her face brightening. She must have found the connection exciting, because she suddenly got very talkative, launching into a lecture on how Rügen was connected to the mainland by a causeway, making it possible to take the train across the sea from the mainland city of Stralsund, which was once part of the Hanseatic League, to Sassnitz, the biggest town on the island.

Akash's curiosity made him an ideal listener. With him nodding enthusiastically in all the right places, Nora, her tongue speeding up like a well-oiled machine, went on to tell us that Sylt, a famous island in northern Germany, was also connected to the mainland, and that it attracted more tourists than Rügen, even though it was smaller, because after all, Rügen was the largest island in Germany. She gave us more information about both islands than we really needed, and since she was going on about Rügen as if it were a distant relation she was really proud of, I decided to burst her bubble.

"Rügen may belong to Germany now," I said, "but it used to belong to Sweden."

I've never liked the phrase "belong to" very much, and using it twice in such a short sentence left a bad taste in my mouth. What's more, it sounded like I was accusing Nora, as a German, of laying claiming to an island that was actually part of Scandinavia, which was awfully childish of me, but it was too late to take it back now. Nora was suddenly gloomy—I saw pain in her eyes. The last thing she wanted was to be associated with a nation that prided itself on stealing territory from other countries.

"That's right," she said apologetically, "Rügen was Swedish territory first, then Prussian, then finally German. But that's true of other islands, too. The northern part of Sylt was Danish territory all through the Middle Ages, but changed hands several times before Germany took it over in the nineteenth century." She concluded on a more abstract note. "Islands cause wars when countries start fighting over them." Hiruko slowly lowered her head, then raised it again, looking very sad.

Unsure of whether this would comfort her or not, I said, "Well, no one's going to start fighting over Rügen or Sylt these days. The fire's burned itself out, and all that's left are the ashes. So, there's nothing to worry about."

"But lots of islands are still smoldering," said Akash, "and could burst into flame at any time. I wonder what makes the difference between islands where the fighting's done, and those where a war could start any time." Hiruko bit her lip and looked down again. After a long, uncomfortable silence, she finally spoke.

"An island is a whale," she said, sounding like she was about to cry, "floating freely in the sea. It doesn't really belong to Country A or Country B."

Maybe I was the only one who thought she sounded sad. The content was pretty cheerful, so it would be logical to assume that the voice was, too. But to me, she sounded sad.

Nanook, who'd been leaning over the handrail, suddenly turned around.

"Wars between big, powerful countries bore me," he said. "But do you guys know about the mysterious Rügen people who lived there long before either the Germans or the Swedes?"

"An indigenous tribe?" asked Akash, his eyes bright beneath those long eyelashes.

"That's right. They were driven to extinction after the Germanic and Slavic peoples came, though. I guess they were just unlucky."

"What's so mysterious about them?"

"Nothing is known about their lives. They've disappeared from history. We Greenlanders had much better luck. Our island is so cold, and so far away from any land mass, that the continental hordes never came to absorb us into their ranks."

"So, you're saying Rügen suffered because its location was too good. If India was on the eastern edge of Siberia, the British probably wouldn't have come. But then again, India in Siberia wouldn't be India, would it, so isn't it kind of strange to think of a country and of its location as two separate things?" Akash seemed to be talking to himself, following a stream of meandering thoughts.

Just then I was caught off guard by a gust of wind, and stumbled several steps backward. This put some distance between Hiruko and me, so that I was seeing her as a silhouette, lit from behind, with a backdrop of the sea, clouds, and a solitary seagull motionless in the sky. Like an actress practicing her soliloquy, she slowly began to speak.

"My country, too, was isolated for a long time. But in a sense, our location was not so bad. The Americans came. They were looking for a gas station, to fill the tanks on their whaling vessels."

A *gas station?* I thought, then realized she must mean a base to refuel their ships. There was something about that in *Moby-Dick*.

"Was whaling that important to America back then?" asked Akash, curious as ever.

"They needed oil from the whales."

"What for?"

"To light up the night."

"Why? To keep ghosts away?"

"No, so they could work in their offices after it got dark."

Hiruko's simple explanation brought to mind a scene of people hard at work by the light of old-fashioned lamps burning whale oil. Some bent over desks, while others operated machines in factories. It had a warm, cozy feel, like something out of a picture book. But in reality, this was when people started sleeping less so they could work longer hours, turning their lost time into the money they needed to survive in a world of cutthroat international competition. America, the country where it all began, sent whaling ships one after another into the Pacific Ocean. And just as many came from England.

"The Pacific Islands were sacrificed for whale oil," said Nora, excited to find a new minority to side with, but what really surprised me was that she seemed to think of Honshu, where Hiruko was from, as an island. You could certainly look at it that way, but Honshu must have had a bigger population than all the Scandinavian countries put together. Was Honshu really just one more island, floating in the Pacific?

I was still mulling this over when Nanook, who had already taken my train of thought a step further, said to Hiruko in fluent Danish, "I know there was an island called Hokkaido. It didn't belong to any country, and lots of different ethnic groups lived there. The same was true of Sakhalin. To the people on Hokkaido or Sakhalin, Honshu wasn't just another island—it was more like a continent, the mainland. So, the difference between continents and islands seems pretty relative to me."

Even though Nanook and I don't look at all alike, the way our minds work is so similar it surprises me sometimes. The biggest difference between us is that while I always try to avoid saying anything that will make Hiruko sad, Nanook doesn't even seem to see her. Yet I end up saying things that depress her a lot more often than he does.

The white wall in front of us was gradually moving closer. Just looking at it, I could feel the powdery limestone on my fingertips. Its pure white made the blue-green of the sea look all the deeper. That combination of white chalk and the deep blue Baltic was something like the relationship between Nanook and me.

By speaking Danish, Nanook had closed himself off in a separate space with Hiruko and me, who understood him, while shutting out Nora and Akash, who didn't. That put me off, so I decided to speak in English.

"If you look at the world from the viewpoint of the sea," I said, "all the continents are islands. America, too—just one big island. In that sense, no different than Rügen."

"Weren't we supposed to stop here for about three hours?"

asked Akash, as if this was something he'd just remembered, and Nora took a tightly folded copy of our travel schedule out of her purse. "Although this boat is not a conventional passenger liner," it said, "our main purpose being to transport mail, we have a few sightseeing programs for passengers. At certain ports of call, there will be events to introduce the local culture of the Baltic Sea region." That word "certain" might be a trap.

"Seems we'll be following the shoreline around to Sassnitz. Ferries and barges dock there."

"You seem to know a lot about this island, Nora. Have you been here before?"

"Only once. But that was a trip I'll never forget. I came to buy Sanddorn berries to make jam. I knew the guy I was in love with at the time liked it. And the berries come from this island."

There's nothing sticky or sentimental about Nora, but she seems to fall in love awfully easily.

"In English it's called seaberry—berries of the sea," explained Akash, whose English is much better than mine.

"Seaberry?" Hiruko repeated. "I didn't know that."

"They're small, bright orange berries," Nora explained, smiling over at her, "but too sour to eat raw. That's why we make them into jam. *Sand* is sand, just like in English, and *Dorn* means thorn. I came all the way from Trier, hoping that if I made him his favorite jam, he'd know how I felt about him."

"And were you successful?" asked Akash. It was a ticklish question that Nora left unanswered.

As the ship slowly turned right, following the shoreline, I saw a ferry docked at the port. Suddenly Susanoo, who'd apparently been in his cabin all this time, appeared on deck with a leather bag slung over his shoulder.

"We'll be on land for three hours," he announced, as if he were our group leader. "Is everyone ready to go ashore?" When you read myths, it's always hard to tell what the gods are thinking, but Susanoo was even more of an enigma. When we first met him he didn't talk at all, so we worried that he might be suffering from aphasia, but then one day words started pouring out of his mouth like a waterfall, and now, after shutting himself up in his cabin since we'd boarded, he was suddenly on deck, ordering everyone around. It would be hard to find anyone less suited to the word "democracy." But then again maybe all the men in Hiruko's homeland were like this.

"That's a nice scarf," said Nora. I've never given much thought to what people wear, but I now noticed that Susanoo was all dressed up in a checkered jacket with a muffler around his neck. The mismatch between his spiffy outfit and that worn-out leather bag, like something a student might carry, made him look unbalanced, and slightly ridiculous.

Was there going to be a reception for us on shore? I had on the same old shirt and slacks I wear when I'm lying on the sofa at home. Akash's crimson silk sari would be fit for an audience with the king. Nora's freshly ironed dress had been chosen, like all her clothes, with quality in mind. What Hiruko had on was harder to describe. For one thing, what I'd call a T-shirt turned into a blouse on her. She had something around her neck that looked like a detachable collar but might not have been, and what seemed like a vest might actually have been sewn on for decoration. I couldn't tell whether the cloth flapping around her legs was a very wide pair of culottes or a skirt. The color was close to gray under a cloudy sky, but wavered between blue and green when it caught the bright sunlight, reflected off the sea. Her outfit looked casual here on deck, but would shine with the formal elegance of linen in a ballroom—just right, perhaps, for an ocean voyage, where there were no vertical or horizontal dress codes.

Slipping into the space next to the ferry, our boat jolted and came to a stop. I stood there watching the deck hands throw the heavy, wet rope over the mooring post until I realized the others had all disappeared, and hurried back to my cabin to fetch my jacket.

For some reason, I've always been fascinated by people throwing ropes, even when I was little. A lasso makes circles, spinning wildly in the air while a cowboy in the center holds it in, and the tension builds until the moment the rope leaps forward to catch whatever it's aiming for. I never liked Westerns but watched them anyway, patiently waiting for scenes of cowboys lassoing cattle. When my parents took me to the port, I watched sailors throwing ropes from ship decks. I was remembering that as I got off the boat and saw a group who seemed to be some sort of citizens' organization waiting for us on the lighter. As soon we stepped on land, a man in his fifties, apparently their representative, stepped forward and said, "Welcome to Rügen Island. My name is Tafel. We've been anxiously awaiting your arrival. Let us escort you to our meeting place."

There was nothing obsequious about him; on the contrary, he was doing his best not to sound arrogant, to hide his sense of superiority.

Having easily picked us out from the passengers coming down the ramp, Mr. Tafel gestured to his followers, assigning one to each of us. Though he was obviously trying to be hospitable, this felt like being "taken" rather than "escorted."

"The restaurant is over there," said Mr. Tafel, walking beside me. "Lunch is the ideal setting for cultural exchange." As I listened to him, I couldn't help worrying about Hiruko, whose escort was hidden in his shadow. With one of them for each of us, we seemed more like prisoners than guests.

From outside, the building where the restaurant was looked utterly drab, but as soon as I stepped through the door I wondered if I hadn't entered an entirely different dimension, unrelated to Rügen Island. Tobacco smoke had seeped into the walls, giving them an odor like dried leaves, and I also smelled something like the disinfectant I remembered from hospital visits as a child.

There was a mural in pastel colors on one wall of the room.

Muscular men wielding pickaxes. Rosy-cheeked women carrying sheaves of wheat. Men driving tractors. Women assembling machine parts on a conveyor belt. Typical social realist motifs, yet the painting itself must have been recent, because I saw cell phones peeking out of pockets.

In the center was an oblong table, the kind you see in meeting rooms. If it hadn't been covered with a white tablecloth, I'd have thought we were going to have a conference. Our seats were assigned, with a place card and miniature flag for each of us. The Danish flag at mine made me hesitate to sit there. I do not represent Denmark.

Nora sat down and, noticing the German flag at her place, frowned and quietly laid it on its side. Akash looked at the Indian flag with a wry smile, then turned away. Nanook's nostrils flared as he grinned at the Greenlandic flag. I would have liked to hear what they thought of all this—it was a shame that, under the circumstances, we weren't free to talk.

For the first time, I realized that the Greenlandic flag is a parody of the one for Hiruko's homeland, with the red rising sun on a white background. Paint the lower half of that red ball white, and the background behind it red, and you've got the Greenlandic flag. My mother always said the red and white were to match the colors of the Danish flag, but I wonder if that's true. She believed that Denmark and Greenland are tied together like parent and child, and that whatever she wanted to believe must be true. But now I'm convinced that someone must have hit on the design for Greenland's flag while playing around with that rising sun. Could there be some deep connection between the two countries that I knew nothing about? Hiruko gazed dreamily at the miniature Greenlandic flag.

"greenland's sun over land of ice rises," she whispered when she noticed I was watching her, "into land of ice sinks." She was right—it's a beautiful design. The same red and white, yet the

Danish flag at my place had a cross, which wouldn't mean much to the nonreligious. But people have been fixated on the sun since the Stone Age, regardless of religion or nationality, because after all, none of us would exist without it. The sun rises over our land of ice, Greenland's flag declares, and sets on it at night. That seemed smart to me, and modern as well.

Sometimes I envy Nanook, being from Greenland. He can get on my nerves, but I have to admit I'm no match for him. It's not just that he's from far away. Hiruko's country is just as distant as Greenland, though in the opposite direction, yet he managed to master her native language on his own. What have I ever done besides lounge on the sofa in my living room? I was about fifteen when my mother bought it for me, and I took it with me when I moved out—now I'm in graduate school, still using it. It's a fine piece of Danish furniture, so my years of lying on it haven't damaged it at all. If it had collapsed under my weight I might have gotten up and done something, so maybe furniture companies should think twice about manufacturing such durable sofas.

I noticed something awful. There was no flag at Hiruko and Susanoo's places. They were both looking dreamily at the flags around them, so either they hadn't noticed, or were pretending they hadn't to hide their feelings.

A waiter in uniform came in and passed around glasses of vodka, so quickly no one had time to refuse.

"Let's make a toast!" Lifting his glass, Tafel, the group leader, cried, "Na zdorovie!" That was Russian, wasn't it? I studied German in high school, so even though I can't speak it very well, I can understand it. But as far as Russian goes, I know only a few words I picked up from spy movies set during the Cold War. "Cheers!" "Do it!" "Okay!"—that's about it. I took a swallow. The clear liquid burned my throat going down. I looked around at the others. Akash and Hiruko gingerly licked the edge of their glasses. After draining theirs in one gulp, Nora and Nanook's faces scrunched up in frowns.

"We are pleased to welcome you to this island of chalk cliffs," said Tafel in German. "Many sea voyagers cross the Mediterranean to the Suez Canal and then head east, a route we might call Islamic Fund-oil-mentalist. We regard the oil-centered world view of today's politicians with suspicion, and thus take special note of the fact that you have chosen a different path. Another common route follows the Atlantic down the western coast of Africa, rounding the Cape of Good Hope before heading east. This Neoimperialistic Route aims to catch Africa like a whale in a huge net, squeezing out its riches to the last oily drop. You, on the other hand, have entered the Baltic Sea, sometimes referred to as a cul-de-sac. This is the route that leads to the future. Let us toast your wise decision."

Darting around like a weasel, the waiter had already distributed a second round of vodka. Tafel raised his glass again. "Na Zdorovie!" he shouted, and was met with a few weak responses. Immediately after drinking that second glass, I began to wish I hadn't, for far from feeling pleasantly drunk, my heart was pounding with anxiety. We were setting sail on the Baltic Sea. Something wasn't right here. Was this really the route we had chosen, of our own free will?

My memories of us choosing this route together were gone, like a sign exposed to the elements so long that you can't read it anymore. The scene that I saw in my mind, of a little robot handing out our tickets, was probably from an anime I'd seen as a kid. I seemed to remember Akash being happy about going back to India, but I'd have to ask him about that later, to see if it was true. Anyway, hadn't we planned to go either through the Suez Canal or around the Cape of Good Hope? And yet here we were, about to set out on an entirely different route. Maybe some political upheaval in the Middle East or Africa had made that original plan impossible. But then why didn't I remember hearing anything about it? I'd noticed a sort of lounge on board, with a computer screen you could read newspapers on. That might be a good place to find out why ships couldn't pass through the Suez Canal, or go near the Cape of Good Hope. I'd have to check once we were back on board.

It was all so mysterious, it made me wonder if we hadn't been chloroformed at the Copenhagen port and dragged aboard, or maybe we'd caught some fever and been brainwashed while we were delirious—things that only happen in spy movies, but still…

I'd gotten so used to the rocking of the boat that even though we were now on land the walls and floor seemed to be gently swaying, giving me an uneasy feeling in the pit of my stomach. Maybe if I ate something, the force of gravity would yank me back into place.

An appetizer of French bread and caviar was served. A row of yellow lemon slices shone sourly on the plate. Nanook and Akash squeezed lemon juice over the black, gleaming fish eggs. Nora looked worriedly at the German flag she'd laid on its side, while stealing occasional glances at the Greenlandic flag and Nanook's face. If she married Nanook and got Danish citizenship, she'd be free from her complicated feelings about her own country's flag. Maybe that's what she was thinking about—at any rate, she looked so distracted I don't think she'd have noticed if she was scooping up blackberries with her little spoon instead of caviar.

Hiruko stared vaguely at the lemon slices. People looking at lemons always seem sad somehow. Oranges would have made an entirely different impression.

Only Susanoo sat with his head up and chest out, ignoring the caviar, and looking at us instead, brimming with confidence as he surveyed our faces, one by one. "There seems to be some misunderstanding here," he declared. "Unfortunately, we don't belong to the social class that pays for the privilege of learning about foreign cultures. We're foundlings, searching for a lost country."

I was startled, but our hosts seemed even more agitated, like flags whipped up in a sudden gust of wind. Tafel sat there dumbstruck, his mouth hanging open, while a pretty woman with the air of a fox turned to Susanoo with an alluring look.

"Lost?" she asked coldly. "What country might that be?"

"One you know nothing about," Susanoo growled softly.

"You're only thinking of yourself," the fox woman said, her voice full of contempt. "You want to return to the country where you grew up. But you can't go back to childhood. Psychologically, you've never broken away from your parents."

"If you're so independent from yours," taunted Susanoo, "then why are you drinking vodka and eating caviar?" I didn't understand what he meant by that, but they certainly did. A man wearing a necktie seemed especially flustered.

"This caviar is not a Russian bribe," he said in a high-pitched voice that didn't match his face at all.

"Then I have a question for you—what, exactly, is cultural exchange?"

"Providing you with information, first about basic culture— what we eat and drink, our words of greeting—then moving on to things such as agricultural policy, and our systems of education and healthcare."

"You mean the culture of this island? Is caviar produced here?"

"No, we do not actually live on this island," the man in the necktie went on. "We're a group formed especially to greet you here, at the entrance to the Baltic. This island doesn't really interest us. So, we'd like you to forget about Rügen, and turn your attention to the Baltic as a whole, and to the larger world that lies beyond it." He concluded by pounding the table lightly with his fist, right in front of Hiruko. She started, blinking furiously as if she'd just been awakened from an afternoon nap.

"dozed off. in dream island i saw. island where i lived i forget not. but search for not. to that island plan to return i have not. what happened i want to know only," she said in Panska, which the man in the necktie didn't understand. When I started to translate what she'd said into English, though, Tafel cut me off, saying sarcastically, "English is not included in our system of education," forcing me to translate Hiruko's Panska into my lousy German. Having napped my way through my high school German classes, I never learned the grammar properly, pronounce things in my own way, and simply ignore the gender of nouns. It wasn't that I'd forgotten whether *isel* (island) is a masculine or feminine noun—I'd never really learned it in the first place. And since *insel* rhymes with *pinsel* (brush), which I knew was a masculine noun, I decided to treat *insel* as one, too. To my disgust, the fox woman threw in an entirely unnecessary comment.

"My, my," she said, lightly tapping her lip with a manicured fingernail, "your island is a man." Most people wouldn't notice a mistaken article in the middle of a conversation. And even if they did, it would be like mist skimming the back of their consciousness, something hardly worth mentioning. Had this woman been an undercover agent, trained to identify spies by the characteristics of their speech? I usually don't get angry when people tell me I'm lazy, but nitpicking about trivial grammatical mistakes can make my blood boil. Since I'm trying to stay on an even keel, I do my best to keep my weak points—like my lousy German—hidden. But when someone makes a comment like this, it's best to laugh it off.

"Ha, ha, since pinsel is masculine," I admitted honestly, making a joke of it, "I thought insel must be, too."

"The brush is the phallus," the fox woman declared, looking perfectly serious, "while the island is the vagina." Frowning in consternation, Tafel quickly defended her.

"I ask you to excuse this lady. You see, gender is now a matter of such great concern in our society that things no one gives much thought to in everyday life sometimes become the subject of serious debate. Of course, if we don't change the small things first, society will never improve."

"You think your society is so advanced," Susanoo blurted out as if a switch inside him had suddenly been turned on. "That's why you planned this cultural exchange, so you could educate us. All I want is to see the chalk cliffs and here you are, trying to enlighten me."

Tafel and his group looked shocked, and Nora stepped in to mediate.

"You've got it all wrong, Susanoo," she scolded. "I'm grateful to these people for introducing their culture to us. Every country has several different cultures, and learning about them is fun. There's nothing more boring than just hitting all the tourist spots."

"She's right," said Akash, his sense of justice newly awakened, "I want to know more about the culture on this island, too. After all, I've never been here before."

"How will finding out about this island help us on our journey?" Susanoo fired back, disgruntled. "It's a waste of time."

I decided to use my brain this time, and say something that would be useful to everyone.

"You're wrong about that, Susanoo—this isn't just a distraction. The people here have special knowledge about the concept of 'east.' And since that's the direction we're heading in, learning from them will definitely put some wind in our sails."

"But if you'll take a look at our next port of call," said a man who, until then, had been sitting there hunched over his plate, "I believe you'll see that most of the people there will probably head west." Straightening his back, he took a handkerchief out of his pocket and wiped the sweat off his forehead. There was a strange-looking flag on it: the upper third was blue sky, the lower third blue sea, and in between was a white stripe with a picture of the sun in the middle, with eyes, a nose, and a mouth.

CHAPTER 3   *Akash Speaks*

An odd flag, yet one I'd seen somewhere before. The top third was the color of the sky, the bottom third the slightly deeper blue of the sea, and in the center of the white stripe between them was the sun. Though it had a face—eyes, nose, and a mouth—the expression was mysterious, beyond human understanding. What country did this flag represent? Being similar to ours, it had stayed in my memory, however faintly. The top third of the Indian flag is saffron yellow, and the bottom third green, with something round in the center of the white stripe in between. When I was a child, I used to wonder what that was. Not a face. And not the sun, either.

When he'd finished wiping his forehead with that strange flag, the man waved it in the air to get rid of the wrinkles, then spread it out on the table to show everyone.

"This is the flag of Argentina," he said. "I was born in a town in Poland, and studied law at the University of Warsaw. Then I crossed the Atlantic on a passenger ship for South America, but soon after I arrived war broke out, making it impossible for me to return to Poland. I hadn't been escaping from the war—I simply wanted to go somewhere far away."

He was an aristocratic type, like you see in the movies. His hooded, introspective eyes were rather close together, his cheeks pale, his nose straight. His thin lips were slightly parted, as if he were preoccupied with his own thoughts. His role in this welcome party was unclear to me.

In fact, the whole group was incomprehensible. Tafel was acting like their leader, but was he really? Had that fox-like woman been hired to keep everyone distracted with that high-pitched laugh of hers, and what about that very ordinary-looking man—had he been chosen for his ordinariness? They must have been randomly selected—all they had in common was their stance as members of the general public, making this aristocrat stand out all the more. Rather than looking down on them, he seemed to know how different he was, and, having given up on being understood, was acting as he pleased, not caring what anyone thought of him.

"Staying in the country where you were born is fine," he said, "But every country has a certain percentage of people who decide not to. In some the number is larger than in others. Quite a few choose to leave Armenia, for instance."

Armenia must have been a touchy subject, because Tafel got awfully flustered and suddenly announced, "This concludes our cultural exchange luncheon," then noisily slid his chair back and stood up.

While I was relieved to be done with that oppressive luncheon, I wanted to hear more from that strange man, and wondered sadly if this was the last I'd see of him. Watching him stroll lightly out of the dining room, carrying nothing, I hurried after him. Just as he was pushing the door open, he happened to look behind him.

"Excuse me," I said, "Please, wait a minute. My name is Akash." Since I didn't know his name, I thought I'd try telling him mine. His brown eyes looked me up and down, assessing me for a minute.

"And mine is Witold," he said, stretching out a pale hand with long fingers, blood vessels standing out on the back. When I gently shook it, it felt cold, like marble.

"I wanted to hear what you'd say next. It's a shame we ran out of time."

"We'll have plenty of time to be bored on the boat."

"Are you going, too?" I asked eagerly, unable to hide my joy. Witold looked around with a meaningful nod.

"Indeed, I am," he said. "I didn't tell anyone in that group at lunch, but I'm leaving here on your boat. I already have my ticket."

"Do you have luggage?"

Pursing his lips, Witold laughed, then unbuttoned his jacket and opened it to show me the inside. Six pockets had been sewn into the lining, with his passport, toothbrush, a notebook, and other things stuck in them. I now understood the reason for his baggy jacket, much too big for such a slender man.

"Is that all you have?" I asked.

"The secret to a good exile is to take as little with you as possible."

Just then Knut caught up to us.

"Are you going into exile?" he asked in a tone so casual the question might have been, "Are you here for an afternoon hike, or staying overnight in a hotel?" I was afraid Witold might be offended, but he seemed rather amused.

"I'll be an exile in the country where I was born, for about a week," he said. So that was it—he was going as far as our next port of call, which was in Poland. All I could remember about it was that the name was hard to pronounce. But wait—weren't we stopping at two ports in Poland? If so, which one was Witold's? Whichever it was, Knut, who'd joined our conversation with an offhand remark, had a better grasp of the situation than I, who'd heard the word *exile* and immediately assumed it was something terribly serious.

The word "exile" always makes me nervous. I've had dreams about suddenly having to leave the house I'm living in for some faraway country, carrying only one suitcase. That's strange, since I've never actually experienced anything like that.

Apparently, everyone has a reoccurring nightmare. And when they find out why, the bad dreams stop. Mine always begins in the parlor of the house where I spent my childhood. I'm sitting at the dining room table, reading a biography of Gandhi—a book from the top shelf of my uncle's bookcase, one I'd never even touched as a child. I'm the only one at home, and the atmosphere is ominous. Hearing violent tapping sounds, I look up to see scores of bees flying straight into the window. Some lose consciousness on impact and fall to the ground, while others dart back, make a big loop, and reorganize. The black swarm forms a human face, its eyebrows slanted upward in anger. The bees are enraged. The expressions of individual bees are almost impossible to read. They're too small, for one thing, and like robots, they can't make those tiny wrinkles on either side of their noses. Hovering together that way, shaping themselves into an angry human face, was so absolutely brilliant it made my hair stand on end.

I see a glass of milk with honey in it on the table. I'm the one who's been drinking it. Naturally, they're furious with human beings for stealing the honey they worked so hard to gather. "Even if we take a little for ourselves," I remember saying to a friend of mine who belonged to a religious sect that prohibits its members from eating honey, "the bees have plenty to feed the next generation." They themselves wouldn't accept that explanation, though.

Staring at the milk in the glass, I wonder how the bees know there's honey in it. White being a color that hides everything within its own purity, I'd been sure I had nothing to worry about, but the bees saw right through the milk. Soon they'll find the air vent beside the window, and come swarming into the room. The thought of them stinging my face scares me. And the thin skin at the back of my neck—that would really hurt. I don't want their stingers in my hands or fingers, either.

While I'm filled with dread the banging of the bees against the window disappears, replaced by a thumping sound, like someone throwing themselves against the door. Definitely not knocking. Some huge animal is trying to slam its way into the house. A cow, I think. A mother cow—terribly upset with me for stealing the milk meant for her calf—is going to attack. I can't live in this house anymore. As long as I'm here, they'll know I belong to a family that drinks milk with honey.

Our neighborhood had families that belonged to various different religious sects, distinguished by the structure of their houses. My uncle once told me they used to be divided by color, with vegetarians living in saffron yellow houses, while those of families who ate mutton but not pork were painted green, and white houses were scattered among them, as if to soften the contrast. White meant neither purity nor surrender, but reconciliation.

By the time I was old enough to explore the neighborhood on my own, though, our society had become much more complicated, so that now the houses of families who ate fish but not meat had roof tiles shaped like fish scales. Those who ate beef, on the other hand, lived in brick houses the color of rare steak. The window frames on our house had yellow and black stripes. This meant that although we didn't eat fish or meat, we consumed milk and honey. You can tell the difference between a Hindu temple and an Islamic mosque at a glance, so why not have houses that tell you which sect the family belongs to, I used to think, but while that might be fine in peacetime, if civil war broke out it could become so dangerous you'd end up abandoning the house you'd worked so hard to build.

My nightmare speeds up as I run out of time. I open all the drawers in the house, grabbing bracelets and necklaces by the handful to throw into a bag. There's an oil painting of a schooner on the wall, but it's too big to take. This makes me very sad, since that picture has meant a lot to our family over the years, but I have to suppress my feelings and leave the chest of drawers and the cupboard behind as well. Where I'm going, it'll be years before I own enough clothes to fill that chest, or eat off plates like the ones in the cupboard. So, there's nothing to do but leave it all here. I have to tear myself away from all these things that have become a part of me and, taking just one suitcase, go and live in some faraway land, never to return to this house, I tell myself, and then I wake up.

I had a comfortable childhood, so I wonder if these dreams come from the wounds of Indian history that haven't yet healed. The scab is dry, but if you tore it off, you'd still find bloody, raw flesh underneath.

Knut and I are quite different on that point. There were no famines or civil wars in Denmark even when his grandparents were young. Exile was the fate of the foreign refugees their country took in. That doesn't mean that Knut is indifferent to other people's troubles, though. He could be lying around on the sofa watching television, but he's taken pity on Hiruko, and apparently plans to accompany her until we reach the end of this difficult journey. Thoughts like these were running through my mind when Witold tapped me on the shoulder.

"I'll see you later on deck," he said as he sprang lightly up the gangway and disappeared into the boat.

The boat was painted black. Looking up at it from the lighter barge, I was struck by its volume. Like a whale—not a very convincing comparison coming from someone like me who's never actually seen a whale, but there was nothing else it reminded me of. You never see anything like that curve from the prow to the bottom in Trier, where I live now, probably because land dwellers have never needed that sort of rounded surface, not in the time of the Roman Empire, when Trier was founded, nor at any time since. Water carved the dolphin's dorsal fin and the whale's tail into shapes especially designed to cut through it. The architect's name, I suppose, is "the sea."

Still looking up, I started to walk, lost my balance, and stumbled. I was sure I was going to fall when I felt a strong arm supporting me from behind. Knut's smell was in the air. A dry, musky animal scent sometimes used in men's cologne. A flame I'd never felt before shot up inside me.

"Be careful," he said. "It's slippery here." I didn't have the courage to look at him. The wet deck was the color of copper.

"Why did you decide to travel with Hiruko?" I suddenly asked to hide my embarrassment. Having regained my footing, I finally managed to look him in the eye.

"Why? Because she interests me linguistically," he answered, not particularly surprised. That must have sounded funny even to him, though, because he laughed and added, "Maybe I was waiting for someone I could tag along with because my own life's so boring."

"I'm going to my cabin to fetch my jacket," I said, afraid he'd ask me the same question if I stuck around too long, "Suddenly it's gotten chilly." I hurried up the gangway, calling over my shoulder, "I'll see you on deck." There's something I want to keep hidden from Knut. I can't talk to anyone about it, and I'm pretty sure no one has noticed it yet. The only one in our group who might have is Susanoo. Thinking of him someday prying open the innermost chamber of my heart with that merciless tongue of his gives me the shivers. My talent is for dressing, not undressing—will he strip me naked one of these days?

When I got back to my cabin, I picked up the blueish-green blouson I'd thrown on the bed and put it on over my red sari. Though I dress like a woman, I prefer blousons that are gender-neutral, both in color and style.

On the floor I saw the thin, twisted straps of a lonely-looking pair of women's sandals where I'd left them by the bed. They would look better with my sari, but I don't want my feet to get cold while I'm standing for hours on deck, so I keep them covered with strawberry-colored socks and sneakers.

I bought the sneakers last year. I saw a documentary about everyday life at a certain university in California that included an interview with an attractive Indian woman wearing a sari and jogging shoes. A professor of English literature at the university, she talked about how every morning she drove her car into the country, where she'd jog along a soft earthen path beside a forest. The outfit suited her perfectly. A sari with sneakers—a new look, I thought, impressed.

Do the women in Hiruko's homeland go running in kimono and jogging shoes? I've seen kimonos in old movies on TV, but unlike saris, they're all so elaborate, or terribly genteel, and I don't remember a single pattern that would have looked good on Hiruko. There was one on sale at the Asia Shop, a Yukata brand kimono with a chrysanthemum and peony design that might have suited her, though. The flowers weren't brightly colored, but simply navy blue and white, which had a calming effect. That one you could probably wear with jogging shoes.

On deck I could feel the boat swaying back and forth through the soles of my sneakers even though we hadn't set sail yet. Of course, I knew that what was below me wasn't land, but immeasurable depths of sea water.

An orange life preserver caught my eye, and without thinking I walked toward it. There was a lifeboat on the other side, hanging horizontally so it could be lowered and rowed away as soon as it hit the water. By "hanging" I don't mean by a rope—it was held in place with metal pipes.

I wondered how many lifeboats there were on this boat. Enough for all the passengers? And how many passengers were there, anyway? The dining hall had six tables, with six people sitting at each, which comes to thirty-six. Of course, there could be other dining rooms, with more people using them. This was a mail boat, so it wouldn't be carrying hundreds like one of those luxury passenger liners, but if you included the crew, it would still be quite a few. Say there were two lifeboats on either side at the prow, stern, and in the center—that would make six in all. How many would each one hold—ten or so?

With these thoughts running through my mind, I measured

the lifeboat with my eyes, and then noticed Witold standing behind me, off to the side. He said something I never expected to hear: "I see you're the type who likes to stand near a lifeboat."

That gave me a jolt—did he know about that secret I hadn't mentioned to anyone? It was true that I always looked for those orange life preservers, and stood right next to them. Sometimes I even imagined myself inside one, floating by myself on the ocean.

"I'm not a very good swimmer," I said. "We didn't have swimming lessons at my school in India." Then, afraid this excuse I'd made for myself would be a blot on the entire country, I quickly added, "But in recent years Indian athletes have gotten Olympic medals in swimming." It's funny the way traces of nationalism pop up at times like this. Perhaps he thought he'd found a receptive audience, because he then took the conversation in an unexpected direction.

"The Olympics..." he said. "I've always wondered—when an athlete gets a medal, and his hometown later ends up belonging to a different country, what happens to the medal?"

"Even if the country disappears, the medal would still belong to the athlete who won it. After all, medals are awarded to individuals or teams, not to their countries."

"Then why do they raise the country's flag, and sing the national anthem at the award ceremony?"

"That certainly is strange, now that you mention it."

"When I was born, my hometown wasn't in Poland, but in Russian territory. It's not all that unusual for Poland to disappear from the map. So, we Poles believe in our towns more than our country. Towns are made from stone and brick, so they don't vanish so easily. Countries, on the other hand, are only promises, recorded on documents—in other words, they're made of paper."

"What's made of paper?" asked Knut, who'd just arrived and heard only the tail end.

"Countries," I replied. "We're all upset because Hiruko's country may have sunk in the ocean, but Witold says it's not all that unusual for countries to vanish. It's happened to Poland, where he's from. But he says that towns don't disappear, even when the country does. Because while countries are made of paper, towns are built from stone and brick."

"Stone and brick," Knut said, after some thought. "But you know, the town where Hiruko grew up might have been made of paper."

"What makes you think that?"

"There was an International Exposition I went to when I was a kid. Each country had a pavilion that showed its image of the future. The Singapore pavilion had skyscrapers of light, Iceland had a volcano made from ice, and the Dutch pavilion was a ghost ship riding on a fleet of one hundred bicycles. Hiruko's country's pavilion was shaped like a huge tortoise shell, with the walls, roof, floor, and even the windows made out of recycled paper. The ceiling was awfully high, but there were no wooden pillars, and of course no bricks, concrete, or metal. Everything was recycled paper. What really surprised me was the car they had on display—its body, the tires—all recycled paper."

"I've heard rumors about East German cars with bodies made of cardboard," Witold said with a wry smile.

"This was completely different," Knut retorted, looking put out. "They had plenty of metal. And they weren't trying to save money, either. They just wanted to show how sophisticated technology can make it possible to manufacture whole cars out of recycled paper."

"And what's so great about paper cars?"

"Well, they're a lot better than metal. Can you imagine how many cars are thrown away every day, just in Europe? If you crushed them all into plates, you'd have a stack as high as the Alps in no time. And since that's too much waste for us to handle here, we force it all on African countries, where there are people who know how to disassemble them, then make the parts into new cars. Recycling—great, you might say. The trouble is that those recycled cars emit tons of exhaust fumes that make people sick. Anyone who's tried breathing on a street in Nairobi will know what I'm talking about."

"Have you been to Nairobi?" I asked, excited to have this glimpse into Knut's hidden personal life.

"No, I just saw it on TV," he replied, looking a little embarrassed, his cheeks dyed cherry-blossom pink—by the sea breeze, perhaps. I apparently didn't need to revise my image of him as a guy who'd rather be lying on the sofa than traveling. That was a relief.

Looking rather gloomy, Hiruko came up the gangway. She was so thin that as she walked, her body twisted slightly right and left like a leaf buffeted by the wind, and I was afraid she might be blown away. When I called out to her she stopped and looked at me, her face expressionless as she came toward us.

"Hiruko, was your house made of paper?" asked Knut. Just at that moment a gust of wind mockingly erased his words. Not cold exactly, but very salty, the wind kept playing with Hiruko, blowing her hair first across her mouth, then her eyes, hiding them as if the Sea Breeze God was trying to steal her face, one bit at a time. Putting an arm around her shoulders, drawing her close, Knut asked again, in a gentler, comforting voice, "Did you live in a house made of paper?"

"In Odense?" she asked, her mouth hanging open in surprise. In unison, Knut and I burst out laughing.

"When you hear the word *house*, you immediately think of the one you're living in now, in Odense. To you, a 'house' is something that's finished moving."

"Were you talking about houses?" she asked.

"Actually, we were talking about whether or not countries can just vanish. Witold says they can, although towns don't disappear so easily. That's because countries only exist on paper—in documents—whereas towns are collections of buildings, made of stone or brick, so they don't disappear all at once. But what about the houses in your hometown? Were they made of stone or brick?"

Hiruko shook her head.

"Even so, can you imagine a whole town vanishing?" I asked. "I mean, even if your house burned down, the town would still be there, wouldn't it?" She nodded with her eyes.

"If houses fall down, people rebuild in the same place," she said sadly. "Our island was small, so there was no other place to go."

"The same is true of London, you know," I said to cheer her up. "The city was destroyed by fire any number of times, but no one gave up and moved out to the suburbs. Their houses burned down, but the city was still there."

I guess that wasn't very encouraging, though, because she went on, sounding just as sad as before. "Our houses were not made only of paper. We used wood, and concrete, too. But still they were ruined. Nature smashes even concrete. Floods, tsunami, landslides, volcanoes erupting. When houses are destroyed, people rebuild in the same area. Because ancestors' bones are buried there. They don't want ancestors' bones to lead a lonely life. Many people think that way. Sometimes everyone digs up their ancestors' bones, puts them in a box, and they all leave the place together. Then, the town itself becomes a ghost."

"They all leave together? Why is that?"

"Because if they go on living there, they'll get sick."

Looking very serious, Witold leaned toward her and, looking deep into her eyes, asked, "Did you come to Europe as a refugee because you couldn't go on living in your homeland?"

"No. I came to study, but while I was gone, maybe my homeland became a place where no human being can live."

"That's something like what happened to me. I didn't leave

Poland back then because I couldn't live there anymore. But while I was away, something terrible happened, and I couldn't go back. So, you can't really call me an exile."

That reminded me of someone. "That's just like Magnus Hirschfeld!" I said, so excited I was almost shouting. "He left by ship for a foreign lecture tour, but while he was away the Nazis took over, and he couldn't go back to Germany." Witold, Knut, and Hiruko were all looking at me expectantly. "Hirschfeld was a doctor, a pioneer in the scientific study of gender. He wrote out identification papers for transvestites, so that they wouldn't be arrested. Back then, the police would stop a man wearing women's clothes on the street, but if he had one of Hirschfeld's ID cards, they couldn't do anything to him."

"What did it say on the card?"

"Something like 'If the bearer is prohibited from cross-dressing, his health and well-being will be jeopardized.' The need to cross-dress, like sexual desire, comes from somewhere deep inside, and repressing it can lead to serious illness—that, basically, was the message."

"So, cross-dressing for health?" Hiruko asked, as if she found this rather amusing. She looked a little brighter now.

"Yes, you could say that. But the Nazis weren't going to stand for it."

"Why not?" she asked. "They wanted everyone to be healthy, didn't they?"

I burst out laughing, but there wasn't a trace of irony in her face.

"The word 'health' can mean lots of different things. The Nazis wanted to turn human beings into machines—men for churning out sperm, women for popping out babies. That, to them, was health. Since war reduces the population, they needed to increase production to make up for the loss." Of course, I was being sarcastic.

"Production machinery—that won't do," said Witold. "I'd much rather see men, women, and all the other sexes as a brilliant display of pornografia."

The sudden appearance of this strange word *pornografia* caught me off guard. Witold's aristocratic features simply didn't fit with those garish photos you see in erotic magazines. That odd suffix *-grafia* did have an artistic ring to it, but why "pornografia" rather than "pornography," and was there a difference between the two? I wanted to ask him about that right away, but first, I needed to finish what I'd started to say.

"If Hirschfeld had stayed in Nazi Germany, they probably would have killed him. He was invited to give a lecture in your country, too, Hiruko. While he was there, he got interested in the traditional theater, where men appear on stage dressed in wigs and elaborate kimonos to play women's roles. He apparently interviewed an actor named On Nagata. Traveling the world lets you see a whole range of sexual experiences first hand."

"And how long did his world tour take?"

"Around the time when he got the invitation to lecture in America, he suspected his life would be in danger if he stayed in Germany, so he accepted the offer and set off by ship. Then he just kept going, visiting lots of different countries until he died about four years later. If you think of all that as one journey, it was an awfully long one."

"The fact that he went first to America seems important to me. In other words, that he went West," Witold said. He smiled, looking pleased with himself, while Knut glowered back at him.

"Okay, I get it—there were people who went West," he retorted. "Toward the setting sun, which makes you imagine the future. And the East is where the sun crawls up over the horizon, so some people think of it as the past. But can't you also think of traveling toward the East as trying to reach a memory? That's what we want to do, so we'll keep on going, no matter what."

"But," Witold objected, furrowing his brow, "what is there, actually, in the East? What could there possibly be beyond Siberia?"

Knut was about to answer when Hiruko cut him off.

"Whales," she announced. "Where Eurasia ends, the Pacific Ocean begins. With Moby Dick swimming in it." Instead of her homeland, Hiruko had named the largest mammal on earth as her reason for heading east.

"Whales? But surely there are whales in the western seas as well."

"In the novel, Moby Dick is found in the East."

"Are you sure?" asked Knut. "Ahab's ship headed northeast from Java, but then didn't he bypass the fishing grounds off the coast of your country and head down into the South Pacific?"

Hiruko looked so sad to hear that, that I wanted to say something—anything—to make her feel better.

"The ship may have sailed into the South Pacific while they were chasing the white whale, but weren't they near Hiruko's homeland when they saw it for the first time?"

Actually, I was only bluffing—I'd never read *Moby-Dick*, and the friend who told me the story didn't mention anything about the routes of whaling vessels. Fortunately, Knut didn't seem to doubt I'd read it.

"You may be right. From Massachusetts down to Argentina they'd be heading south, but as you say, after they rounded the Cape of Good Hope they'd definitely be heading toward Hiruko's homeland."

"See—if you followed the white whale, you'd come close to where her country was. Even if national borders have changed slightly since then, the migration routes carved into the whales' memories stay the same. Those routes are probably more reliable than our maps of the world."

Unsure of where this was going, I stopped talking and looked down at the peaks and valleys on the ocean's surface. As I watched, they started to look like a detailed model of a mountain range. Which reminded me of a model of the Alps I once saw in a museum in a small town in northern Italy—I was surprised to see how many mountains there were between the really famous ones that are over thirteen thousand feet high, like Mont Blanc, the Matterhorn, the Jungfrau, and I remember wondering if they all had names as well. The sea has peaks and valleys, too, but they're always moving, changing every second, so there's no way to name them.

Waves are merely wrinkles that appear on the surface of water. Much more substantial than the ones you see in cloth waving in the wind, though, because they give us a sense of all the teeming life far below. Seaweed swaying like ominous hands, flat fish whipping up clouds of sand as they move forward, octopuses darting behind rocks, schools of tiny fish escaping predators by switching directions in perfect unison, like needles mastering synchronized swimming. I've heard that light doesn't even reach the deepest parts of the sea. I once saw a picture of a deep-sea fish whose eyes had atrophied since it no longer needed to see. The patches where its eyes had been looked like windows that had been filled in with concrete, then painted over. How much water was there, sandwiched between the dark bottom of the sea and the surface I was now looking at?

"I know it's only fiction," said Knut, "but I got scared while I was reading *Moby-Dick*, especially the description toward the end of Ahab blindly chasing the white whale without looking at a map or a compass. When you think of it, though," he went on, laughing, "since oceans cover the entire earth, a ship will always be floating on one of them, so in that sense, it's pretty safe. It's not like a long time ago when people believed the earth was flat as a plate, and worried about slipping over the edge."

We heard Nora's sharp, rhythmical steps, walking toward us.

"I see you decided to come along," she said cheerfully to Witold.

"I'm happy to join you on this trip, even if it's just for a while," he answered like the gentleman he was. Then the wind blew, the waves roared, and I didn't hear what they said next.

Witold is probably attracted to strong, dependable women like Nora. Perhaps he had a wife like that, who went with him to Argentina. Even in a climate so unlike Poland, she'd have made sure his favorite cabbage soup was on the dinner table, and found a pillow with just the right firmness so he'd have sweet dreams every night. It must have been hard, picking through prickly cactus in search of cabbage for Polish soup in an alien land. Witold looked like an aristocrat. But even working-class men of his generation wouldn't have helped clean the house, and since Witold wouldn't have been able to hire a housekeeper right away, his wife must have mopped the floors of their old colonial-style house. No matter how hard she scrubbed the wind would keep blowing sand across the floor, making it grainy and rough like her chapped skin—the texture of life in exile, which probably brought her to tears in secret.

Of course, all this was in my imagination. I don't even know whether Witold was married. Yet seeing that sort of sophisticated intellectual type is enough to make me wonder how his wife must have suffered, which shows how strong my tendency to see things from a woman's point of view has become.

Knut and Hiruko were looking into each other's eyes as they chatted, while Witold's attention was focused on Nora, leaving me the odd man out. This sometimes happens at student parties in Germany, when couples form and drift off together. At times like that, rather than just standing around, I try to work my way into someone's conversation.

"Why did you decide to go to Argentina?" I asked, peering into Witold's face. "You said it wasn't to escape from the war, didn't you?"

Perhaps he didn't understand the question, because he stared vaguely into space without answering. Had inhaling Nora's feminine fragrance paralyzed his mind? Taking a closer look, I saw slight alterations in his face. The whites of his eyes were moist, his nostrils flared, his lower lip sagging.

"Are you all right?" I asked. "Are you seasick, or are you high on a drug called pornografia?"

The mention of "pornografia" seemed to wake him up—his face looked a little more normal.

"You want to know why I traveled abroad?" he replied. "Well, I thought that, by getting away from the environment in which I was brought up ..."

So far, so good—he'd started to give me a serious answer, but then his voice trailed off. As I waited for him to go on, I quietly leaned over for a whiff of Nora's clothing. She was practical—logical, too—and I wondered if even that type of woman uses perfume, or whether she might naturally be exuding some intoxicating feminine scent that Witold had gotten drunk on. All I smelled was the salty sea breeze. The sea frightened me, the way it kept relentlessly washing the air, as if telling us that not a single human being was really there.

Though I'm now en route to becoming a woman, I'm not sure I'll ever emit a feminine fragrance naturally, so I use rose- and vanilla-based perfumed oil. And since people tend not to trust you once they catch you using artificial scent, I only dab on a drop or two.

"What happens when you leave the environment you were raised in?" I asked Witold. That brought him out of his daze, and he seemed to have finally found what he wanted to say.

"When you're in your own country," he said, "you're patriotic without thinking about it. If your homeland is in a vulnerable position, that vulnerability seems admirable, praiseworthy. Take Poland for example. It's in a terrible location, surrounded by great powers, but telling yourself how bravely it fought until it finally won independence fills you with a nationalistic pride that brings tears to your eyes. Spend your childhood listening to adults talk about Poland's valor, and you grow up into a nationalist in spite of yourself. It's the same old story, like a sentimental pop song, demanding your tears."

Hiruko chimed in. "I am the same," she chanted. "I heard many stories of how our country was best in the world. Our children were fastest at multiplying seven times seven, and no nation's umbrellas worked as well as ours." Witold nodded, examining her chest with an appraising eye.

"I believe you. People shut inside their own boundaries are satisfied with these songs of praise, and because no one doubts them anymore, they seep into your very bones. But in Argentina, no one cared about what made Poland great. A life surrounded by foreigners can cure you of the disease called 'our-country-is-best-itis.' That's why I wanted to go to Argentina."

He said all this quickly, in one breath, then turned back to Nora and started eyeing her until I thought I'd better pull him back toward the topic of exile.

"I've experienced something like that, too," I said. "I didn't notice it so much in India, but that old story about Gandhi and his spinning wheel makes me feel a rush of pride even now." I seem to have honed my verbal skills to compete with that alluring fragrance women exude—I use the power of words to attract men to me rather than them. Just as I'd expected, Witold moved away from Nora.

"Gandhi and his spinning wheel?" he asked, his eyes shining.

"That's right. Remember when you showed us the Argentine flag at lunch? The Indian flag has a similar design—three wide horizontal stripes with something round in the middle. On the Argentine flag it's the sun, but the Indian flag has a wheel called the Ashoka Chakra. King Ashoka was a Buddhist, and the design is based on a ship's steering wheel, meaning that the Buddha will take the helm and steer us on the correct path through life, so that we'll avoid peril. I didn't know that until I came to study in Germany—I heard about it from a German friend who's really into Buddhism. Of course, I'm not sure how far to trust his explanation. There aren't many Buddhists in India, so I'd never had a Buddhist friend to talk to about things like that."

As soon as she heard the word Buddhism, Nora's face brightened. "You mean there's a Buddhist motif in the flag, even though Buddhism isn't so important in India?" she asked enthusiastically. I didn't want to ignore her, but just then I remembered something more important.

"The Indian flag tacked on the wall in my uncle's house had what was clearly a spinning wheel in the middle, rather than the Ashoka Chakra. When I asked my uncle about it, he told me that old flag dated back to just before we got our independence from England, and that the spinning wheel was a symbol of our new nation. Gandhi taught us that until we learned to spin our own thread, and make our own clothes, we'd never be spiritually independent, my uncle had explained with tears in his eyes. I'm not sure whether you'd call that patriotism, but I definitely felt his passion, and it's been with me ever since."

"England got wealthy," said Nora, rejoining the conversation, "buying cheap cotton from India to support its textile industry." In her element, she went on: "Because industry didn't develop in India, the people who actually worked in the cotton fields stayed poor. Gandhi wanted them to keep their cotton instead of selling it, and become independent by spinning it into thread, then weaving the cloth to make their clothes themselves."

"Stories like that," said Witold, nodding and smiling at her, "of how your country cast off the fetters of foreign rule to gain independence, are matches that light the flames of nationalism."

Apparently not noticing that the point he was making ran

counter to hers, she returned his nod, and went on: "There are similar situations, even today. People who grow cotton, spin it into thread, then make it into clothing are trapped in poverty."

I always get irritated watching a man and a woman assume they're on the same wavelength even though they don't understand each other at all. Listening to Witold and Nora talk in parallel lines, my mind looked for a way to bend those lines so they'd cross.

"Even cosmopolitans have a switch that can light the fire of nationalism. In my case, that might be a spinning wheel. Gandhi is probably keeping his wheel turning somewhere above the clouds, sighing now and then. The world has changed so much that now no one knows how to make clothing from cotton they've grown and picked themselves. In southern India, the spinning wheels still turn. But the cotton they're making into thread was grown in Turkey or Africa, and that India-spun thread will be dyed in China, then made into clothing in Bangladesh. Children pick the cotton and work the sewing machines, day and night."

A seagull had appeared in the clear blue sky, its head swiveling around to check out each of us, as if to say, "That one's not going to throw me any bread, nor is this one, or the one next to her." It flew on by while the tips of the waves, as white as the bird's feathers, washed over the lifeboat, splashing loudly.

CHAPTER 4   *Nora Speaks*

It was getting close to dinnertime, so we ended our conversation and went back to our cabins. Under a low ceiling, the narrow corridor was lined with doors. My hair smelled of salt, and the sea. All that time while the wind was blowing through it, Nanook hadn't appeared on deck, which worried me, so I stopped in front of his door and, after some hesitation, knocked. I heard what sounded like a chair being turned over, and then he opened the door, his tousled hair hanging down over his forehead.

"What do you want?" He looked sleepy.

"It's almost dinnertime. You're coming, aren't you?"

Irritated, he squinted at me and lowered his chin. "I'm not hungry," he growled, then turned away.

"Are you sick?" I asked. It always gets to me when a man says he has no appetite, so I'm afraid I sounded more angry than worried.

"There's nothing wrong with me. I'm just not hungry," he said, stepping back, starting to close the door.

"It's not normal for a young man like you to have no appetite," I said.

"That sounds to me like sexual harassment." He looked like he was joking, but there was a thorn in his voice. Which was understandable—that *should* in a sentence like "A young man *should* eat a lot" turns me off too.

"Sorry. Your appetite is your own business. We should all be able to eat what we want whenever we like, as much as we want— that's the modern way, I know, but still . . ."

"But what?" He answered the question for me. "But it's more fun to have dinner together—that's what you wanted to say, isn't it?" He'd gone beyond aggravation and was now making fun of me. "So, you think this guy Nanook you're so fond of belongs to a small tribe in Hokkaido? With a sunken hearth in the middle of the floor, and the whole family sitting around the fire eating rice porridge together. That girl with the baby on her lap looks awfully young—could she be its mother? There's another kid, a little older, plunked down next to her; his father's handing him some porridge. Is the guy next to them their older brother, all grown up, or an uncle? A couple of other little kids, and Grandma and Grandpa at the back, smiling. In that picture on your kitchen wall they each have a bowl, filled from the same big pot hanging from a hook over the fire—your image of the ideal family."

I did have a picture like that in my kitchen, of an Ainu family eating together. It was a sketch by Isabella Bird, who traveled through Asia in the late nineteenth century. And he had seen it, even though he hadn't really seemed to be looking. Not only that—he'd saved it, as a snapshot in his mind.

That day when I discovered him lying in the ruins of the Roman baths in Trier with a sprained ankle and took him home to treat it, his face was a blank, and I couldn't tell what he was thinking. Usually when I have friends over, they check out the titles in my bookshelf, then ask me about that picture on the kitchen wall, but Nanook was like someone from another planet. Nevertheless, he'd seen it, and stored it away in his memory.

"I'm glad you remember my sketch of the Ainu family so well."

"Nothing to be glad about—I was trying to tell you how ridiculous you are, idealizing an ethnic minority living in a world of ice and snow."

If he hadn't met that odious, arrogant doctor in Copenhagen, my Ainu sketch would have stayed in the back of his mind, and he never would have mentioned it. As an experiment, he and the doctor switched personalities for a time, and in the process, he learned some awfully nasty lessons, the worst of which was, "Gather as much information as you can about someone's personal life and then use it as a weapon against them." The personality switch had ended long ago, so Nanook should have been back to his normal self by now, but he was still a long way off from the man I'd known.

"I'm not idealizing them," I protested. "I just like that sketch."

"I am not an Ainu. Some anthropologists say the ethnic minorities scattered around the northern regions of Eurasia might be related, but it's racial prejudice to lump them all together into one big happy family of noble savages."

"You don't understand. I'm just kind of drawn to the idea of a family living in nature, helping each other out."

"Nature? Family? I survive on the hot dogs I buy on Copenhagen street corners, which I eat alone. I have nothing to do with either nature or family."

"But what about your childhood in Greenland? I remember you talking about your grandfather."

"I never sat around the hearth with my grandparents, if that's what you mean."

"But your grandfather used to make a hole in the ice to catch fish—didn't you and your family eat what he caught?"

"Yeah, sometimes. But we didn't have a hearth with a big pot over the fire. Pots are for cooking vegetables or grain. You don't really need them when your diet's mainly meat or fish. My mother started growing vegetables after it got warmer because of climate change. But that meant that our culture had been destroyed."

"If hunting dies out, can't you replace it with something new?"

"Maybe. But anyway, I'm not trying to say that hunting is a tradition we have to carry on. We did it because we had to, killing only as many animals as we needed, then carefully preserving the meat so it would last. We didn't waste anything—we used the hides to make our clothes and shoes. If we'd had vegetables and grains, we wouldn't have stuck to hunting." As he talked Nanook had softened up like root vegetables cooking in a pot over the fire, until finally he smiled and said, "Fish and grain don't go together naturally, so sticking one on top of the other that way strikes me as kind of strange."

"Sticking fish and grain together?"

"That's what sushi is. Putting a piece of fish on top of rice and squeezing, forcing two things that don't belong together into one. But it's pretty weird for someone who worked part-time as a sushi chef to be saying sushi's strange."

"It's not such a surprising combination, though—kind of like eating potatoes with steak."

"Would a lion who's just killed a deer go looking for vegetables to eat with it?"

That made me laugh. There's a game where the first one to laugh loses, but I didn't feel I'd lost.

"It's entirely possible that a lion would eat the hot dog and leave the pickles and bun, but a father lion would never go out to a hot dog stand by himself and leave his family behind. Lions always share their kill, don't they?"

"I see," Nanook laughed. "You're saying that we should act like the lions. You want us to all eat together, sitting around the same table, whether we're hungry or not, because being together is important—isn't that what you mean?"

"Is that wrong? We're traveling together, so why not eat together? Of course, if you want to be alone sometimes, that's okay too."

"I don't especially want to be alone."

"Really? We were all talking together on deck, but you didn't come, so I was worried."

"Who do you mean 'we'?"

"Akash, Knut, Hiruko and me. And Witold."

"Witold? Who's that?"

"The Polish man who was using a little Argentine flag as a handkerchief when we had lunch on Rügen Island."

"A revolutionary?"

"No, a novelist, I think."

"Did he give everyone a lecture on deck?"

"No, we were just talking."

"Was Susanoo there?"

That was when I realized that Susanoo hadn't been there. I'd been wondering where Nanook was the whole time, but until now, I'd never given Susanoo a thought. Maybe I was feeling his absence as a little respite, though. Just imagining him stomping onto the deck I hear ropes slamming against the mast, and the deck starts pitching and rolling under my feet. To me, he's a sign of stormy weather.

"Susanoo wasn't there," I said, "But he's probably coming to dinner. I'm going back to my cabin to change first, so I'll see you in the dining hall." With that, I left Nanook.

The pale, wan little piece of soap melted in my hands as I washed carefully between my fingers, and up to my wrists. I left the bathroom, and as I stood in the middle of my cabin thinking over my conversation with Nanook, I realized that there was no warmth or weight in the light coming through the porthole, and the cabin, bathed in this ersatz light, was starting to look like my childhood bedroom as I'd seen it in a dream. Though I'd made the bed, there was a slight indentation in the pillow, shaped like my head. It made the pillow look twisted—in pain—and the wrinkles in the coverlet formed the eyes, brows, and mouth of an angry face. When I returned to the bathroom my toothbrush was leaning suggestively forward, and even the cup it was in seemed to be chuckling to itself. I looked in the mirror. People tend to think of me as a rational person. The face in the mirror certainly wasn't irrational.

On deck I'd been wearing a heavy blue blouse. Perhaps I'd chosen that color so I'd fit in with the sea and the sky. For the dining hall, I prefer a white one, although not necessarily to match the tablecloth. Actually, it's just a plain, white cotton shirt—nothing feminine about it. As I was undoing the buttons, I saw the image of a child in the mirror behind me. Working a sewing machine, making clothes. This girl, who looked about ten or so, was sewing the blouse I was now taking off.

She stopped and looked up. A face like a childhood Akash. Had she seen me? I couldn't tell because, expressionless, she looked down again and went back to pushing the pedal on her sewing machine. The skin on her foot had turned pale and powdery, so dry it was peeling off in flakes. Couldn't be. I'd never buy anything made in a factory that exploited children that way. Quickly, I turned the blouse inside out to check for the Fair Trade tag in the lining.

The cotton, soft on my skin, murmured, "Be comfortable in your own body." I can't stand the cheap sheen of polyester—cotton, to me, is warm, and honest. Which is why signs of its crueler face were so disturbing—had this old friend betrayed me? Last year I bought a copy of *Huckleberry Finn*. I'd read it in German as a child, but decided to try it in English. Back then I didn't understand that the people working in the cotton fields were slaves, but this time, that was all I could think about. Cotton fiber was drenched with blood flowing from whipped backs, and sweat from unpaid labor—I felt bad having it next to my skin. Huckleberry Finn was dead, the Civil War ended a long time ago, cotton exported from America is no longer picked by slaves because there's no slavery, I told myself, but the word *slave* kept jumping out at me from the pages of *Huckleberry Finn*, so I gave up and, deciding to read something entirely different, I'd picked up a biography of Gandhi. The ghost of cotton was apparently haunting me, though, because here I found the same motif, in a detailed account that went on for pages, of Gandhi's anger at seeing Indian laborers forced to pick cotton for minuscule wages. When they could no longer import cotton from America, the British coerced India into producing it for them, turning India into a country whose survival depended on selling cotton to England, the book said. The British bought cotton from India on the cheap and turned it into cloth in their own textile factories at great profit. But the Indians who produced it never got any richer. That gave Gandhi the idea that his countrymen had to make their own clothes, taking over every stage in the process. India had long been independent, and wasn't a poor country anymore, I thought, trying to comfort myself, yet depression seeped into my skin every time I wore cotton. Even so, no other fabric appealed to me.

With the ghost of cotton lingering on the pages of every book I picked up, I decided to read *On Cotton*, which I'd seen in the visitors' library at the Karl Marx Haus when I first started working there. At the time, I'd warily asked a colleague why it was there, and she'd casually replied, "Probably because Marx considered the relationship between cotton production and slavery to be such a serious problem."

"But that's all in the past, isn't it?" I'd retorted angrily. Taken aback, her eyes widened.

"This book is about both the past and the present," she'd said.

Though I was hoping it would show me that slave labor now played no part in cotton production, that old ghost had set a trap for me, and I fell right in. The book told me in detail about how before a cheap T-shirt can be sold in Europe, people in Africa, India, China, and Turkey, so poor they give up their health and all their leisure just to eat, have to grow the cotton, spin the fiber into thread, then weave it into cloth and dye it. Each step in the process sucks out their lives, transforming them into the soft cloth we feel against our skin. Would I no longer be able to wear cotton clothes? Of course, polyester may take an even heavier toll on the people who make it. But the pain that's been collecting since the nineteenth century is concentrated mainly in cotton. All that suffering had left a residue of resentment that weighed on me. I could always wear silk, but it surely had its own dark history.

While I was mulling over all this, the "green button"—the officially recognized label of the Fair Trade movement—appeared like a savior. It guarantees that the basic human rights of the workers who produced the garments were protected. If I bought only clothing with a green button, I'd finally be able to escape the ghost of cotton.

Yet walking around town, I still sometimes bought things that caught my eye from street vendors. They seduced me, you might say. Even when there was no breeze, the sleeves of a blouse would float up, beckoning, as if calling to me, "Hey there!" I'd go over for a look. "I'll bet I'm perfect for you," the shirt would add, "Why don't you try me on?" If it was neon-colored polyester I'd keep on going, but sometimes it would be plant-dyed cotton, in the natural colors I love. Taking it in my hands I'd see how even the stitching was, and it would indeed fit me perfectly, as if made to order, not too tight in the shoulders or wrinkly around the bust. Cheap, too, so I wouldn't regret having bought it on impulse. At the cash register, I'd hear the rustle of paper as the woman bagged it for me—a sound that gave me an inexpressible sense of satisfaction. Then I'd get home, realize I'd forgotten to check for the green button, and discover, after a frantic search, that it wasn't there. At that price, it couldn't possibly have been Fair Trade. The words "child labor" would flash through my mind. Why had I bought this shirt? It was because of people like me, always hunting for bargains, seduced by sleeves calling from hangers, thrilled by the rustling of a paper bag, that clothes like this kept on being sold, while children in faraway countries were forced to sew them day and night instead of going to school.

Cheapness is now a value in itself. Because I earn a good salary at the Karl Marx Haus, I have no need to seek out cheap clothes. The person I see in my mirror is careful about quality, and always checks for the Fair Trade button. But whenever I turn away, I succumb to the thrill of buying something cheap on a whim. Then when I've worn it for a day, I'll catch a whiff of nasty chemicals, or feel something prickling at my shoulder blades—there's always something that puts me off, and I end up tossing it in the back of a drawer, never to be worn again until I finally deposit it in one of the containers. Not the one for burnable trash, but the one with a heart on it, for clothes you want to donate to the Third World. That term Third World, supposedly dead, now huddles silently in the dark abyss of that huge container.

With all these thoughts running through my head, it had taken me a long time to get changed. I raced out of my cabin and down the corridor, and when I opened the door to the dining hall, more than half the passengers were already seated. I heard fragments of several different languages mingled in with the clinking of china and glasses. From the Venus table, to my right, friction between Russian-sounding consonants formed a carpet for lively mañanas from the Mars table opposite to land on. The people at the Saturn table, who didn't seem to have a common language, used gestures—a woman wearing glasses decorated with yellow feathers skillfully used both hands to form triangles and diamonds, and a man in a clown suit responded by tossing his dessert fork in the air and catching it on the back of one of his hands. A guy in a black turtleneck sweater was expressionless and still as a stone, yet when I passed by, he wiggled his earlobes. At the Jupiter table, toward the back, they were speaking English, in a slightly higher register than anyone else.

While this mixture of languages melted into a before-dinner symphony, the only one at our Earth table, right in the middle, was Susanoo, leaning back in his chair, silently drinking water.

No one else had come. If I'd dawdled a little longer, I wouldn't have had to be alone with him. Hating to be late, I'd practically run down the corridor, but everyone else was even later, meaning that Susanoo was the only punctual one in our group.

"We were all talking on deck," I said, trying to sound agreeable, "Were you in your cabin all this time?"

Susanoo frowned. "What were you talking about?" he asked sharply, then thrust out his glass and barked, "Give me a refill."

With the pitcher right between us, shouldn't he pour for me before refilling his own glass? Being polite to a woman—even superficially—had apparently never occurred to him. I don't have much use for "ladies first." I can't stand men who hold the door for me, or help me with my coat, then during meetings refuse to listen to a thing I say. Even so, when that silly "ladies first" rule is so totally ignored, it gets on my nerves. Which is a contradiction. Perhaps the environment Susanoo was raised in didn't have a "ladies first" rule. If so, I'm the self-centered one, for being so critical of him. Still, I couldn't bring myself to pour him a glass of water.

"Sorry," I said, "I have a pain in my wrist, so I'm afraid that pitcher's just too heavy for me." Accepting my rather lame excuse, Susanoo refilled his own glass before reluctantly pouring for me.

"What were you talking about on deck?" he asked again.

"Cotton. The workers in the fields were treated terribly."

"You mean on American cotton plantations? Slavery was abolished a long time ago."

"No, in India."

"Gandhi?"

Fortunately, just as we got to this point, Akash appeared.

"Akash, what were you guys talking about on deck?" With a *you can't get anywhere with a woman* sort of look, he rubbed me out of the picture, turned to Akash, and repeated his question. I'm sure Akash wasn't happy to be seen as another man.

"We were discussing flags."

"Flags?"

"That's right. For some reason, the Indian and Argentinian flags are quite similar."

Nanook then walked in and sat down next to me. That made me feel warm inside, though he didn't seem to notice.

"The Irish flag resembles the Indian flag," he said, ignoring me, turning to Akash. "It's got three colors—a white stripe sandwiched between orange and green, to cancel out the tension between them. Whether they're hoping for real reconciliation, or are satisfied if things just stay quiet, nobody knows. And the stripes are vertical, which is different from the horizontal ones on the Indian and Argentinian flags." While he was talking, he tore off a piece of bread and put it in his mouth. After claiming not to be hungry, it seemed he couldn't even wait for the soup.

I saw Knut come into the dining hall. He stopped to talk to someone at the table to the right of the entrance—the one I privately called "Russians-of-all-types." I couldn't see who it was from where I was sitting, though. The dining hall in the sanatorium where Thomas Mann's *The Magic Mountain* takes place has one table for aristocratic Russians and another for the more ordinary sort, but here there's only one for all of them.

At our table, the discussion of national flags continued.

"So white means neutral, does it?" Susanoo asked. "But on your flag, it stands for ice, right?"

"With the ground completely frozen over," said Nanook quietly, "it's more like cold war than reconciliation."

"In myth, the gods never reconcile," Susanoo announced. He sounded arrogant, perhaps because what he said was so out of place.

"Are you still talking about flags?" asked Knut, who'd been standing there, listening, but now pulled out a chair and sat down.

Glowering over at him, Susanoo retorted, "They don't interest me at all. What they tell you about a country is a sham, it's all made up, after the fact."

"But isn't it good," Akash gently protested, a frown on his face, "to show your hopes for your country through colors and symbols?"

"What good is hope, when we're all drowning in the sea of fate," Susanoo shot back. "Nora," he said, staring at me. "I have a question for you. The black, red, and yellow in the German flag—what do those colors mean?"

He meant it as a jab, to provoke me, but I sidestepped at the last minute.

"Nothing in particular," I said casually.

"That can't be—ridiculous. They must stand for something—freedom, equality, whatever."

"No, they don't."

"You mean your flag's empty?"

That sounded so harsh I felt I had to defend it.

"Well, I wouldn't go that far. We have scholars researching the historical significance of those colors. None of them has come up with a definitive explanation, though, and there's nothing about it in the legal code, either."

"In other words, you don't know the meaning of your own country's colors." This sounded like an attack. So now it was my duty to explain the German flag. I was feeling disgruntled, as if I'd gotten the short end of the stick, when I saw Akash look over at me and wink.

"Actually," he said cheerfully, "each color represents a political party. Red is revolutionary, and black is conservative, as is yellow. You may be wondering why there are two separate conservative parties. Well, the black one is rooted in Christianity, while the yellow one has grown out of social media. But I'm sure you've noticed that something important is missing. Of course, it's the Green Party, dedicated to protecting the environment. So why is there no green in the German flag? The reason is quite simple. The Greens were late for history class, and unfortunately, there were no empty seats left when they arrived." He chuckled, as if this sounded funny even to him. But although Akash was only joking, Susanoo took him seriously.

"So that's how it is," he said, impressed. "The Germans see their country as a collection of political parties. You've put your time there as a student to good use—you're very observant." Susanoo held out his wine glass to be filled. The liquid the waiter poured into it looked like blood.

"Who were you talking to?" I asked Knut. He didn't seem to know what I meant, so I stuck my chin out toward the Russian table by the door.

"Witold," he said simply.

"But there are three Russian couples, aren't there?"

He stretched out his neck and squinted for a better look.

"There were yesterday. Now Witold's joined them, but there are still three men and three women."

"Witold must have locked one of the Russian men in his cabin so he could take his place at the dinner table," Nanook joked.

"Maybe Witold's been there all the time and we just didn't notice."

"No, that's impossible," Akash objected. "Witold wasn't even on the boat when we were in Copenhagen." Susanoo's thoughts seemed to have wandered off to some faraway place. Relieved, I turned back to Knut.

"So, what were you and Witold talking about?"

"I told him I envied him, being fluent in Russian, and he asked what languages we spoke. I told him German, English, Panska, and Danish."

"Did he seem interested in Panska?" asked Nanook. Knut nodded.

"I'm going to complain about this!" Susanoo suddenly roared, standing up and striding off with his wine glass in hand. Akash hurried after him. We watched them disappear through the door to the corridor leading to the kitchen.

"I'm afraid to ask what that's all about," said Nanook, "but it won't help if we all make a fuss. Tell me more about Witold and Panska."

Knut told us that when he'd finished explaining about Panska, Witold had said, "Oh, so it's like Esperanto."

"No," Knut had objected, "Panska isn't an artificial language someone made up in his study—it came into being naturally."

"But Esperanto isn't as artificial as most people think," Witold had replied, getting quite emotional. "The people who actually speak it bring it to life, and it's changed through the years."

At this point in the conversation, a well-built Russian woman at the table had turned to Knut and said in a teasing tone, "Witold gets fired up at the mention of one of his countrymen. That's because his country's so small."

I took a sip of water. "She probably said that because Zamenhof, who invented Esperanto, is also Polish. But the part about Esperanto not being entirely artificial is interesting, don't you think?" Knut stared at me, flabbergasted. "Don't tell me you didn't know that Esperanto originated in Poland?" I asked.

"No, I knew that," he said "But just now I was talking to Nanook in Danish, and you understood everything." He was staring intently at my hair, as if he thought I had mysterious linguistic powers hidden somewhere in it.

"Well, when people travel together for a long time, sometimes they pick up each other's languages."

Susanoo and Akash were arguing as they came back to the table.

"What's wrong?"

"Susanoo demanded Japanese sake instead of wine," Akash said, looking frustrated.

"As we head further east," Nanook drawled, "wine will disappear and the sake will start flowing, naturally."

Despite the cheap fare, wine was served both at lunch and dinner. With a carafe sparkling like polished crystal in each hand, the waiter came around, asking the passengers if they preferred red or white. Though the food was simple, the freshly ironed tablecloths and napkins, the elegant way the wine was poured, and the well-timed appearance of soup, main course, and dessert made the meals seem high-class.

By the time Hiruko finally appeared, the waiters were already bringing our soup.

"We were talking about how Esperanto wasn't just created in a laboratory," Knut said to welcome her—in Danish, I think, but it was getting hard to tell Danish from German or English unless I really concentrated.

"language in laboratory born equals eternal infant not," said Hiruko.

Akash didn't laugh. Though he's equally fluent in English and German, for him there's still a wall between German and the Scandinavian languages.

I heard the word *soup* from somewhere far away, and watched it change into *suppe*, then *zupa*, then *sopa* as it floated above my head.

The main course was beef rolled with bacon and onions inside, with a sour cream sauce. Just as we'd all stopped talking and picked up our knives and forks, Susanoo announced, "After dinner, the boat will be stopping at Szczecin. We'll be there for less than three hours, but that should give us plenty of time to see the town."

The way he said it, as if he were our leader, got on my nerves.

"Yes, I'd say the old town is beautiful," I replied, "though I've only been there four times," then realized that it had actually been three, not four, and felt embarrassed at having added an extra visit, as if I were showing off. Putting down his fork, Knut leaned toward me, full of curiosity.

"You've been there four times?" he asked. "You'll have to show us the sights."

"The streets in the old town are lined with Hansa-style houses. Seen from the front, the roofs aren't triangular. They're sort of stacked up in blocks."

"Stacked up in blocks?"

"The roofs look like two of those old *kaidan-tansu* pushed together—one on the left side and the other on the right," Nanook explained. Hiruko looked surprised, and asked Nanook something in a language I didn't understand—probably her native language, which Nanook studied by himself. He nodded to her, then turned back to me. "A *kaidan-tansu* is a kind of chest from the Edo period, shaped like a staircase. Once they had the staircase, they wanted to use the spaces below the steps as drawers, so they came up with this really unique piece of furniture."

"Nanook," said Knut, sounding a little envious, but teasing at the same time, "how do you know about furniture from Hiruko's country that was used such a long time ago?"

"I found an English book about furniture of the Edo period at a flea market. It didn't cost much, so I bought it and read it in my spare time. You're right—it was a long time ago, but even if there're none of those old chests left, a book somebody happened to write about them won't disappear so easily."

As I sat there looking at Nanook, I completely forgot that I was supposed to tell Knut about Szczecin.

I thought Susanoo might be dejected, because I'd told the others about Szczecin, and Nanook had explained what a *kaidan-tansu* is before he had the chance to, but he wasn't.

"Listen everyone," he said, still talking like our leader, "you mustn't be late. Be sure to be back on board fifteen minutes before we set sail again." It wasn't arrogance, exactly—more a sense that he felt solely responsible for making sure we reached our destination, which seemed kind of creepy.

"Today's dessert is paczki," the waiter said as he passed the plates out. A filled doughnut, like what we call a Berliner or a Krapfen. When dessert comes, we all retreat into our own worlds. The group sitting around the table comes undone, then dissolves. Consuming his paczki in three bites, Nanook wiped his mouth with his napkin and made his escape. Susanoo stared silently down at the fried doughnut on his plate, not even picking up his dessert fork. Akash took a single bite before turning around to chatter away in English with his new Indian friends at the Jupiter table. Knut and Hiruko glanced at each other between bites.

As if drawn toward the door to the kitchen I stood up as soon as I'd finished my paczki, wiping my hands as I headed that way. The aluminum swinging door waiters were always rushing in and out of seemed very light. Just as I was about to go through, a waiter with a tray under his arm emerged, looking straight ahead, on his way to clear the Mercury table, where everyone had already left. The people who sat there didn't speak, so they always finished first. At our table, Hiruko and Knut were staring into each other's eyes, having what looked like a romantic tête-à-tête. Acting like lovers, but probably talking about something linguistic, like adjectives.

Beyond the swinging door was a straight, narrow corridor. Passengers were not supposed to be here. If someone saw me, I'd tell them I was going to meet Chen, a friend of mine who worked in the kitchen. I actually had a colleague by that name once, a woman from Hong Kong who told me she'd worked on a luxury liner when she was young. This mail boat certainly wasn't a luxury liner, and Chen had vowed never to work on a ship again, but lies are easier to tell when they have a smidgen of truth mixed in.

On the left-hand side of the corridor, about halfway down, was a cubbyhole too small to be called a room, where there was a stack of plastic crates, the kind that hold a dozen bottles of beer, about six feet tall. The young man working there looked up at me. He was around twenty or so, and reminded me of a Senegalese singer I like. Not sure what to say, he opened his mouth and an Ä with a distinctively German ring to it came out, so I spoke to him in my native language.

"What are you doing?" I asked.

"I'm pouring out the wine," he answered in fluent German, then picked up a cardboard box and deftly sliced off a corner with a knife he had in his other hand. He then tilted the box to let the red wine splash into the bucket at his feet. "Bottles are heavy," he went on. "It's important for the food and drink on a ship be as light as possible. That's why we choose boxed wine. Boxes wouldn't look very classy in the dining room, though, so I empty the wine into buckets and take them to the kitchen, where it's poured it into carafes. The carafes are polished to look like crystal, and the waiters take them around from table to table, filling the guests' glasses."

He closed his eyes as he talked, apparently imagining elegant meals in the dining hall. In the blue bucket, the red wine looked like dirty water. He opened his eyes again and picked up the next box.

"Are you from Pfalz, too?" he asked. "Our new manager, perhaps?" His speech had a lilt to it, as if he were humming.

But he wasn't from Senegal after all. Born in the Palatine region of Germany, he'd felt friendly toward me, mistakenly thinking I might also be from there, and imagining, furthermore, that I might be his new manager. I was afraid I'd be chased out if I told him honestly that I'd just wandered in here out of curiosity, so I decided to keep things vague.

"Something like that. My name's Nora, and I live in Trier. Do you do this kind of work every day?"

"For now, anyway," he replied as he cut another box to pour

into the bucket. "I'm hoping they'll give me something more interesting to do next week. My dream is to manage a big hotel someday." He gently laughed.

He didn't look as if he'd grown up in hardship, but he must have been awfully patient to keep doing such boring work without a word of complaint.

"Good luck," I said. "I hope your dream comes true." I left him, feeling bad.

To the right a little further on was a staircase leading to the floor below. Carefully, I went down it. A musty, metallic odor hung in the air. In the gloomy fluorescent light of a room without windows, about ten huge washing machines were running at the highest speed. The noise surrounded my head like a helmet I couldn't take off. To one side baskets full of white cloth were piled up as high as the ceiling, and way in the back I saw what looked like a giant loom. Something big like a tablecloth could probably be put through it, and come out wrinkle-free on the other side. Next to a workbench was a huge pile of folded tablecloths, and the little man sitting on the stool beside it looked very tired.

"These washing machines are very big, aren't they?" I yelled in English, loud enough for him to hear over the noise. The man nodded with a friendly smile. Assuming he'd understood me, I added, "Is the waste water poured into the sea?"

When he answered, "Hanoi," I knew he hadn't grasped what I'd asked, but that didn't necessarily mean we couldn't have a conversation. After all, he'd just told me he was from Vietnam.

"These are tablecloths?" I asked.

He nodded.

"Do you think washing all these tablecloths in detergent, then pouring the dirty water into the ocean is the right thing to do? I think we can all manage without tablecloths." Forgetting that he couldn't understand English, I said what I'd wanted to say.

The man nodded enthusiastically. His shoulders then dropped, and, putting his hands together like a pillow, he rested his head to mime sleeping. Perhaps he was trying to tell me how sleepy he was, because he had to work such long hard hours.

"I understand," I said. "You have a rough time. How many hours do you work a day?"

The man put up one finger, but I couldn't believe he meant only one hour. He must have been asking me to wait a minute, because he then stood up, ran to the last washing machine at the back of the room, pulled a brown shoulder bag from behind it, and got out a photograph, which he brought to show me.

"Hansa Market in Hanoi," he said. But why would there be a Hansa Market so far away, in Vietnam? If Hanoi was part of the Hanseatic League, did it also have a port on the Baltic Sea? It could be that Asia was really quite close, and we'd been traveling all this time without noticing it. I looked at the picture. Brightly colored cloth and trinkets hung from stalls on both sides, while a woman, her back to the photographer, rode a small motorbike down the narrow path between.

I turned the picture over, and saw *Hang Da Market* written on the back. So that's it—what had sounded to me like "Hansa Market" was probably the name of a real market in Hanoi, I was thinking when the man reached out and pointed first to the numbers written below Hang Da Market in ballpoint pen, and then to his own chest. His phone number, perhaps. He spread out both palms facing up to show me he was giving me the photograph as a present, so taking it with me, I thanked him and left the laundry room.

CHAPTER 5   *Hiruko Speaks (2)*

Knut's hand was thick and fleshy. It covered mine like a warm blanket, whispering, "Everything's fine. You can stay here. There's no need to go anywhere." But where was "here"? Since leaving Szczecin, we'd been sailing along the coast of Poland, heading for Gdansk. We went slowly, but never stopped, even for a second. "Here" kept shifting, little by little.

Last night, Knut and I stayed behind after dessert. Everyone else left right away, as if they'd suddenly remembered something they had to do. But what could that be on a mail boat? Do human beings have pressing duties no matter where they are? I didn't want to do anything except talk to Knut. He seemed pretty free himself. Free, but not bored.

Long sea voyages are supposed to be for wealthy retirees, while the young get so bored they're yawning before they have time to get seasick. On a luxury passenger liner we'd probably be in the jewelry store picking out rings, or thinking about what to wear at banquets and concerts, or taking yoga classes for our health, or listening to lectures on the Hanseatic League or the Teutonic Knights. But this boat didn't have anything like that. The sky and sea showed us blue, white, and gray patterns, mixing them together for us while we chatted in the on-deck theater, but there were no other onboard activities. Maybe that's why meals were such a big event. Our eyes were drawn to the purplish tinge on red cabbage leaves, and the perfect roundness of green peas, as if they were works of art in a museum, and the rhythms of the other passengers' languages flowed into our ears like modern music, or old folk songs sometimes.

Tonight's dessert was not paczki, but slices of canned pineapple with fresh cream.

"What does this pineapple slice look like to you?" asked Knut as he carefully cut his into four pieces with his dessert fork. "This is a psychological test. Try to come up with five things before I finish counting to ten." He then slowly started to count. I said whatever came to mind.

"halo during solar eclipse, wedding ring, life preserver, wall that medieval city surrounds, doughnut."

"An interesting list," he laughed.

"psychoanalysis result?"

"You're thinking of marriage, but you're afraid of drowning so you're looking for a life preserver. Sightseeing in Gdansk, which you're looking forward to, reminds you of city walls. And you remembered the doughnut we had for dessert last night. These last two suggest that you have sweet, happy things in mind. But deep down, you can't shake off thoughts of a solar eclipse, an image of the end of the world."

"solar eclipse equals end of the world not."

"That's true, but no other spectacle makes us imagine it so vividly."

Knut said we'd had doughnuts for dessert—what could that mean? I didn't remember eating a doughnut. But then I realized he must be talking about the paczki we'd had. I'd always thought of a doughnut as something with a hole in the center, like the ones I'd had as a child, quite different from that round, deep-fried bread covered with sugar.

"doughnut even without hole?"

"Is having a hole a condition for qualifying as a doughnut?"

"doughnut equals thing with hole."

"That makes pineapples doughnuts, too."

"captivated by holes."

"Why?"

"without hole the other side i see not."

"What you say is always inspiring. So, what kind of world do you see on the other side? Utopia?"

"taiwan, the philippines, thailand."

"Countries that export pineapples. Taiwan's near your homeland, isn't it? Can we find the country we're looking for by going through the hole in a pineapple slice?"

"very small hole. impossible through to go."

"You mean you'd be able to, but not me. I've been putting on weight lately."

"body can go through not, to the other side can see. looking only. same as holes in lotus root."

"Does lotus have roots? I thought it was just floating on the water, like duckweed."

"many holes in lotus root. through holes bright future can see. for good result, night before exam we eat."

"You mean you eat the roots of that plant the Buddha uses as a cushion? Instead of paying your respects to Buddha's seat, you *eat* it?"

"respects we pay. also eat."

"Claude Monet did over two hundred water lily paintings. That shows how much he loved ukiyo-e, but you just ignore that, and eat the roots?"

"love we ignore not, but holes we eat. along with roots."

Knut laughed. "Have you ever thought of the pronoun 'you' as a hole?" he asked.

"hole?"

"The referent of 'you' is interchangeable. Which means it's empty. I can use it for Akash, or for Nora. 'You' can be anybody. But when I'm talking to *you* specifically, it seems strange that the word *you* could refer to someone else."

"third person we can use. in native tongue, by second-person pronoun i was called not, by name i was called. after school today, hiruko will what do? my friends always asked. my mother also."

"So, no one said, 'What are *you* going to do after school today?'"

"third person—hiruko—always used."

"And how did that feel?"

"friendly, warm, close."

"Why?"

"when 'i' or 'you' hear, coldness, distance feel. my name hear, to my heart straight comes."

"Really?"

"in childhood, myself always hiruko called. first person 'i' not, third person hiruko always. world without 'i' or 'you.'"

Knut's face crinkled up with silent laughter.

"There's something to that," he said. "I've heard that when I was little, I used to refer to myself in the third person, too. Not 'I'm hungry,' but 'Knut's hungry,' or 'Knut wants to go outside and play.' Sounds awfully childish now."

"cute."

"My mother used to talk to me in the third person, too. She'd say stuff like, 'Knut shouldn't eat too much candy before dinner,' or 'Knut's going to take a bath now.' She used the third person to control me."

"cute."

"There's nothing cute about it. It was a violation of my human rights. She used the third person to force me to do what she wanted."

"child equals bundle of desire. whole box of cookies eats, dinner eats not. with mud on face plays, bath takes not."

"I was that kind of kid, all right," he said, laughing. "Even so, I always wanted her to use the first and second person. '*I* want *you* to eat a good dinner, which is why *I* don't want *you* to eat too many sweets beforehand.' That's how I wanted her to talk."

"in that case, your answer?"

"I probably would have said something like, '*You* are entitled to your opinion, but *I*'ll do what *I* like.'"

"so, whole box of cookies ate, dinner ate not? with mud on your face played, without bath taking to bed went?"

"Maybe so."

"children's rights equal to eat too many sweets not."

Knut laughed again. "You have a point. Human rights are different from doing whatever you want. Children have a right to go to school, but not to eat as much candy as they want. I guess that means that human rights are what someone other than yourself decides is fitting and proper, then forces on you."

"contents of rights equals desire not. if humankind only third person used, egoists might disappear, world a better place might become."

"I'm afraid not," Knut said. "Desire is something the first person forces on the second person. If people got rid of all their first-person-singular desires, they wouldn't be human anymore."

"the world grammar has not. first-person singular has not. human beings equal part of that world."

"That's your first-person singular talking."

I never get bored talking to Knut. When we're all sitting around the table at dinner, I go out of my way to talk to everyone else as well, but when dessert comes and we all retreat into our own worlds, I can relax and talk only with him.

Akash sounded excited, talking with his countrymen at the Jupiter table. Although I couldn't follow their conversation, I caught words, like Russia, India, and weapons.

Susanoo, staring vacantly around the table, suddenly announced, "As you're all aware, our next stop is Gdansk. A town worth seeing, I believe, but make sure you know how long we'll be stopping at the port before you leave the ship."

And then, everyone got up and went their separate ways.

Hoping for a second helping of dessert, Nanook sidled up to a timid-looking waiter. Nora disappeared through the door to the kitchen without touching hers. I remembered how restless she'd seemed when dessert was served the night before, how she'd stood up like a sleepwalker and headed for that same door. The next time I looked over in that direction she was gone, so she must have slipped into the world beyond.

"Nora's fallen in love with the cook," Knut said, as if trying to read my thoughts, "and has gone to meet him on the sly." I stared at him, unable to believe what I'd heard. I could imagine Nora and the cook discussing organic vegetables, but a rendezvous in the kitchen? And what sort of man was the cook, anyway? When I tried to picture a face under that tall, white hat, I saw Nanook.

"in nanook only is nora interested."

"You think so? She may have fallen in love with Nanook when she first met him in Trier, but she's probably over that by this time."

"because nanook a different person became? with that doctor his personality exchanged?"

"I don't think he's really a different person. He's matured."

"even if contents changed, nora nanook only sees."

"You mean she loves his appearance, and not what's inside of him?"

"different. nanook she first met equals original. now his way he lost. but if he to nora returns, original will reappear. nora believes."

"In other words, Nora's fallen into a common misunderstanding."

I noticed the headwaiter, standing near us as if he was anxious to clear the table. Leaving what was around it, I ate only the hole in my pineapple slice and stood up. Knut then asked me two questions in rapid succession.

"Do you mind if I eat your pineapple? Can we go sightseeing in Gdansk together?"

"two questions. one answer. JA!"
"Okay, I'll pick you up at your cabin when we land."
"JA!"

Each taking one of my hands, the letters *J* and *A* started walking. Though pronounced differently from country to country, together they always encourage me with a YES that tells me it's fine to keep on walking with other people. To make the sound "ah" you have to open your mouth wide. "Um," the affirmative I used as a child, was a passive rumble deep in my throat. When someone asked, "You want to play?" I'd answer, "Um." "Want to join our team?" "Um." "Come over to my house?" "Um." "Can I hold your hand?" "Um." In a dim, distant past, all those tentative "ums" were linked together on a slender white string. The moment my plane to Scandinavia left the ground, that string was cut.

While Knut was eating my pineapple, I left the dining hall. A boat is different from a plane or train—when you go back to your cabin, it feels like you're the only one on board. In the metallic silence of the corridor, a door to my left opened, and Susanoo stuck his head out.

"You look awful limp and squishy," he said when he saw me. "Are you seasick?" Back in the dining hall he'd been barking out pronouncements in English as if he were officially in charge of us, but now he was suddenly talking in a rough, local dialect. Those words "limp and squishy" made me realize how uneasy I felt, as if my bones didn't quite meet at the joints. My feet weren't quite flat on the floor, so when the boat rolled, my kneecaps shifted, making my body sway from side to side as if I were carrying a heavy load, making it hard to stay standing up.

"*Nangee*," I said, imagining the characters 難儀. I wasn't sure I should have drawn out the "ee" sound at the end so long, but it felt good in my mouth. I thought I'd heard people add that to other words when I was little. 面倒 (*mendō*), for instance, or 憂鬱 (*yūutsu*) are so square they look like little machines, but an extra "ee" on the end (*mendōee, yūutsuee*), softens them a little. The "ee" is like a slender thread that reaches into your heart. Some people might say it's just a dialect, or a personal tic. Let them.

"What're you gonna do this afternoon?" asked Susanoo.

"I'm going sightseeing in Gdansk with Knut."

"*Ah-kyaa.*"

"Huh?"

"*Akan.* Can't."

"*Nashite?* How come?"

"Cuz yer bones ain't right."

"*Nashite?* Why?"

"Ain't you read the *Kojiki*, the Record of Ancient Matters? You're Hiruko, a shadowy excuse for a first daughter. Turned out bad—can't have babies."

"And what about you—you useless *nomeshikoki*, always smashing things up."

"Don't make me laugh."

Hearing a dry cough behind me, I turned around to see Nanook, standing about three steps away from us.

"You guys use strange words when you're talking by yourselves. I can't make them out."

"This is a battle between dialects—Fukui vs. Niigata."

"Hmm, sounds interesting. Can I get it on tape?"

"It's already over," Susanoo fired back, retreating to his cabin and shutting the door behind him. Not especially disappointed, Nanook shrugged his shoulders and looked over at me, his head tilted to one side. Though he and Knut are about the same height, Nanook is slight, with a slender neck. If Knut were to become a father someday, I'm sure he'd be like a big, shaggy bear from a children's picture book, while Nanook as he gets older will probably look more like a coyote.

"You come from Niigata, right? Does the *nii* of Niigata have the same etymological root as the Danish *ny* and the English *new*?"

I'd never even thought of that, and didn't know what to say.

"Ny-gata is close to Russia, right? If we crossed the continent all the way to the eastern edge, we'd come to your hometown first, before we reached the capital city, wouldn't we?"

"Niigata's actually pretty far away. There's a place called Tsushima that's much nearer. It's close to Pusan, a port city on the continent."

"But if you cross Siberia until you get to the eastern cities of Khabarovsk and Vladivostok, you can take a flight straight to Niigata Koku, right? I like reading travel guides, so I know how to get to lots of places I've never been to. I've seen pictures of Niigata Koku, too. But wait, it isn't *koku*—you have to draw out the vowel sounds, so it's *kōkū*. It's hard to remember which vowels are short, and which are long. *Koku* is a kind of flavor, like umami, but *kōkū* means airport, right?"

"Airport is *kūkō*, not *kōkū*. *Kū* means sky, and *kō* is port."

"That's right—I remember now. Sounds romantic, a port in the sky."

"Our boat is about to arrive at a port on the water, not in the sky—the watery port of Gdansk."

Nanook's friendly chatter could go on forever when he was on a topic that interested him. The way he got things mixed up made me laugh, and then a vision of my homeland as I'd never seen it before would start to glow on the horizon in my mind. At times like that, it seems a shame our conversation has to end.

"Fukui, where Susanoo's from, is on the Russian, rather than the American side, isn't it?"

"That's right."

Just then Akash came down the corridor.

"America vs. Russia?" he asked, apparently having overheard us. "Were you talking about the Cold War?" His dark eyes shone with curiosity.

"No, not the Cold War. The western coast of the archipelago

Hiruko's from faces Russia, while the eastern coast faces America. But that didn't happen because of the Cold War—it's been that way since the Ice Age."

"Actually, back in the Ice Age it wasn't an archipelago yet. It was still a peninsula. After that it was cut off from the continent and became a string of islands, probably due to a rise in sea levels. And if that's true, as the sea rises even higher because of global warming, the whole archipelago might sink into the Pacific Ocean someday."

"The Cold War wasn't cold at all compared to the Ice Age. But Akash, which country does the coast of India face?"

"There's no sea between India and Russia. Just a long stretch of very dry land. Pakistan, Afghanistan, Turkmenistan, Tajikistan, Kirghizstan, Uzbekistan, Kazakhstan—too many countries to count."

"How about America?"

"America is beyond England, which is behind Russia, which in turn is behind Kazakhstan, so much too far away to see."

"Maybe we could catch a train in Russia," Nanook said cheerfully, blinking, "and just keep on going east, through all those countries that end in –stan."

"No, that's not a good idea," Akash quickly replied. "After going through all those borders, you'd be a nervous wreck. It's best to pick a route with as few borders as possible." He rubbed his chin.

"There are no borders at sea," I said quietly. "So, as long as we're on this boat, we won't have to cross a single one."

"That's right," said Akash, looking at me. "It would have been best to go through the Suez Canal, then across India." He let out a lonely sigh.

"You can't go through the Suez Canal," said Nanook, putting a hand on Akash's shoulder. "Now that the Mediterranean is closed off, you can't cross it to get to the Middle East, or on to Africa, either." He looked serious. Oddly enough, I didn't remember ever talking to the others about which route we would take. That part of my memory was a total blank, and then I was suddenly on this mail boat. I wondered if that's what had happened to everyone else, too. I had a question in my mind, and this seemed like a good time to ask it.

"Even if the Suez Canal is closed off, couldn't we have sailed along the coast of Africa down to Cape Town, and gone east from there?"

Nanook and Akash immediately clammed up, probably because they didn't know why we hadn't gone that way, either. But what if they actually did know, and were afraid to say? Or maybe they didn't want to hurt my feelings? From somewhere below, the engine let out a deep groan. Akash sighed. "The seas along the African coast are closely guarded," he said, sounding a little brighter, "so you'd have to stay pretty far out. No passenger ship would take that route now. And freighters won't take on passengers, either. Being stopped by a patrol boat sure wouldn't be much fun, even if it was a mistake."

"What would patrol boats be looking for?" I asked. "Pirates?"

Nanook looked startled for a moment, as if he couldn't believe my ignorance. Then, his expression softening, he explained. "They're watching for ships from the forces trying to keep a United States of Africa from forming."

"What forces?"

"The military of country A, who believe that the movement didn't spring up naturally, from within the continent, but was instigated by country C, who are actually pulling the strings."

"Even if we're not spies from country A," said Akash, looking worried, "from Africa's point of view, we'd definitely be outsiders. So, it's best to stay away from the coast." He looked over at me. "What do you think?"

I knew nothing about international politics, so I blurted out the first thought that came to me: "Africa doesn't belong to our private UN." By that I meant Knut, Nanook, Akash, Nora, Susanoo, and me.

"You're right about that," Akash agreed. When he was talking about a dark subject, his voice deepened, making him sound more like a man.

"There's nothing we can do," said Nanook apologetically. "We're only a small group of people who happen to live in Europe—a subsubsubcommittee, you might say, or a tiny cell. As long as Africa is closed off, the only bridge left to us is Russia. Why don't we cross Siberia and charter a small plane, so we can rediscover your lost archipelago from the air?"

"The minute you first catch sight of islands from a plane is so exciting," said Akash, cheerful once again. "If you're up high enough, you can even see the curve of the earth—our earth, covered by blue water, interrupted by a string of commas and periods, which are the archipelago." Listening to Akash, I felt excited, yet uneasy...

I saw an expanse of blue with Sado Island floating in it, shaped like a Z, the last letter in the alphabet. As we got closer a lush green broccoli forest rose up, and I could make out countless gleaming triangular waves between Sado and the main island. Shifting my eyes from the sea to the Shinano River, I scanned the buildings lined up like match boxes on either side, searching frantically for one that looked familiar. Then the runway appeared, and even though we hadn't landed yet I was already feeling the rough surface of the tarmac under my shoes when the air pressure suddenly dropped—my ears hurt and then the landing gear screeched, scorching the pavement. I was thrown forward but, somehow managing to keep my torso upright, I kept my eyes on the dull airport scenes unfolding beside the plane, looking for something, anything, that would take me back to the life I once knew. As I desperately hunted for evidence showing how special this place was to me, I suddenly realized that Knut, who should have been beside me, had disappeared, along with Akash and Nora, who were supposed to be in the seats in front, and that Nanook wasn't sitting across the aisle, either. I felt the blood drain from my face. Having returned to my country, I had lost everything. Then I woke up from my daydream.

I was sitting on the bed in my cabin. I couldn't remember how I'd gotten there.

I didn't want to return to the country where I was born. Or to forget about it, either. I just wanted to find out what had happened to it. My country, my *kuni*. In my mind, 国 slowly dissolved into くに. I wanted to go to that くに with this group of friends. When we arrived, this *kuni* of mine would not be lost in nostalgia, but transformed into an unfathomable mystery.

My mind wandered off to Eastern Siberia and beyond, but a knock on the door brought it back into my body. I turned the knob, pulled, and ran smack into the wall of Knut's chest. He's so much taller than me that if I stand too close, his face is so far up I can't see it. I took a step backward and there he was, all suntanned. The patches on his cheeks that had been red under the bright sun on deck were now turning brown. Maybe the skin at the corners of his eyes had hardened, because the wrinkles there looked shiny.

"Ready to go?"

"ready."

"Is there something on my face?"

"side-by-side preferable to face-to-face for us."

"What do you mean?"

"explanation later will come. now we go."

When we left the ship, we were surrounded by taxi drivers speaking English, asking if we wanted a hotel or to tour the old city.

"We don't have much time," Knut said quietly, "so let's take a taxi to the fort." He then turned to a taxi driver with a scraggly mustache and a hunting cap on his head, and started negotiating the fare in English. Leaving Knut to haggle, I breathed in the sea air.

A faint odor of cigarette smoke hung in the air. A nostalgic sort of smell. When we were settled in the back seat, the car slid into the traffic, and Knut turned to me.

"Was there a fort in your hometown?" he asked. A question I wasn't expecting.

"no."

"Was there a wall around it?"

"no."

"But didn't big countries ever try to attack you? China, for instance."

"china attacked not."

"How about Mongolia?"

"mongols twice came. but mongols poor swimmers were, afraid of drowning, never again came."

"So, the ocean itself was a sort of wall to keep people out. What about borders between towns?"

"border with yamagata equals mountains. border with gunma equals mikuni tunnel."

"So, mountains and tunnels… Kind of hard to see the outline."

I had never once looked for the outline of my homeland. Since I'm not a bird, I can't see the area where I live from the air. Human beings have to walk on their own two legs, so they see only what's in front of them. They can gaze up at tall buildings, or at cliffs along the shore, or stop in at the souvenir shops that line the port, but they can't check the shape of the country where they live from above. If they're planning a trip, they may look at a map of the city they'll visit, but if they're already living in a place, they usually don't bother.

"So, when you imagine the place where you grew up," Knut persisted, "what shape does it have?" That reminded me of a funny T-shirt I bought when I was in high school, just before I left with some friends for an overnight trip to Iwate. There was a picture of a dinosaur in the shape of Niigata Prefecture across the front, the bright green of young rice plants, running on its hind legs.

"the shape of niigata prefecture equals the shape of dinosaur on hind legs running."

Knut laughed, showing his straight, white teeth. "So, the dinosaur is running across the Pacific Ocean. Which way's it going?"

"on the map, to the right."

"East, then. So no matter how far eastward we go the dinosaur will be running away from us—we may never catch him."

Today I'd talked to both Knut and Nanook about my home prefecture. I'd hardly even mentioned it while living abroad, since so few people around me knew the names of individual prefectures. There's a funny story about a man from Shiga Prefecture who lived in Riga for over forty years—so long that he was completely at home there. When a scholar of Japanese literature from Moscow asked him which prefecture he was from, he said Riga, rather than Shiga, quite naturally. When I was a child, which prefecture a person came from was so important that we even used the special word "extraprefectural." The man next door, a Mr. Honma, was always moaning about his daughter's "extraprefectural marriage" as though it was the greatest tragedy of his life. Thinking he'd said "extraterrestrial marriage," I imagined the daughter boarding a spaceship, traveling way outside the earth's atmosphere, which seemed kind of scary. I realized my mistake when I heard that she was actually living in the city of Aizu-Wakamatsu, which was in a different prefecture. But since you could get there by car in about an hour and a half, why was her father so upset? This seemed very strange to me at the time, so I asked my teacher if the prefectural border was like the pictures of the Berlin Wall in our history textbook, guarded by soldiers with guns.

"No, not at all," she laughed. "Anyone can freely cross the

border between prefectures." Then, suddenly looking sad, she added, "But in each prefecture's past, there are heavy burdens, as well as lighter ones." Around that time, the school bullies had beaten up a new boy from a nearby prefecture.

After I was accepted at a Scandinavian university, I overheard my mother talking on the phone. "My daughter's going to study overseas," she said, and I remember thinking, that's right, I'm crossing an ocean. Yet even though Scandinavia was much farther away, it somehow didn't feel as sad as an extraprefectural journey.

"That's the Weichselmünde Fortress." Knut's voice sounded higher than usual. He then turned to pay the taxi driver, adding "We'd like you to take us into town when we're done here." I got out of the taxi. The fort had a huge stone gate, and a round, gray tower, the kind you see in picture-book castles. We walked through the gate into the grounds, and saw buildings that looked like Hansa merchant houses, with roofs the color of red salmon, clustered around a circular wall with the tower looming above. Somewhere beyond was the ocean, though I couldn't see it.

I'd heard that forts were tall and imposing, built to watch for enemy invaders from the sea, but the Weichselmünde Fortress, peacefully absorbing the sun's rays, looked as if it had never heard the word "war." Everything was perfectly calm.

"similarity to picture book towers."

"Yeah, you wouldn't be surprised if a princess stuck her head out and waved." No sooner had Knut said this than a cute little blonde girl looked out from the second floor.

"Papa!" she called, waving. Did a princess actually live in there? Startled, I heard footsteps behind me, kicking up gravel. It was our taxi driver. Between gasps, he shouted up to his daughter. Perhaps he was scolding her for climbing up so high, telling her to come down at once. He was speaking Polish, which I can't understand. but he didn't sound too angry. This probably wasn't the first time she'd surprised him from inside the tower.

The taxi driver ran around to the back, then soon returned with his little blonde princess and a smaller brown-haired boy with a toy drum, a replica of the ones in military marching bands, strapped to his tummy.

"I'm awfully sorry. My children are always wanting to climb up the tower." Like many taxi drivers, he seemed used to speaking English.

"I'd like to climb up there, too," said Knut. "Where can we buy tickets?"

"I'm afraid it's off limits to the public. It isn't safe."

The girl stared at my face as if she'd never seen anything quite like it, making me uncomfortable.

"Are these your daughter and son?" I asked her father.

"I'm his daughter," the girl answered in English before he had the chance, "and this is my brother Oskar."

"You speak English very well for someone so young," said Knut, squatting down to her level.

"I'm going to be Queen Elizabeth," she answered, "so I'm studying English now."

Tired of hearing this, perhaps, her father didn't react, turning instead to us.

"That tower used to be a lighthouse," he explained.

"Wonderful," said Knut enthusiastically. "I love lighthouses—they're so peaceful. They're not there to sink ships, but to guide them safely into the harbor."

"This one wasn't so peaceful," replied the taxi driver with a rueful smile. "Sweden, Russia, Saxony—we've battled so many enemies from this fort. Speaking of which, are you by any chance Swedish?"

"No, Danish."

"And your wife?"

"I'm from Greenland," I answered, trying not to laugh. Switching countries with Nanook seemed like fun. It was much easier to imagine myself as a native of Greenland than as a wife. Startled, Knut blinked furiously, but the taxi driver looked so serious that my little joke about being Knut's Greenlander wife immediately lost its bite.

"This fortress is a symbol of our homeland," said the taxi driver. "Of course, not all our enemies attacked from the sea. Some came from inland, pretending to be peaceful citizens, and gradually increased their numbers until they finally took over."

"Are all foreigners enemies?" I asked indignantly, wondering if he saw me as an enemy, too. The taxi driver ignored my question.

"Protecting the homeland is a difficult task. Nevertheless, it must be done."

"If all Europe was at peace," Knut said gently, "you wouldn't have to worry. That's the fastest way to safety."

"But can you guarantee that what's good for Europe will be good for our country?" asked the taxi driver sharply, glaring at Knut.

"More than what's good for Europe, or for your own country," Knut replied, "isn't what's good for ordinary people most important?"

"'The people' is an abstract concept I can't believe in. What I really feel in my heart is my homeland." Before he could go on, the little boy cut him off, beating on his tin drum as he screamed in a voice so shrill it almost split our eardrums. Flinching as if I'd been doused with cold water, I watched the taxi driver scold his son, roughly yanking his ear, while Knut put a hand on his shoulder to stop him. I'd never imagined a toy drum less than a foot across could make enough noise to rattle a fortress. I examined the pattern of red and white triangles on the drum, wondering where I'd seen it before.

"It's his job to warn everyone by beating on his drum!" the girl cried, appealing her brother's case. So, this boy, who'd started drumming the moment he heard his father say *homeland* might be a messenger, sent to warn us adults. And his sister was a miniature diplomat, valiantly fighting for peace. The taxi driver shook his head.

"This boy will never grow up," he sighed as if he'd given up on his children. "All he can do is scream and make noise. And this girl of mine always takes his side."

"But maybe we should thank them," I said, wanting to stick up for them. "They're warning us that the whole idea of 'homeland' can be dangerous."

"What's wrong with loving your homeland?" Disgruntled, the taxi driver raised his eyebrows and stared down at me.

"Keep thinking your homeland is always right, and that everyone around you is an enemy, and someday it will dissolve and disappear."

I myself had no idea why I'd said that. The taxi driver looked at me for several seconds with his mouth hanging open, then quickly checked his watch.

"Shall we go back to the old town?" he asked. "Do you mind if the children ride with us?"

Knut, who's much bigger than me, sat in the front next to the driver, while I climbed into the back with the children. The boy smelled like a mixture of sand and milk. Just a moment before he'd been screaming, but now he was perfectly quiet, sitting stiffly in the seat, clutching his drumsticks. His face seemed to say, "It's no good talking to me, you can't convince me of anything." He would probably never mature. He refused to absorb the worldview of the grownups around him and would probably never become one himself. He would stay as he was, beating his drum, letting out his high-pitched shrieks. When the world was at peace, and there was no longer any need for his warnings, he might begin to think about growing up.

CHAPTER 6   *Nanook Speaks*

That was definitely my name. But the handwriting was so bad—like nails scattered across the page—that it took a while to make it out. Below it was a message from Captain Doeff, in English and Russian:

> I beg permission from the Mayor of Kaliningrad for the above-named person, a passenger on my ship the Baltic Light, to see the sights of your fair city for one day.

To the right was the captain's photograph, grinning and holding up two fingers, making the peace sign. The whole thing looked like a joke—would immigration really accept this flimsy pamphlet as a visa? The woman who'd asked me if I wanted to go sightseeing in Kaliningrad the day before had brought it to my cabin. So, without even knowing what country I was a citizen of, simply because I was a passenger on his ship, Captain Doeff was saying I should be allowed to go ashore, and that he'd take full responsibility for me while I was there. I ran into Akash in the corridor, and I asked him what he thought.

"If the ship's captain takes responsibility for his passengers as an individual, any one of them can enter the country, regardless of citizenship? Unbelievable. Still, it would be nice if that's how things were in the future." His nostrils widening, he took a deep breath. "It might be a diplomatic trick."

"What do you mean by that?"

"Kaliningrad is eager to have relations with foreign countries. But the Russian government would rather they not. Being an exclave, Kaliningrad is pretty free, because it's hard to keep under surveillance, yet if they go too far, Russia will crack down on them. Since this fake visa of yours doesn't have a Russian immigration stamp on it, if the government accuses Kaliningrad of letting too many foreigners in, they can blame it on the ship's captain, and claim that he petitioned them as an individual."

"Does that mean I'll be entering the country illegally? Can they arrest me?"

"No, with this personal request from the captain, it's not illegal, and city officials aren't obligated to arrest you. Besides, they really don't want to. In fact, they'd really like to welcome you in, but officially, they can't. This visa is a trick to help them out of this dilemma."

"Sounds like a dangerous gray zone."

"Not especially. What's really gray right now is the weather."

Soon after I'd left Akash, I met Susanoo.

"Be careful of thieves and other criminals," he said sharply when I'd told him I'd be going ashore. I wasn't worried at all, but just to make sure, I asked, "Is there a lot of crime in Kaliningrad?"

"There aren't many foreigners around now, so you'll stand out. What if you're rushed to the hospital with an injury? Be careful."

"I hadn't realized you were so worried about our safety."

"All I think about, all day long, is making sure you guys get to your destination."

For some reason, Susanoo always acts like our leader. I wonder if he thinks he's starring in a play with us. Since I don't have the script, it's like I'm standing on the stage blindfolded. Susanoo has the role of our commanding officer., responsible for making sure we get to wherever we're going, but is he the only one who knows where that is?

If we're in a play, the main character would be Hiruko, rather than Susanoo. If not for her, we wouldn't have started out on this trip in the first place. A drama about the journey of a woman in search of her homeland, rumored to have disappeared. With this plot, it should be a tragedy, but Hiruko seems pretty carefree lately. "I don't really need a homeland as long as I can keep traveling with this group of friends," she says—hardly lines for a tragic heroine. She'll have to stand on deck, crying when she sees the ocean where her homeland vanished, or fall down weeping tears of joy as she kisses the earth of the home she thought she'd lost, so she's got to try a little harder. None of the rest of us will have a chance to act out scenes like that, and besides, our personalities don't suit the role. Rather than accepting a tragic fate, Nora would use her logic to fight it, while Akash, bathed in the light of each passing day, would take in both good luck and misfortune like the weather. Knut, who has no ambition, would be even harder to make into a hero. He has no ideal he's struggling to reach, or any particular goals in life. Since his father's disappeared, maybe he's had nothing to fight against. Then again, he might be playing dead, curled up like an opossum so he won't have to deal with his overprotective mother—either way, he seems determined not to be heroic. Yet he doesn't shut himself up in his room playing computer games all day, either. "I've got nothing else to do," he says to himself, "so why not go traveling with this woman I like?" which seems to me like a pretty cool way to live. Of course, it's upsetting at the same time, because compared to Knut, the way I'm always escaping from Nora's clutches is definitely uncool.

When I first met Nora in the Kaiserthermen, the Roman Imperial baths in Trier, I was glad to have a woman who'd bandage up my sprained ankle, but then somehow we lost our balance, fell into each other's arms, and were swept away on the muddy river of sex. I'm usually pretty shy, so I hesitate before moving in, and if the girl slowly comes closer, and we gradually get together, it feels good in the end, but with Nora, all of a sudden we were one, and there I was, desperately thrashing around, unable to think of anything but getting away.

Nora loves European history, so she's probably looking forward to a full day of sightseeing in Kaliningrad. And I'm sure she's secretly hoping I'll be at her side. If I didn't get off the boat and into the streets fast, she'd catch me. I took a big step forward and hit my head on a metal pipe that twisted like a huge snake as it ran down from the ceiling to the floor. A whole networks of pipes, some big and fat, others skinny, lined the wall of the narrow corridor. What they were for, I had no idea.

"Are you all right?" asked Akash from behind. "What's the rush?"

"Have you seen Nora?"

"She said she was going back to her cabin, to get ready for sightseeing."

"That's good."

"You aren't trying to avoid her, by any chance?" he asked. I heard laughter in his voice.

"Of course not. I just want to see the town by myself, without anyone butting in."

"Oh, I see. Have a good time, then."

"Aren't you getting off?"

"Russian society draws clear distinctions between men and women, which worries me a little. The women are all in skirts and high heels, and the guys wear shirts that show off their muscles. Men don't grow their hair long here, and of course they don't wear skirts. Someone like me would really stick out."

"But the president said they protect minorities."

"That's a joke."

"He said in an interview that by making it illegal for people of the same sex to kiss in public, he was protecting them from violent attacks by antigay gangs."

"Should I be grateful for his concern? On the contrary, doesn't that show that there's a good chance I'd be beaten up?"

"Why?"

"I was born a man, but am relocating to the opposite sex. Some might see that as an affront to masculinity."

"So, you're just going to stay on board the whole time?"

"A few hours lying on my bunk reading won't be so bad. But I envy you. You're so brave."

"Not really. There's plenty of things I'm afraid of."

To Akash, I might seem like a fearless young man who can go anywhere, anytime he pleases. Here I was, about to walk the streets alone in my white sweater. The light glinting off the ends of the strands of wool was the sun's tears. Pure white, that would never be stained red with blood. Was I really a bold, reckless youth who never flinched in the face of danger? Absolutely not, as I knew too well. I couldn't even take off this sweater, even though I could hardly stand its itchiness around my neck. If I stopped now, Nora would come running over and ask me to go sightseeing with her. And coward that I am, I'd cringe and run away like a rabbit. This sweater was actually a gift from Nora. Rabbit man in a white sweater, like the Inaba rabbit from Japanese myth. That didn't necessarily mean I saw Nora as a crocodile, but whispering *usagi* (rabbit) *wani* (crocodile) over and over again in Hiruko's language, I felt a chuckle coming on, and my tension disappeared.

I remember how I laughed when I first learned the word *usagi*. Being interested in criminal terminology, I already knew the word *sagi*, which means "swindler," and figured *sagi* with a *u* in front of it must be a variation. After all, the White Rabbit of Inaba who appears in the Record of Ancient Matters plays a trick on a bunch of crocodiles. Words in Hiruko's language usually don't sound at all like what they mean, but occasionally sound and meaning will be almost too close. The way *sagi* rolls off the tongue doesn't seem the least bit tricky, while *wani* sounds a lot like *wana*, the word for "trap." In the story about the White Rabbit of Inaba, those jagged teeth that line the crocodile's jaw clamp down on the rabbit's leg, just like a trap.

I got off the boat and walked along the pier, where I saw a huge gray warship looming over me like a fortress. I was standing there looking up at it when Hiruko came over.

"Nanook," she said, "are you going to see the town by yourself?"

When we're alone, we speak in her native language. There's nothing I enjoy more. Susanoo doesn't want to have much to do with me, but Hiruko is always happy to chat.

"I am going to see the town alone," I said. "He who chases two rabbits catches not even one."

Hiruko looked surprised. "What does that proverb have to do with sightseeing?" she asked.

"If I go with a woman, that makes two rabbits. But without her, only one. A single rabbit is enough for me."

I thought what I'd said was perfect—I'd used the right counting word, the one for the "small animals" category, which is *hiki*, and I'd even remembered the orthographic changes you have to make, so that one rabbit is *ippiki*, while two is *ni-hiki*, but Hiruko laughed like rain sprinkling down on the pavement.

"You really like proverbs, don't you?" she said. "But Nanook, for rabbits you use the counter for birds, so it's *ichi-wa, ni-wa*, not *ippiki, ni-hiki*."

"Rabbits are not birds," I said angrily.

"They are grammatically."

"Why's that?"

"Because their long ears look like wings, maybe."

"I see."

"But some say it's because of a priest who thought it might be okay to eat a bird now and then, even though Buddhists aren't allowed to eat four-legged animals. And since he really liked rabbit meat, too, he convinced himself that rabbits were birds by using the same counter for both."

"Ah, he told a lie to keep up appearances, so he could eat rabbit without a guilty conscience, and when people followed his example, the lie became part of your culture."

"Are you saying we're all liars?"

"Not necessarily, but no matter which counting word you use, rabbits will never be birds."

"That's true," Hiruko said, "We shouldn't mix animals up that way."

She looked upset, as if that wayward priest has set her whole culture on the path to destruction, so I decided to change the subject.

"What's the counting word for warships?" I asked.

"Ships are complicated. For oil tankers you use 隻 (*seki*), but it's 艘 (*sō*) for a boat like the one we're on, and 艇 (*tei*) for sailboats." Looking down, she drew the Chinese characters for me with her shoe, which didn't leave a mark on the pavement, and besides, the characters were pretty complex, so I couldn't really tell what they looked like. Then, slowly raising her head, she saw that creepy-looking gray warship.

"The counter for this one might be *kan*," she said, not sounding very sure of herself.

"Is that the same *kan* as in the expression that means 'this is the end'?"

"You really know your old sayings! I'd completely forgotten about that one."

"Are you going to see the town with Knut?"

Sometimes when I speak Hiruko's language, I feel myself getting closer to the rhythm of Panska, her homemade language. That might be an interesting research topic for Knut: "Similarities and Differences Between Self-Taught and Homemade Languages." Sounds pretty cool.

A gust of wind blew Hiruko's hair up. She patted it down with both hands.

"That's what I was planning," she said. "Knut was supposed

to meet me here—I wonder what he's doing. Think I'll go to his cabin and see."

I was left in the shadow of the warship. I envy Knut, being able to talk to Hiruko anytime. When I'm with her, we can turn even a monster like this into wordplay and laugh it off, but alone, I felt like it was about to crush me. It made me so mad, I decided to tell it off in English.

"Hey, Dreadnought, I wanna spit on you. Your color, your shape—I hate everything about you. Pleased with yourself, are you, all decked out like a killing machine? You could've picked a cuter design—a pink body, say, covered with flowers and smiley faces. Your enemies would get all warm and fuzzy inside and then, when they're least expecting it, BAM! —you fire your cannons at them. You'd win the battle for sure. Why didn't you think of that, asshole? And what are you doing, sleeping in port where the whole town can see you? You gobble up their taxes and then just sit there till you rust—a pretty miserable life, don't you think? Built but never used—what a waste. Of course, it's better for everyone if killers like you never get to do their dirty work."

I saw a boy, then another and another. They looked to be between the ages of thirteen and seventeen, with shaved heads and shiny fake-leather jackets. Some had tattoos on their wrists or at their temples. I remembered a word from Hiruko's language—*kimpira*. I'm not sure, but I think it started out as underworld slang for kids like Fagan's pickpockets, then came to refer to young punks in the mafia. Anyway, I liked the sound of it—*kimpira*—so it stayed with me.

All six of these *kimpiras* were blond, with pale, washed-out faces. Their eyes looked hard as sapphires, but dry and hollow, like they'd never been on either the giving or receiving end of any kind of human warmth.

Six of them, and six in our group. Unlike these kids, we didn't dress alike, or have the same haircut. We came from all over, lived in different cities, had different jobs. Yet there were things that tied us together. I thought of Akash's dark, friendly eyes, and of Knut and Hiruko passionately discussing adjectives until their lips grew moist. If I knew my life was about to end, I'd want to take all my memories of these friends with me to the grave, even the ones of Nora lecturing me on how the sheep whose wool this sweater was made from ate only organically grown grass, or of Susanoo ordering me to watch out for criminals like an army officer.

But it was silly to get so sentimental when I knew I wasn't in any real danger. These six *kimpiras* were just trying to get a rise out of me. They stared at me with unevenly furrowed brows and clumsily menacing smiles, spitting out words. Judging from their gestures and the looks on their faces, they must have been cursing me out, but since I couldn't understand what they were saying, it didn't sound like that at all. These kids couldn't destroy the beautiful cadences of the Russian language no matter how hard they tried. As I listened to the sounds, I imagined *Swan Lake*, the ballerina's powerful leaps, the delicate lines of her fluttering arms.

I didn't get angry or scared, so they must have realized I was an outsider who didn't even understand their language. This had them stymied for a while until finally one bright-eyed lad got an idea, and called out "Taekwondo!" and the rest of them followed with "Karate!" and "Kung Fu!" They'd decided I was an Asian upstart they could goad into a fight by throwing all the words they thought we had in common at me. That must be it. At any rate, they clearly believed I was from somewhere in East Asia. I wanted to tell them there are no martial arts in Eskimo culture, but I didn't speak Russian.

But why were there no martial arts in our tradition? Or, looking at it the other way around, isn't there something strange about the way Hiruko and Susanoo's ancestors came up with all these different styles of fighting—karate, judo, aikido—and then spent so much time practicing them? Suddenly there's a bear in front of you and no way to escape—you'd have to fight it, but what kind of person would imagine all the possible angles of attack and how he'd respond to each one years before the bear even appeared, and then spend hours and hours perfecting them? An overachiever or a neurotic, probably. Hiruko and Susanoo's ancestors must have tended toward pouring all their effort into learning skills that were only useful in imaginary situations. If that's how they used their energy, wouldn't they already be exhausted long before the world ended?

When I'm in danger, my brain starts working really fast, cranking out enough ideas for a five-page essay on a theory of culture in a split second. When the ice cracked under their feet, or they suddenly met a bear, my ancestors had to decide what to do right away, so even if our everyday lives seem pretty leisurely, in an emergency all the nutrients go straight to our brains. The kids I was facing might be as dangerous as a bear, so my brain was going at full speed. There are so many books about the Roman Empire—why didn't I write one about Hiruko and Susanoo's vanished culture? I saw the guy I'd been back when I wanted to go to university waving to me from somewhere off in the distance, calling "Come on back." But before I answered him, I'd have to get through this crisis.

First, I had to see them for what they were. And then, guess their names. That would really scare them. There are stories all over the world about some evil spirit who loses his magical powers when the hero or heroine says his name. Nora must have read "Rumpelstiltskin" from Grimms' Fairy Tales as a child, and I'm sure Hiruko knows "The Carpenter and the Troll" and Akash, the British story "Tom, Tit, Tot."

But then again, a tundra wolf couldn't make a bear shrink in fear by announcing, "You're a bear." And if I were to tell these kids, "You're all *kimpira*," it wouldn't scare them any more than splashing water in a frog's face.

But was *kimpira* really the right word? I had a feeling I'd gotten it wrong—wasn't it *chimpira*? Both were local words, rooted in Hiruko and Susanoo's homeland. *Kimpira*, I now remembered, was a popular dish there—thin strips of carrot and burdock root, sautéed in sesame oil; it was *chimpira* that meant a young recruit to the mafia. Here in Russian territory, neither one would do me much good, though. I needed a more international sort of slur. How about racist? These punks were definitely racists. And anyone would be insulted if you called them that. In Danish it was *racistisk*, and in German, *rassistisch*—if I repeated them over and over, like variations on a theme, these Russian kids would surely get the message. That's what I'd do—call them a bunch of racists. The word in Hiruko's language was *jinshu-sabetsu-shugi-sha*, so long and complicated it made me proud just to be able to pronounce it, so I really wanted to throw it in with the simpler Danish and German words, but I knew that vanity of that sort would be useless in a fight.

"Racist! Racistisk! Rassistisch! Racist! Racistisk! Rassistisch!" No matter how many times I yelled my three variations, I got to reaction from the kids, who just kept shouting back:

"Taekwondo!" "Kung Fu!" "Karate!" "Sumo!"

Sumo wrestling had somehow gotten into the mix. You morons, not all arts are martial! I saw a piece of wet rope at my feet. About nine feet long, cut with a sharp knife at either end, it had probably been used to tie up cargo. That reminded me of string games from my childhood. They have them in Hiruko's country, and Eskimos have played them for generations. Of course, they're not for self-defense, but they definitely require technique. And some of my ancestors played string games not only with their hands, but with their whole bodies.

I picked up the rope in both hands and pulled it taut. That got to them: they took two or three steps back, and I heard one whisper, "Bruce Lee." Smothering my laughter, I tied the two ends together to make a loop, and with the rope wrapped around both wrists, stuck my head through. An old woman who was really good at full-body string games used to live near us, and she'd sometimes demonstrate this trick. Trying to remember how she'd done it, I first crossed my arms over my chest, then bent over and stuck a foot through, keeping an eye on the *chimpira*, standing still with their mouths hanging open, but just as I was feeling like I had them where I wanted them, bowled over by my Eskimo full-body string game, I heard a deep voice from behind, along with footsteps, and suddenly a middle-aged man about six and a half feet tall was standing between me and the *chimpira* gang. At the sight of him, they turned back into children, spinning around and racing off at top speed, waving their arms in the air.

"Sorry about that. Are you all right?" the man asked in English with a serious, worried look. He was wearing a brown corduroy jacket.

"I'm fine, thank you."

"Are you hurt?"

"No."

"I'm afraid the little ones are bored. They're not really violent, though. Still, you must have been shocked."

They don't look so little to me, I thought as I unwound the rope, but I must not have been paying attention to what I was doing, because I lost my balance and fell down flat on my ass.

"Are you sure you're all right? Did they tie you up?"

"No, I was showing them a sort of arty rope trick. Since I don't speak their language, I thought it might be a good way to teach them something about my culture."

"I'm always telling them to study English..."

"Don't worry—it's really my fault for not knowing Russian."

"There are lots of young people here who are quite good at foreign languages. Actually, I'm a teacher, and those boys go to my school."

"I see—so that's why they ran away."

"As an apology, I'd like to treat you to a cup of coffee."

I decided to accept the offer from this teacher, whose told me his name was Sergei, and we started off, side by side. I'm pretty tall myself, but Sergei's face was so far above me I had to tilt my head to look up at him. His freshly shaven chin stood out against the gray sky.

Sergei's parents lived far to the east, in Vladivostok, and were apparently terribly worried about him being here in Kaliningrad. I'd only just met him, and already he was telling me about his parents.

"Every time I talk to my mother on the phone, she pleads with me to come back home. She says there're plenty of teaching jobs in Vladivostok, so there's no need for me to stay here. And my father agrees with her. He's pretty quiet, though, so he doesn't usually come out and say it."

"Why are they so worried about you living in Kaliningrad?" I asked.

"Because there are European countries all around it. After Lithuania became independent from the USSR, Kaliningrad was cut off from Russia. Then Poland and the Baltic countries joined the EU, leaving Kaliningrad alone, surrounded by Europe."

"What's so dangerous about Europe?"

"I was born in Vladivostok, so in high school, I was obsessed with Europe. Vladivostok is officially in Russia, but it's actually on the eastern edge of Asia. Being born in Asia felt like bad luck to me, and I always dreamt of living in Europe one day."

"I see."

"Fortunately, I married a girl from Kaliningrad. When I found a teaching job here, my dream came true. But after I started living here, I discovered that my neighbors and colleagues at school didn't admire Europe at all; in fact, they resent the way Europeans dismiss Russia as a backward country. They say we should take pride in being Russian, and go our own way, separate from Europe."

"Russia is backward?"

"That's right. The Europeans say that Russian politics is opaque, so you never know what's really going on, and that the Russian people are prejudiced and narrow-minded. Europe acts like it wants us to be friends, but if we join them, we'll be treated as second-class citizens. Lots of Russians say that rather than letting Europe humiliate us, we should stay on our own path."

"But can you really go it alone?" I asked. "You need friends on a journey."

Sergei's face lit up, and he looked warmly down at me. I was expecting him to go on talking about the political situation, but what he said next, softly, almost to himself, was completely different.

"I get hungry for kimchi."

That really took me by surprise.

"Things we used to eat all the time in Vladivostok," he said, "are really hard to find here in Kaliningrad. Actually, there's something I miss even more than kimchi—Korean carrot salad. When I was growing up, we had it at least once a week." He sounded happy, remembering his favorite dish.

"You mean ginseng?"

"No, it's made with ordinary carrots. You can buy Korean salad in any shop in the Russian Far East, but people make it at home, too. You sauté julienned carrots with onions and red chili peppers, add garlic and a little water, put it all in a glass jar and let it chill in the refrigerator."

I'd never heard of Koreans making salads like that, but, afraid our conversation might wander down a blind alley if I asked him about it, I decided to steer us back to a more general topic.

"It sounds like your diet changed completely when you came here," I said.

"It's not just a matter of food. I miss seeing people who look like you, too. In the Russian Far East, I saw Asian-looking people all the time so I never gave it much thought, but here I hardly ever see anyone with features like yours."

As Sergei was smiling down at me, examining my face so intently it embarrassed me, I thought I'd better tell him the truth. I hated to disillusion him just when things were getting interesting, but if I let him go on believing I was Asian, it would get harder and harder to confess that I really wasn't.

"To be perfectly honest, I'm from Greenland, not Asia."

Pursing his lips, Sergei gave me a puzzled look. "But Inuit are also Asian, are they not?" he asked. Now it was my turn to be puzzled. "At least in the history textbook we use at my school," he went on, "it says that the Inuit are of Asian extraction. Do you really think you have to know how to make sushi, and write those terribly complicated Chinese characters to qualify as Asian?"

"Actually, I used to work in a sushi bar, so I do know how to make sushi, and I can write Chinese characters, too."

"Now you've got me thoroughly confused," he said, "which makes things all the more interesting. So, you're from Greenland, but you know how to write those intricate Chinese characters?"

"Well, not all of them."

"How many are there in all?"

"I don't know."

"You don't know?"

"It's impossible to know for sure. Every day some of them disappear without anyone noticing. So, you'd really have to count them all every day to get the right number, but since there are far too many to count in a single day, nobody knows exactly how many there are."

"Good heavens. Can't you even make a rough estimate?"

"About 100,000."

"Really? You have to memorize that many? Asian students must be very diligent. I envy their teachers."

"It's not that bad. You can get along fine with about 2000."

"I grew up in Vladivostok, which is about as close as you can get to East Asia, and yet I can't write even one of those Chinese characters. The only foreign languages that interested me when I was young were English and German. And ironically, now that I'm living in Europe, I'm shut up inside a sort of Russian cocoon. Sometimes the Russian language even seems like a castle wall, protecting me from the outside world."

"No western European country's going to attack you so they can expand their territory."

"You're right about that. But little by little, the West tries to pull us in their direction, financially, and by spreading democracy. And if the Kremlin gets angry enough to fight back, the border areas could become battlefields. That's what really scares me."

Shivering in the cold air, I looked around. I saw a man some distance away, walking with his head down. Although he was the only one around, I felt like we were being watched. Sergei stopped, straightened his shoulders, and intoned, "He who truly knows what he possesses and what he does not possess is a rich man."

"Huh?"

"That's a Ukrainian proverb."

"Do you like to collect proverbs, too?"

"Yes, I see we have something in common."

I remembered what Sergei had said about Russians wanting to go their own way rather joining Europe and becoming second-class citizens. "How about this one, then?" I translated an old saying I half remembered into English for him. "It's better to be a bird's mouth than a bull's anus."

Sergei snorted with laughter, then, like the teacher he was, corrected my mistake.

"Birds have beaks, not mouths."

The coffee shop door was wooden, with an anchor on it in

relief. When he opened it, and we went inside, I felt a gust of warm air on my face. The whole place reeked of strong foreign tobacco; there was a counter with no empty seats, and tables scattered haphazardly around that all seemed to be occupied as well. Strolling in as if it were his own living room, Sergei went straight to the back, where he found an empty table and motioned for me to come over. It was in a corner, giving us a good view of the entire shop, including the counter and the door, which opened and closed now and then. I must have been awfully nervous, because I suddenly felt relieved, knowing we couldn't be attacked from behind.

Sitting face to face, our eyes were finally at the same level. At the table diagonally in front of us, a woman was looking down her nose at the man she was with, as if she thought that would make her seem more beautiful. He leaned forward as he talked to her, doing his best to please her, but she kept pushing him away, giving him curt, one-word answers.

"I envy you, traveling by boat," said Sergei, lovingly tracing the outline of the anchor on the cover of the menu with his finger, "Did you sail all the way from Greenland?"

"No, from Copenhagen. Do you have an airport here?"

"Certainly. The Khrabrovo Elizabeth Petrovna Airport. It was supposed to be the Immanuel Kant Airport—they took a vote when it was built, and that's the name that won. Kant is the most famous native of Kaliningrad. But in the end, he was thrown out."

"Why is that?"

"Probably because he was German. Prussian, actually, because Kaliningrad was part of the Kingdom of Prussia when he was born. At any rate, the patriots thought the airport should be named after a Russian. And some objected even more strongly on the grounds that he was a philosopher. They attacked him as a parasite who spent his life shut up in an Ivory Tower writing books nobody could understand."

Naming airports after philosophers seemed like a great idea to me. Think how high a sky linked by Kierkegaard Airport, Spinoza Airport, Descartes Airport, Lao Tzu Airport, and Kūkai Airport would feel. But wait—Kūkai Airport (空海空港) looks kind of strange. It has two skies (空), a sea (海) and a port (港), so it's hard to tell whether the port is for air or sea. If someone asked me why I'd picked that name, I could only say it was because I liked it.

Just then, something came to me, as if someone had tapped me on the shoulder.

"Did you say your parents were living in Vladivostok?"

"That's right."

"Have you been back there recently?"

"No, it's so far away I haven't even been back once since I moved here. It's more than six thousand miles away."

"But you talk to your parents on the phone, don't you?"

"Yes, quite often, in fact."

"Have they said anything about the situation in the Far East?"

"Such as?"

"Disappearances, for instance."

"Now that you mention it, they did say something about rarely seeing a certain expensive kind of crab at the market these days. It's a pretty rare species anyway, though—I don't think I've ever had it myself."

"Has anything else gone missing from the sea, besides crabs?"

"I don't think so."

For some reason I couldn't get up the courage to ask him directly about Hiruko's homeland. If Sergei had heard about a whole country vanishing into the sea, he surely would've brought it up himself, and if there hadn't been any stories like that on the news and I suddenly asked him about it, he might think I was hallucinating. Since he had no idea what my question was really driving at, he veered even further away from the topic of sinking islands.

"I haven't eaten crab at all since I've been living in Kaliningrad. After all, this city was built by the Germans. They're mostly merchants and civil servants who can work all afternoon on a lunch of bread and cheese. They think the tongue is for debate, not tasting crab."

"Does a tongue that can talk about philosophy," I said sarcastically, "really need to know how to taste crab? Tell the truth— aren't you sorry the airport wasn't named after Immanuel Kant?"

"Oh, I didn't mean to insult the Germans," he replied, looking embarrassed, "or the Russians either, for that matter. But I need to vent my frustration with both the West and the East at least once a day, to keep my stress level down."

The door opened and Nora marched in, her chest puffed out like the diva in an opera making her appearance on stage. I tried to dive behind Sergei, but it was too late. She saw me right away, and came swooping over like a hawk spotting a rabbit.

"Is this where you've been hiding?" she said. "There was no answer when I knocked on the door of your cabin, so I figured you'd already left, but I never expected to run into you here. I guess I got lucky."

Sergei's face brightened as he listened to the German words flow from Nora's mouth.

"Here, have a seat," he said in fluent German as he pulled out a chair for her. "The wood looks hard, but it's actually quite comfortable." Then, turning to me, he asked, "Is this a friend of yours?"

"We're traveling on the same boat," I answered in halting German.

Nora then introduced herself, adding, unnecessarily, "We're on a quest." Afraid Sergei would get the wrong idea, and think "we" meant just her and me, I quickly blurted out, "There are six of us in all, traveling together." He'd already forgotten about me, though, and was busy showing her the menu, leaning over to explain that the coffee beans here were from Brazil, the cakes made with local products like chestnuts and plums. Moments ago he'd been going on about how the Germans can work all day on a cheese sandwich, and now he was trying to reel Nora in with talk about gourmet German cakes—wasn't that a contradiction? And furthermore, he'd used the Russian name Kaliningrad with me, but now he'd suddenly switched to Königsberg, its German name. I guess Nora wasn't too irritated, because she was nodding along, but her eyes were on me the whole time.

"During Prussian times, Königsberg was a more important city than Berlin," said Sergei, but Nora, who had no strong feelings for either city, simply replied, "Oh, yes?"

"I am a high school teacher."

"Oh, yes?"

"My subjects are English and history, but the German language has fascinated me ever since I was a child."

"Really?"

"As I was telling your friend Nanook, our airport was supposed to have been named after Immanuel Kant."

"Oh, yes?"

"A great philosopher, one all your countrymen can proud of."

For the first time Nora's brow furrowed. "I can't say I approve of what he wrote about Eskimos, though."

I resented this lame attempt to show she was on my side.

"There's nothing about Eskimos in Kant's writings," I said. I wasn't entirely sure if this was true, but I once had an American friend who was really into racial prejudice, and he definitely would have mentioned something about it. Nora looked surprised, but didn't back down.

"Well, maybe not Eskimos specifically, but he wrote terribly racist things about non-Europeans in general."

That seemed to pull Sergei back down to earth. "I myself often think about what, exactly, a European is," he said. "And how

Europeans are different from non-Europeans. It's not going to make me any happier, but walking around town, that sort of thing naturally comes to mind."

"Do you like taking walks?"

"Yes, I do. It would be easy to go abroad from here, but for some reason I hardly ever leave the city these days. I envy the way you and your friends keep on traveling, crossing borders."

"Why?" Nora and I asked in unison.

"Even though I'm living in a port," Sergei said with a weary smile, "I don't feel I can get away—not very far, anyway. The Baltic seems like a pond, closed to the outside."

"Why not try thinking of it as a table instead?" I suggested. "Made not of wood, but salt water. With lots of countries gathered around it, holding a meeting. We have our meals at round tables in the dining hall on board ship. The Baltic seems a little like that to me."

Nora turned to me with a dreamy look in her eyes. Sergei hurriedly changed the subject.

"I know a shop that sells fine amber jewelry at reasonable prices—would you like to go?" he asked. He assumed that, being a woman, Nora would naturally go for any kind of jewelry, and that made me mad.

"Nora won't buy jewelry," I retorted, "unless it comes with a certificate guaranteeing that the miners dug out the stones under safe, humane, working conditions."

Her mouth dropped open, and she laughed silently. "You know how fanatical I am about Free Trade," she said, sounding both surprised and quite pleased. I wasn't trying to make her happy, though. What I really wanted to do was pour a bucket of water over Sergei's head.

"I now see," he said to Nora, "how concerned you are about workers' rights."

"And protecting the environment," I added for good measure.

A boring jewelry store was the last thing I wanted to see, but the idea of them going without me turned me off, too.

"I read a newspaper article about illegal amber mining," Nora said to Sergei. Her smile had vanished. "It's as bad as harvesting coral—both are terrible for the environment. Nature mustn't be packaged and sold for financial gain."

"But of all the amber that's sold, only a tiny fraction is mined illegally," said Sergei, "and not by people who want to destroy the environment. In fact, they're risking arrest so they can make a little money to support their families." I hadn't expected a school teacher to be so sympathetic to the plight of illegal amber miners. He'd stuck up for those students of his, too, telling me they weren't violent, just bored. I wondered if it pained him to hear outsiders badmouthing members of his own community. Pulling his bag over, he took a photo out of his wallet and put it on the table.

"This is a piece a friend of mine found," he said. "It's no wonder the ancients thought of amber as bits of the sun that had fallen into the sea."

I stared at the picture, struck by its beauty, completely forgetting our conversation up to then. In the center of the gleaming, golden-brown amber, an insect with long legs and large angel's wings was curtsying like a tiny ballerina. Purely by chance, it had fallen into a fragment of light that had surrounded it, preserving its body just as it was, in eternal sleep.

"This is a prehistoric fly."

I saw myself in that fly, bent over, struggling to free myself from a rope wrapped around me. If I were trapped in amber in that pose, what sort of human beings would discover me one day, as far into the future as we were from prehistoric times? Maybe those humans of the future would no longer be able to even imagine what the word "race" had once meant.

CHAPTER 7   *Hiruko Speaks (3)*

The sea breeze blew up behind my ears, teasing me, mussing my hair. My cheeks itched. My skin was dry. Countless points of light reflected off the handrail in a mad dance, piercing my retinas, turning a corner of the sea into a gleaming carpet. The heavy clouds that had covered the sky were gone, but the light brought not joy, but daggers. Its brightness stole the pinks and blues from the passengers' clothes, making them appear almost white. Only the color of the sea grew deeper.

The rumbling of the engine was strong enough to feel beneath my feet, yet the scene in front of me moved so very slowly. As if this ship were only a tiny boat. We inched along a bank lined with identical trees. The church spire beyond them had barely moved. Behind my earlobe, I heard a voice.

"Where are we going?"

The noise of the wind and waves had drowned out Knut's footsteps.

"eastward," I answered, but Knut, his head tilted to one side, corrected me.

"No, north, I think. We're following along the coast of Lithuania where it bulges out, so north." Standing beside me, Knut put his beefy hands on the handrail, then immediately let go. In my own hands I felt the chill he must have felt in his.

"direction our eyes cannot see. east and west cannot see. countries cannot see. people and towns only can see."

"Kaliningrad was really interesting. It's too bad we won't be able to see Vilnius."

"reason?"

"Because it's too far inland. My life seems to consist of sightseeing and nothing else. When you haven't got a problem to focus on, all you can be is a tourist."

"i also equal tourist."

"No, you don't."

"at kaliningrad the sights i saw. in latvia, at riga, the sights i will see. an immigrant, people think. but a tourist i am."

"That's not true. You're a noble traveler, in search of a place that's been lost."

"homeland misplaced. where to look i know not. in unexpected place may find. in latvia, in riga may find. why latvia? answer in the wind is blowing."

Knut laughed, along with the wind. Things I could never explain in my native language come out naturally in Panska. And Knut has no trouble understanding me. If I were to say the same thing to Susanoo in my native language, he'd scowl and bark, "What're you trying to say? I can't understand you at all."

How long would this boat trip last? Would we get off, and switch to a train someday? Imagining the first day of a train trip made me uneasy. The tracks run straight toward the east, so once you're on board, there's no escape. The train barrels on, until one day the tracks end, where the land meets the sea. In that sea floats the answer. Had my homeland disappeared, or not? On this mail boat, traveling slowly from port to port, I could forget about the destination, delay the final conclusion.

A gust of wind blew a swath of crimson silk into our line of vision. Akash's face followed, then his voice, asking, "How was Kaliningrad?" Like stage curtains opening, Knut and I stepped right and left, inviting him in.

"We rode on Tramway 5," said Knut. "It's a trolley, but people say it's more interesting than a bus tour."

"The new Russian Orthodox Church, with shiny golden onions on the roof," I chimed in, nodding in agreement. "Behind it, the old gray German Protestant Church. Police Headquarters. Kaliningrad State Technical University. A socialist department store."

"You must have done a lot of research before you went."

"We had a guide, an old man in his fifties, who spoke to us in the tram. He had us pegged as foreigners, and started pointing things out to us through the window, telling us all about them, even though we hadn't asked him to. He said he had relatives in America, and seemed happy for the chance to speak English. Kind of a nuisance, maybe, but I'm glad we met him." Knut smiled at me like a co-conspirator—someone who'd been there.

"So, Tramway 5 passes through all the major tourist sites," Akash said, sounding impressed.

"Every city has at least one trolley or bus route like that."

I watched as a stream of images of Kaliningrad flowed by in my mind, stopping at the most vivid one, of a certain public square.

"There was a square called Hansa Platz," I said. "In the center was the Triumphal Column, and beyond it, a church. Empty public squares scare me."

"Why?"

"Because I see a crowd gathered there. Except they're not really there. Because they're dead."

Knut looked shocked at the word *dead*, but when I smiled at him, he smiled back, then turned to Akash and asked, "Didn't you go sightseeing in Kaliningrad?"

"No, I didn't." He hung his head and was silent for a while, as if he couldn't find the words for what came next. "I was afraid it would be dangerous," he finally said. "But I guess Kaliningrad's not that much worse than any other city."

Susanoo came striding over as if he'd been waiting for us. "Did you make it back all right?" he asked in English.

"Of course we did," I said. "Has something terrible happened?"

He snorted with laughter, then, switching to our native language, said ominously, "You forget that certain places are off limits to women and children. You think you're free to go anywhere you please, but remember—I'm the one who has to keep everyone safe, and your reckless behavior drives me crazy." Maybe he used our native tongue because he knew how weird that would sound in English, and didn't want people to dislike him more than they already did. But I'd had enough.

"Some women and children might prefer to make their own city," I said sarcastically, "so it's safe for anyone to walk the streets, rather than having someone like you protecting them."

"Women and children may be safe in Kaliningrad," he fired back, trying on a coat of borrowed logic that didn't suit him at all, "but people who don't fit into any of the three established categories—man, woman, and child—never are."

"People who don't fit into your framework?" I asked angrily. "You mean women who don't wear makeup?"

My rage had as much effect on Susanoo as splashing water in a frog's face.

"That's exactly what I mean," he calmly replied. Tilting his head slightly, he looked me up and down, then went on, still in our native language. "Though you don't have the feminine charms of most women of our homeland, you don't seem to have rejected femininity altogether, so you probably won't be attacked by a hate gang."

Knut didn't understand the meaning, but Susanoo's tone must have sounded insulting to him. "Would you mind saying that again, in English?" he asked quietly, taking a step forward.

"*Fmm*, I'd rather not." The *fmm* was in our native tongue—the rest, English.

"Why?"

"Because if I express my thoughts unfiltered, I'll be regarded as a barbarian. So when I speak English, I say only things that are acceptable internationally. My true feelings I reserve for my mother tongue."

"Keep on that way and you'll end up with a split personality."

"*Fmm*, the whole world has a split personality—haven't you noticed? But keeping Hiruko safe is what's important, don't you think?"

"Whatever—just tell me what you said to her."

Susanoo refused, so I explained the gist of what he'd said in Panska—that while I wasn't as feminine as most women in our homeland, I wasn't flagrantly rejecting traditional femininity either, so I wasn't in much danger of being attacked. Knut's eyebrows shot up in anger, and Akash quickly took him by the arm.

"Did he deny Hiruko's beauty, as a woman?" he asked in English. "I've heard him talk that way before. He's like a big brother who can't see how pretty his kid sister is. Men always find foreign, exotic women more attractive. And there's nothing wrong with that. You and I can see Hiruko's beauty, even if he can't. We're family, maybe from far away but close all the same."

I was surprised to hear that he thought I was even a little bit pretty. If there was anyone in our group with truly polished feminine beauty, it wasn't Nora or me, but Akash. Today his lips were painted a deep cherry red, lifted at the edges like tiny arrows sending out joy. But when his mouth settled back into a straight line, his dark eyes, looking straight ahead, were so serious they seemed almost sad.

"beautiful equals adjective," I said. "if for each person one adjective, beautiful to Akash i give."

"I'd like you to give me the adjective 'hungry,'" said Knut, laughing as he put his arm around my shoulders. It was almost time for lunch.

As the waiters started passing out little hors d'oeuvre plates of pickled herring, the noisy hum of passengers' voices receded like a wave going out at low tide, and was replaced by the sound of metal forks clinking against china. Just below the silvery herring skin was a thin, oily layer the color of dark chocolate, and below it, the firm, white, vinegary flesh. The slabs were too big to fit in my mouth, but when I tried cutting one, the skin slipped under my fork and the flesh crumbled. Looking over at Knut, I saw that he was using his fork like a bear's front claws, skillfully stabbing, separating, and carrying the pieces to his mouth. Movements so elegant they reminded me both of an animal and of the kind of upper-class English gentleman I'd only seen on TV.

Quiet gasps of surprise spread like ripples through the dining room, and I looked toward the door to see Captain Doeff dressed in his uniform, taking his hat off to greet us.

"Ladies and gentlemen, good evening, I'm Captain Doeff." A burst of applause from the Russian table, followed by the Spanish table. Our table halfheartedly joined in. This was the first time the captain had appeared in the dining room. "Are you all enjoying your voyage? Is the sea beginning to seem like your living room carpet, the sky your ceiling? The lamp we call the sun is unfortunately out of order, it often doesn't shine at all." Captain Doeff's heavy torso danced lightly to the rhythm of his English. "For generations," he went on, "my forefathers spent their lives with one foot—the left—in Amsterdam and the other on board a ship. Even so, those left feet were often left floating in midair."

A burst of laughter from the English table.

"Riga, our next port of call, was not a foreign destination to my forebearers, but rather part of their own neighborhood. Before setting out, fathers would say to their children, 'I'm going over to Riga now, so wait for me here in the sandbox.' It wasn't regarded as a journey at all. That word was reserved for faraway places like Cape Town, or Batavia."

"He's Dutch all right," Knut whispered in my ear. Captain Doeff must have had sharp ears because he immediately glanced over at Knut, then gave me an embarrassed smile. Though he was probably still in his forties, his skin was like leather from long exposure to the sea air, with deep wrinkles around that smile.

"Among my ancestors was a merchant," he said, "who was stranded in Batavia after his ship was caught in a bad storm. Something of a daydreamer, he whiled away the long, boring days by writing a sort of fantasy adventure tale for his children back in Amsterdam, in which a fictional island called Dejima appears."

Startled, I wondered if I'd misheard. If he was talking about the place we call 出島, then why had he said it was a fictional island? Or was it me who had it wrong? Maybe I'd dozed off during history class one day in junior high school, and had been mistakenly thinking Dejima was real ever since. The same sort of thing had happened before. Until recently I believed that we didn't fight the Mongols when they came to attack us eight centuries ago because a violent wind suddenly arose and sank all their ships. Then I belatedly learned that I'd been asleep when our history teacher had said, "Most scholars have serious doubts about that old story. Sad to say, our ancestors probably fought a bloody battle to keep the Mongols at bay." Even now, my eyes were getting heavy as I listened to the captain. Not because I was bored. Just the opposite—when I hear something interesting, images start bouncing off each other, setting off a chain reaction inside my head that makes it swell up like a balloon about to burst.

"Are you all right?" asked Knut, placing his pleasantly cool hand over mine. That cleared up the weather in my mind. This was no time to be napping. I needed to hear everything this descendant of Dutch merchants had to say.

Still talking, Captain Doeff strode toward our table. I couldn't tell what sort of face I was making, so I looked down.

"In the story my ancestor wrote to stave off his boredom in Batavia—which is what we called Jakarta while it was under Dutch rule—there's a fictional archipelago, consisting of three large islands and countless small ones."

Three main islands because Hokkaido wouldn't have been part of our country back then, I thought. An oddly bright light was shining on one part of my brain, while the rest was wrapped in mist.

"The people of this archipelago were full of contradictions. They were fascinated by the outside world, eager to speak with foreigners, and to trade with them. They wanted to know everything—what sort of pictures were being painted in Europe, how doctors cured their patients, how ships were made, and the common folk were just as curious as the scholars. Yet at the same time, the idea of foreigners actually coming into their country terrified them. They were afraid that outsiders would make their society fall apart."

Though all this sounded vaguely familiar, I couldn't remember when or where I'd heard it, or even if this was exactly what I'd heard. Was the captain making up a story, or telling us about history—or spinning a tale that was neither, following the rules of some game? Feeling a need to find out which, I looked up, and my eyes met the captain's. He seemed relieved when I didn't say anything, and, turning toward the Spanish table, went on.

"Not all Europeans were born to be missionaries. Some, like my ancestors, enjoyed life without the help of God. Of course, I'm sure many were devout Christians, but being savvy merchants, they understood the difficulty of exporting things people don't want. Apparently, what the natives of this archipelago desired was not God, but textiles, sugar, and spices. They were also interested in European paintings, clocks, and medical books. In my forefather's story, a very odd hotel also appears, one built especially for

Dutch merchants like him. It was a man-made island, the whole of which they were free to inhabit. It was called Dejima. The *De* stands not for 'Deus,' but for 'delivery.'"

"These forefathers you speak of who rejected God and stayed in that Dejima Hotel were toadies, were they not?" asked an icy cold voice. A gentleman with a scarf around his neck, sitting at the English table. From his pronunciation, I guessed he'd graduated from a British public school. I envied him. With an upper-class accent like that, anything sounds convincing. Not the least bit rattled, Captain Doeff continued in his heavily Dutch accented English.

"They didn't deny God, they simply realized that He was unsuitable as an export. It's better to export tomatoes than God. You make more money, and your customers will be much happier."

Before the English gentleman had a chance to reply, a voice came from the Spanish table.

"Your ancestors trod on a picture of the Virgin Mary to show the locals that they had abandoned their Christian faith. You can't get much more servile than that."

"I agree," said the English gentleman, nodding. Captain Doeff was still unfazed.

"Servile?" he said. "My ancestors were clever and brave, but as they were neither knights nor samurai, they had very little interest in honor. Honor is a kind of disease that makes some of your bones grow stiff and hard."

The Spanish table grew noisy. A young man with black, wavy hair down to his shoulders stood up to face the captain.

"Have you forgotten God?" he asked accusingly. The voice was surprisingly gentle for such a harsh question. Captain Doeff, now a little nervous, spread out both hands, motioning for everyone to calm down.

"Don't take everything so seriously," he said. "I'm not saying that God is a fiction. This is only a fantasy written by one of my ancestors, in which a fictitious island called Dejima appears."

I almost broke in to say that this was also actual history, not just a story, but swallowed hard and bit my lip. I wanted to hear what he'd say next. Besides, there might be difficult circumstances I knew nothing about. Maybe he'd be fired for telling us about Dejima, and had been forced to turn it into a fairy tale, to keep his job. I couldn't even imagine the political background behind his decision to come to the dining hall and tell us this story tonight.

The captain glanced over and, seeing that my lips were firmly closed, went on.

"My ancestor also learned about the local culture. He made a dictionary, and following the tradition of that country, he wrote three-line poems with five, seven, and five syllables."

"Why five-seven-five?" asked the English gentleman. "Mightn't that be some black magic the savages cooked up?"

"Five for the planets, perhaps—Mars, Mercury, Jupiter, Venus, and Saturn."

"But you said the middle line has seven syllables, did you not?"

"They added the moon and sun, to make seven."

So that's it, I thought, impressed. I remembered analyzing haiku poems in my National Language classes in junior high and high school, but no one ever told me why they were written in that five-seven-five syllable pattern. Or maybe I'd dozed off again, and missed the explanation. People tend to have pride in their own country's culture, but because your homeland is also the place where you've spent the most time napping, you can end up with lots of mistaken notions about it.

The Englishman, confident that his dismissal of five-seven-five as mumbo jumbo had been a real fastball, was thoroughly disgusted when Captain Doeff had so nimbly caught and returned it. "Though what you say is undeniably interesting," he said, determined to get his own back, "only a toady from a country with no literary giants like our Shakespeare would go so far as to actually study a primitive, non-European genre of poetry. Besides, the Dutch aren't the only ones to have written strange tales about the Far East. I'm sure you've heard of Jonathan Swift, another of our great writers."

"Swift was born in Dublin," Akash broke in. This pitch from an unexpected direction unsettled the Englishman for a moment, but he soon recovered and returned the ball.

He told Akash: "Swift's parents were an English couple who'd moved to Ireland." Then, as if he didn't consider Akash worth bothering about, he turned back to Captain Doeff.

"Unlike the fantasy your ancestor produced, *Gulliver's Travels* is read the world over. Swift writes about Dejima, in Nagasaki. Your ancestor simply pilfered it from him."

Nanook suddenly leaned over and whispered to me in Danish, "They're saying Dejima isn't real. Aren't you going to set them straight?" Nora looked worried, and Knut quietly put his hand on my shoulder. Blinking, Akash asked innocently, "Was Dejima a real place?"

These friends of mine were well read, and knew about all sorts of things, but they'd probably never heard of Dejima. The oceans covering the earth are so vast, with so many islands floating in them that the chances of a ship in search of knowledge coming across a tiny scrap like Dejima are very slim.

"Dejima actually existed," I said in my native tongue, and Susanoo, who until then had been ignoring us as he calmly ate his herring, suddenly looked up.

"There's nothing fictitious about it," he said in English, making no attempt to lower his voice. "That doesn't change the fact that myth is more real than history."

Startled, the English gentleman looked over at Susanoo, but must have decided that he wasn't worthy of his attention, either, because he turned back to Captain Doeff.

"*Gulliver's Travels* is a book nearly everyone reads, so you haven't got a leg to stand on. The Lilliputians, one-twelfth the size of normal human beings, the giants twelve times our size who inhabit Brobdingnag, Nagasaki and Dejima—these are all Swift's creations, and the Dutch aren't the only ones who've stolen from him. Of course, there was no concept of copyright in his time, and it's much too late to sue the plagiarists."

"Have you forgotten," asked the captain with a grin, "that Lemuel Gulliver studied medicine in Holland, at Leiden University, and therefore spoke Dutch? That's why he was able to talk to people in Nagasaki. If he had known only English, he would have been in a pickle. A man who can't communicate with the characters in his own story—that would be a real comedy."

I was getting more and more confused. If all the islands in *Gulliver's Travels* were imaginary, so were the people who lived on them, and all their descendants, too.

"I don't remember Gulliver landing in Nagasaki," I whispered to Nanook. "Was there a scene like that? With geisha and samurai?" Nanook had read practically everything, and had a good memory besides.

"No," he answered, "I think it was just the emperor and an interpreter. I'd like to tell them myself that Nagasaki is a real place, but I've only read about it in books—I've never actually seen it with my own eyes, so you've got to say something."

I knew he was trying to encourage me, but I'd already lost my confidence.

"I'm not sure myself anymore," I said in English. "Maybe my whole past is fiction." I'd meant to say it in Panska, but the channels in my brain got switched, and it came out in English. Hearing me, Susanoo put down his fork with a loud clink.

"The A-bomb was dropped on Nagasaki," he said, also in English. "Can you drop an A-bomb on an imaginary place? That proves it's real."

The dining hall went silent. Glaring angrily over at me, Susanoo went on in our native language. "Imagine you're descended from the gods of myth. The people around you are all ordinary human beings, living in mundane reality, and only a select few—yourself included—are direct descendants of the gods. Just think about that."

I was almost swept away by his delusion, but caught myself just in time.

"Don't try to hypnotize me," I managed to say. "I'm not a mythical character. I'm an ordinary person with a regular job. I'm descended from the interpreter, not the emperor. And so are you." Hearing us speak in our native language made Knut nervous.

"What were you saying?" he asked in English.

"And what is your opinion," asked the English gentleman. He was clearly speaking to me.

"My opinion of what?" I asked.

"What do you think about fiction? You've said nothing all this time, but this discussion is directly related to you."

I felt that unless I spoke, I wouldn't be able to breathe. I hadn't figured out what I wanted to say yet, but as if driven, started to talk.

"Since I started living in Europe, I've sometimes felt like an imaginary person. Everyday life goes smoothly as long as I successfully perform that role. Everyone's been kind to me, I've found a job, and my human rights are protected. But imaginary people aren't supposed to have human rights. So can you see why I feel some uncertainty about my own existence?" My surroundings disappeared, and I felt perfectly calm, as if I were alone in my cabin, reading aloud from a book. "If I were to return to my homeland someday, the moment I set foot on it, Europe might start to seem like a fictitious place. But then the people closest to me now—the friends I'm traveling with—would turn into characters in a made-up story, and I'd be left in a lonely place called reality. I'd hate that. In order for us to stay together, won't we either have to stop turning people we don't know into fiction, or all become fictitious ourselves?"

When I'd finished, I heard cheers and applause from the Spanish table. Then the clapping died down, but just as it seemed to be fading away completely, it grew louder and more rhythmical, joined by the stomping of feet, and the strumming of a guitar one of the traveling players must have had hidden away, while couples from his table put on fox and rabbit masks and stood up to dance to the jingle-jangle of a tambourine. This was apparently part of a preplanned program. Captain Doeff bowed dramatically and left the dining hall. Couples from the Spanish table now got up and started dancing in each other's arms. Though I'd never done it myself, whenever I saw people dancing like that in a movie, I thought I'd like to try it sometime. My eyes met Knut's. He definitely wasn't the dancing type.

"Knut, let's dance," Akash suddenly said. I was surprised to see Knut readily accept the invitation.

"No," I blurted out, quickly getting to my feet, "Knut wants to dance with me." I stood in front of him and put my arms around his waist. Watching to see how the others did it, we swayed back and forth, edging our way among the other couples toward the traveling players' table.

"This is really something," Knut whispered. "You love to dance—I had no idea."

As we circled around, I saw pictures changing like a slide show: Akash's crestfallen face, Nora's shining eyes, Nanook, hunched over, trying to sneak out quietly. After a while I closed my eyes and pressed my temple against Knut's flannel shirt.

After dinner, Knut and I were sitting at a table in the coffee shop, looking at a map of Riga, when a woman we didn't know walked over to us. I remembered a painting called "The Unknown Woman," which I saw as a child. I don't think I'd ever seen a Western style oil painting before. My mother and I took the Joestsu Shinkansen all the way to Ueno Station, then caught a taxi, so it must have been at one of those luxurious old-fashioned department stores in the Ginza or Nihombashi. We were there to buy clothes for a relative's wedding, but there was also an art gallery, where they were holding an exhibition of paintings from the Tretyakov Gallery. There was even a small zoo on the roof. I've never forgotten that "Unknown Woman" I met in that strange, wonderful building. Looking down from a horse-drawn carriage in her black fur and velvet coat, she seems arrogant at first, yet gazing at her face a while, you realize she isn't, not at all. She's in a higher position than the observer so that she'll be safe, not because she feels superior. There's melancholy in her downcast eyes, and her youthful lips are firmly closed, as if she wants you to know she never resorts to flirting or flattery. Though a trace of childhood remains, she is neither innocent nor pure—the difficult relationships she's been through have left shadows. I was puzzled, wondering who she might be. Mysteries we can't digest stay with us the longest.

The woman now coming toward us looked exactly like that woman in the painting.

"The dancing was fun, wasn't it," she said, and, remembering how I'd danced with Knut, my cheeks flushed. When the music started, I didn't want to stand by watching Knut dance with Akash, so I'd asked him myself. We'd always exchanged words before—quietly swaying together was something new. The core of my body grew hot, and the shapes in my mind melted away, leaving only a flowing stream. I didn't remember seeing the "Unknown Woman" on the dance floor, but she seemed to include herself in the "fun," so she must have been there.

"My name is Anna." she went on. "You and your husband are very well matched."

"Actually," Knut said, flustered but serious, "I'm a linguist, not a husband."

"I see," she said, accepting his disjointed reply without cracking a smile, "a splendid occupation." Then, looking intently at me, she went on. "What they were saying about your country being fictitious, that it doesn't really exist, is all nonsense. There's no need for you to put up with lies like that." Her voice was so intense it was almost frightening. She'd apparently come over just to tell me this. "My grandfather had a friend who was a cameraman," she went on, "and he traveled to your country once, to film a scene for a movie. It was unusual to go so far away back then, so we all went to the airport to see him off. The film that scene appears in became very famous—I've seen it myself, several times. The city with a multilevel highway snaking through it like a roller coaster is supposed to be a city of the future, which, of course, would be impossible to actually film, so they chose a location in a country that actually existed. Which proves my point—it's not an imaginary place."

While I was pleased that someone I didn't know was so determined to prove my country's existence, I wasn't sure if the fact that it had been used as a movie counted as hard evidence. Besides, I couldn't shake the notion that the witness providing this evidence had come straight out of a painting. "It's *your* existence that surprises me," I wanted to say, but didn't.

"Thank you for providing circumstantial evidence suggesting that my homeland is not fictitious." This clumsy expression of gratitude was all I could manage. Still unsmiling, Anna nodded. It wasn't a lovable face, but she didn't look cold, either. This is it, I thought, the expression I saw for the very first time in that painting, "The Unknown Woman." Anna didn't fit the stereotype of feminine beauty—her face was stubbornly her own. While she made no effort to attract people, she didn't haughtily look down on them, either. That balance fascinated me, but after examining her face for a while, I began to feel uneasy. She looked like she was living on the edge, with nothing to spare, hiding her anxiety, concealing her depression with bright colors, secretly clenching her fists to stifle her anger, refraining from laughter to conserve her strength, somehow managing to survive while wiping her tears away in private from time to time. Yet not only did she keep her back straight, her eyes focused on what was ahead, but now she was trying to help me, a perfect stranger.

"And when you saw that city in the movie, what did you think of it?" I asked.

"It was all gray concrete," she replied with a rather vague look considering she was the one who'd brought it up. "I don't remember it very well." I was wondering if maybe she'd only wanted to talk about this old film because it brought back memories of her grandfather and his friend, and whether it might be time to end the conversation when Knut suddenly stood up and, like a chivalrous knight paying homage to his lady, took her hand, bowed and kissed it.

"You've given us valuable information," he said, "and we're very grateful."

Anna dissolved into laughter. "There's no need to thank me," she said, her face screwed up with embarrassment—a feeling that didn't match her face at all. And in fact, she wasn't embarrassed, but pleased at having been acknowledged in this way. Knowing he was only kidding around, I was surprised at how happy Knut's grand gesture had made her, and equally surprised that he knew exactly how to please a woman like Anna. Still in dramatic mode, he asked politely, "I wonder if you'd mind sharing the title of that film your grandfather's friend worked on."

"*Solaris*," she answered coldly. I couldn't see why her voice should have suddenly grown so cold. But the name Solaris definitely had a chilly ring to it.

"That planet was Mercury, was it not?" said Knut, still very polite.

"I wouldn't know," Anna replied, growing colder all the time.

"The Mercury table in the dining room," I said, suddenly remembering, "is where the people who don't talk sit. They're as silent as water."

Anna looked startled, as if she'd just remembered I was there. "Those people didn't stop talking because they like the quiet," she said, giving me a bit of unexpected information. For some reason I was afraid to ask what she meant by that, so I said nothing.

"Are you two planning to go sightseeing in Riga?" she asked, looking us over with a fresh confident smile.

I nodded, and Knut quickly followed suit.

"Riga was an important place to me."

"How so?"

"Back when Europe was divided into West and East, Riga was where I went when I wanted to drink in the atmosphere of Western Europe. There were streets that reminded me of the Hanseatic culture of northern Germany, Italian cafés, lots of art nouveau buildings, and in the suburbs, mansions that millionaires from New Jersey might have lived in."

I'd been so caught up with Anna's face that I hadn't noticed until now, but she spoke English with an American accent. Her speech also had the affected lilt of an Eastern European intellectual, though, so I prayed she wouldn't realize how uncultured I was. Knut, on the other hand, wasn't the least bit nervous.

"So, you know Riga well," he said. "Are there any sights you'd recommend to us?"

"The first place I'd like you to see," she said with a mischievous smile, "is 221B Baker Street."

"You mean Sherlock Holmes's place?"

"That's right."

"You mean he lived in Riga, not London?"

"There's a series of Russian films about Sherlock Holmes. Riga was one of the locations they used. Probably because they couldn't shoot in London, but no matter—to me that will always be the real Baker Street. Do you know *A Study in Scarlet*?"

"Of course."

Leaning over our map of Riga, Anna deftly took the pencil out of Knut's hand, and made an X on a certain alley.

"Here," she said, "is where you want to go." Then, as if she'd suddenly remembered something she had to do, she turned and walked away.

She'd left as abruptly as she'd appeared. Knut and I looked at each other and laughed.

"Anna likes movies."

"To her, the evidence that something is real can be found in film. If that's true, she didn't need to take a sea voyage—she could've just gone to the movies. But is it really true that part of Tarkovsky's *Solaris* was shot in your country?"

"not the place i lived. roppongi, in the capitol city. or nearby, i think."

"Roppongi? It has a nice rhythm. What does it mean?"

"six trees."

"Sounds cool. I'd like to go there sometime. But if I did, I might find just six trees standing there, and nothing else. Still, that would be better than a futuristic city, with gray concrete multilevel highways covering the sky. Maybe it's the present, which was the future back then, that's perfectly preserved in that scene from Tarkovsky's film."

I closed my eyes, and saw six big cherry trees. Concrete highways circled in and out like a Möbius strip. Below, Knut and I were dancing. I couldn't hear any music yet. When the music starts, this will seem more like reality, I thought.

CHAPTER 8   *Knut Speaks (2)*

I was strolling the streets of Riga, hand in hand with Hiruko, when a huge building floated up in front of us like a bank of cumulus clouds. Hiruko gasped and shouted, "moscow university!"

"We're in Riga," I said, "so what's Moscow University doing here?" Hiruko let go of my hand and rushed toward it.

"finally, to moscow we come," she murmured, half to herself. "in moscow. train we must ride, eastward, eastward. to sea we cannot escape."

A little running wouldn't bring us any closer—that monster of a building wasn't going to let us near it that easily. Still, I hurried after Hiruko.

"This is Riga," I said with my hands on her shoulders, gently shaking her from behind. "So that can't be Moscow University. And anyway, how do you know what it looks like?"

"my aunt in youth at moscow studied," she said, looking up at me, her eyes covered with a thin film of tears. "to me photographs she sent. my favorite aunt."

The structure looming over us looked as if the Empire State Building in New York, or maybe the Woolworth Building, had grown straight out of the Palace of Versailles, and was standing there saying, "Look at me! I'm bigger than America and France combined."

"moscow university," Hiruko repeated. Which would mean that we'd somehow ended up in Moscow. That might not be so bad after all. From here we could take the Trans-Siberian Railway all the way to the east. Then maybe we could cross over to Niigata, Hiruko's home, on a fishing boat. Our journey was nearing its finale.

While I was lost in thought, a skinny young guy in a bright blue jacket walked up to us.

"This is Riga," he said with a grin, "and that's the Latvian Academy of Sciences. But the building itself is a copy of the Lomonosov Moscow State University." Hiruko tilted her head, looking puzzled.

"The building was a present from Stalin," he explained. "There's another one just like it in Warsaw, my home town. When I was a kid people used to say that Moscow, Warsaw, and Riga were like sisters. Weird, huh? The Three Sisters—like Chekhov's play. But it wasn't just cities. I later found out there are Seven Sisters—seven buildings in Moscow alone that look so much alike people call them sisters. One is the Hotel Ukraina, another the Foreign Ministry—the contents are all different, but to look at, they're practically identical. That generous Russian dictator must have thought it would be a waste to keep all his beauties in Moscow, so he decided to give copies away to other countries, as presents. He built the eighth sister in Warsaw. We said no thank you, but he gave it to us anyway. The ninth is right in front of us—the Latvian Academy of Sciences. The tenth is in Bucharest, and the eleventh in Prague."

The kid rattled off this heavy history like a DJ announcing the Top Ten on the Hit Parade.

"Authority like a huge tomb," Hiruko said in English, "playing the role of a Palace of Science. But aren't there some free-spirited people inside the Academy?"

He muttered something to himself in a language that wasn't English.

"You're Polish, aren't you?" I asked. "Are you here as a tourist?"

"No," he said, looking embarrassed, "there's this girl in Riga who makes her own pendants and earrings, and she's got a booth in the

Central Market where she sells the things..." He sounded very vague—by the end his pronunciation was as mushy as gruel, and I could hardly understand him. I almost asked him if he'd come all the way to Riga just to see homemade jewelry, but decided not to. Maybe there was something he didn't want to tell us. Like that he had a steady girlfriend back in Warsaw, but was sneaking off to see this girl in Riga he'd met recently... I must have gotten that wrong, though, because he didn't seem to have anything to hide.

"Her name's Inese," he went on. "And the Riga Central Market's really a cool place. It's actually a row of hangars big enough for a whole airplane to fit in, and each one is full of stalls. They probably sell more kinds of food than the big markets in Budapest or Vienna. There are places to sit down and eat, too. You see so many different people, and can taste so many things from faraway places—it's like traveling on the Silk Road."

"Sounds great," I said, "Let's go."

"Let's go—sounds good," said Hiruko at the same time. The young man told us his name was Bruno.

The building was so huge that I hurt my neck looking up at the geometrical patterns on the ceiling. The salty, pungent smell of dried fish. The black holes where their eyes used to be looked a little creepy. They were hanging down, five to a string, with handwritten price tags dangling. Pale green watermelons with dark green stripes running down the sides like cracks. One booth had pretty glass bottles filled with red or yellow liquid—cooking oil, maybe—with lovely sprigs of herbs inside, like artificial flowers. A man with an embroidered brimless cap on his head was selling big loaves of round, flat bread. The label on a square of cheese, so pale it was almost white, caught my eye.

"This label is in Cyrillic," I said.

"It's Kyrgyz cheese."

"Are even products from Central Asia labeled in Russian?" I asked Bruno, finding this a bit strange.

"That's right," he said. "They may be far from here, but they're still part of the Soviet Union, so the trade routes are there." He was using the present tense on purpose.

"But wasn't the USSR dissolved a long time ago?"

"No, it's still around, haunting us like a ghost. You see it in the network of roads food travels to get here. This market is a federation of flavors from Uzbekistan, Azerbaijan—lots of different places."

Hiruko stopped in front of a row of canvas bags filled with spices, so I stopped there, too until Bruno, who'd gone ahead, came back to get us.

"I'm going to get a present for Inese," he said. "Do you want to come along?"

"Sure," I said. "An amber necklace, maybe?" That was the first thing that popped into my head.

"You've got the color right," he laughed, "but what I'm getting her is thick and syrupy."

A tiny woman with a green scarf on her head was sitting alone on a wooden stool waiting for customers. About fifty jars were lined up on a shelf, each with a piece of paper taped to the front, covered with tiny handwriting. I took a closer look and saw these labels, too, were in Cyrillic; in the curves of the letters I thought I saw passion, or perhaps even deep-seated hatred.

"Honey!" cried Hiruko. Hearing her, the woman with the scarf got wearily to her feet, then broke into a wide smile at the sight of Bruno, patting him on the arm with her suntanned, wrinkled hands. Maybe she wanted to touch his shoulder but was too short to reach that high.

"She's Russian," Bruno told us, "and she's been selling honey for over fifty years."

The woman carefully examined our faces.

"Honey is a cure-all. The labels tell you what each kind is especially good for. This is the third time I've bought honey here."

Picking up various jars, Bruno explained that this one was good for stomach ailments, while that one soothed a sore throat from a cold. Another kind helped wounds heal faster, and still another guaranteed a good, deep sleep at night.

"So, which one are you going to buy for Inese?" I asked.

"One that'll help her circulation. Most days, she sits at her booth from morning till night. These hangars were originally built to house Zeppelins, not human beings, so she complains about being cold."

Bruno said something in Russian to the woman with the scarf, and took a jar from her. Then she started looking for a different kind, running her fingers over the jars on the shelf until she came to the one furthest to the right, which she picked out, wiped on her apron, and handed to Bruno. She reminded me of fairy-tale witches. Not that she looked scary or cruel, but in her wrinkled face I sensed the long years she'd spent alone, patiently gathering honey from the natural world, tasting it, and drawing magic from it, a little at a time.

Bruno paid her, and handed the second jar she'd given him to Hiruko.

"This one's a present for you guys," he said.

"Thanks," I said, "What kind of healing powers does this kind have?"

Smiling over at Hiruko, who seemed surprised at this unexpected gift, Bruno replied mysteriously, "Seems eating it can get you to the moon."

I puzzled over the meaning of this riddle all the way back to the boat. As we were climbing the steps, Hiruko, who'd apparently been thinking about it, too, suddenly shouted, "Honeymoon!"

As if to invite me in, Hiruko opened the door to her cabin, and when I'd entered, after some hesitation, closed the door behind me. It smelled good inside, like jasmine, maybe. We sat side by side on the bed. The surface of the honey looked as hard as amber, not likely to let a finger through. A metal spoon might do the trick, though. There should be a spoon and cup around here somewhere, I was thinking when I saw Hiruko stick her forefinger in, whirl it around, and slowly pull it out again. The droplets clinging to Hiruko's finger regretted parting with their compatriots in the jar for a moment until they finally cut ties with their old life and were lifted up to disappear between a pair of pale pink lips.

"like a dream," said Hiruko. Dreams can be nightmares, though, so this didn't necessarily mean "sweet." Perhaps that's why my own forefinger hesitated until Hiruko suddenly grabbed it and stuck it into the honey. I felt resistance at first, as if the honey was trying to gently peel the nail off as my finger descended further, to the second joint, but after Hiruko let go and I tried to pull it out again, the honey clung wistfully to the joint, refusing to part with it. Yanking it out seemed heartless, but I wasn't going to let my finger steep in the jar forever. Wrapped in translucent golden goo, it was so much fatter now that it hardly seemed my own. When it started to drip I rushed to stick it in my mouth, but missed the mark. I tried coaxing the droplets outside my lips into my mouth with my finger, and ended up making my face even stickier, so I finally stuck out my tongue and licked. The taste was sweet, with traces of the pungency of tree bark, and the bitterness of pollen. The moment my eyes met Hiruko's, as if on cue, my heart began to expand and press up against my throat above and down on my bladder below, so I could feel it pounding—*ba-boom, ba-boom, ba-boom*, throughout my entire body.

"Words like *hony* and *honi* have the meaning "golden" hidden in their etymology," I said, pretending everything was normal.

"bees the flower cosmos love," said Hiruko. "pistils and stamen of cosmos equal golden."

"The gold of the flowers seeps into the bees' bodies, making their honey golden, too," I said. "Maybe it's the color they carry away."

Not noticing that I was gasping for breath, Hiruko calmly said, "golden words here," as she reached out to wipe the honey off my face. The moment her delicate fingertip touched the side of my lip, my heart burst and, grabbing her wrist, I puller it close to my chest. Her torso drifted down on top of me, as lightly as a cosmos blossom.

We were a little late for dinner. Nearly all the guests had already started in on their appetizers, and the sound of their chatter mingling with the clinking of forks against plates made the dining hall as noisy as a beehive that's been poked with a stick. While we were sitting down Akash shot me a glance. He seemed to know what we'd just done in Hiruko's cabin, which was embarrassing. Seeing that we'd arrived, the waiter swooped over with tongs in hand, and skillfully picked out slices of pickled fish with a bay leaf on top, along with raw onion, to put on our plates.

Nora and Nanook were too busy arguing to notice us:

"Why are you staring at me?"

"Because you're acting strange."

"What am I doing that's strange?"

"Well, you always said you loved pickled mackerel, and now there's a piece of it right in front of you but you won't touch it."

"The kind I like is called *shime-saba*—cured mackerel. I never said I was crazy about all kinds of pickled fish. Knowing how good *shime-saba* tastes makes this stuff all the harder to eat."

"That sounds to me like nationalism."

"It is not. Mackerel is not my nationality."

I nearly burst out laughing, but the two of them kept at it, deadly serious. Akash was watching them, his chin rocking back and forth like a skiff on the waves as he searched for words to patch things up between them. Fork in hand, Hiruko stared into the distance with moist, dreamy eyes but didn't touch her fish.

Nanook didn't seem to see anyone but Nora.

"Could you stop," he griped, "trying to remember everything I like or dislike? My specialty is pretending to be someone I'm not." They glowered at each other.

"You hide what's in your heart," she shot back, "because you're afraid of being rejected."

I glanced over at Susanoo, who, even though his German must have been much better than mine, didn't seem to even hear Nanook and Nora as he gloomily ate his fish. When the waiter wanted to be genteel, he would sometimes say "Votre hors d'œuvre" in French, but genteel wasn't really Susanoo's thing. Holding a bit of fish down with a dainty little fork so he could cut it into even tinier pieces, then gracefully carry them to his mouth, didn't suit him at all. It was easier to imagine him climbing out of the sea with a fish so huge he'd need both arms to hold it, then slamming it down on a boulder, taking out a hunting knife, and cutting off slices to eat raw. The words "appetizer" and "main course" were meaningless to him. Salt water would be his chosen seasoning, and if he could avoid it, he wouldn't use a fork, or chopsticks, either. He regarded any country's customs as amateur theatrics, and secretly laughed at anyone who took them seriously. And it wasn't just fish, carved up to fit this silly "hors d'œuvre" convention. Nanook and Nora's tiff, Akash's concern—to Susanoo, it was all just noise, not worth bothering about.

"what about thinking?" Hiruko asked, hitting my elbow with hers. That's not very good manners, I thought, and even though I hadn't said it out loud, Hiruko seemed to read my mind.

"to you," she said in Panska, "elbow equals symbol of competition and hostility. to me, friendship memories. in high school, with elbows friend next to me sitting communicated. voices teacher heard, but elbows silent."

The message from an elbow is completely different from what words or the expression on someone's face tells you. When Hiruko's elbow hit mine, I felt something round and hard, as if I'd touched a stranger's soul.

"The elbow isn't a very romantic messenger, though."

"romantic equals sweet," she replied. "appetizer always sour." She took a bite of mackerel, and her lips puckered at the taste. Though he didn't understand Panska, Akash knew exactly what that meant.

"This fish really is sour, isn't it?" he said in English.

Speaking Panska and Danish, Hiruko and I were in our own world, while Nora and Nanook were still arguing in German, and Susanoo was sharing silence with his mackerel, so Akash may have been searching for a crack he could slip through in English. If the UN General Assembly was like this, what would become of the world? Gatherings of people speaking different languages are fine—the trouble is that each person responds only to what he or she understands. If aliens from outer space were to see us, they might think we were all discussing the same topic, when actually, several distinct conversations were flowing along like parallel streams.

"Sour for appetizers, bitter for coffee, and sweet for dessert, but hot and spicy is entirely missing in Baltic cuisine," Akash murmured to himself. He'd practically given up finding someone to talk to when Nora overheard him, and forgot all about her fight with Nanook.

"In the Ayurveda diet," she said in German, "I hear that several different flavors have to be included in the same meal, but how many exactly—four? Sour, bitter, sweet, hot?"

At the word Ayurveda, Akash's face lit up as if he'd suddenly run into a childhood friend.

"There're actually six," he replied, also in German. "Besides the four you mentioned, there's saltiness, and astringency. A meeting with one representative of each flavor is considered healthy. But to tell the truth, my tongue's much simpler—I'm satisfied if everything's spicy."

"Baltic cooking is anything but," Nanook said in German. I noticed that the irritation lines had already disappeared from his forehead. Lover's spats seem deep but they're really pretty shallow. The Baltic, on the other hand, seems shallow, but is actually very deep, probably due to all the history that's accumulated on the bottom before vacationers started splashing around. Besides, it has to be deep enough for big ships to cross it.

I heard a woman's voice behind me.

"Excuse me, but I thought I heard someone speaking German."

Twisting around in my chair, I looked up to see a round-faced woman with her hair done in rows of waves. She used the polite German of people educated in Eastern Europe. When no one responded, she said in English, "I'm so sorry, I must have misheard," and turned to leave.

"No, you didn't," I blurted out in German. "You were correct. Some of us speak German. This table has several languages. English, German, Panska, and Danish." The rhythm of my German sounded like Hiruko's Panska. Smiling, the woman introduced herself.

"My name is Hella Wuolijoki. I was born in Estonia, but we often spoke German at home while I was growing up, and I am quite well read in German literature. Though it may seem impudent of me to say so, I have come to feel that German is my own language."

She was from the Mercury table, next to ours. I thought I'd seen her before, but as their shared language was silence, I didn't have a clear grasp of their individual personalities.

"I go to a German university," Akash said warmly, "so to me, the German language is like my father. Marathi is my mother. Do you also feel that German is your father? And that Estonian is your mother?"

"Yes, I do. I was strongly influenced by my aunt as well, though. It was under the guidance of Finnish, my mother's elder sister, that I became a writer. As Finnish is much better known abroad than Estonian, my mother, I myself am thought of as Finnish, married to German."

"You mean you married a German man?" Nanook asked gingerly.

"I never married him, but we were lovers."

Nora's eyebrows shot up. "Are you by any chance," she asked, her eyes moving as if she was searching through her memory, "the writer who hid Bertolt Brecht from the Nazis while he was in exile in Scandinavia? The famous Finnish communist?" The way Nora said it, the word "communist" sounded more like "community."

"That's exactly right."

Was this a ghost ship we were on? We'd already met a Polish writer who was supposed to be long dead. There's a legend about a ship that sails forever, carrying the spirits of people who can't die because they have unfulfilled wishes, or resentments they can't let go of, or things they needed to say but couldn't. I had no memory of dying myself, and I really didn't want Hiruko to be a ghost. But sometimes I've been afraid the people closest to me might actually be ghosts. Was this boat a place where the living and the dead could come together and talk? A mail boat because it carried letters between this world and the next? Or did the difference between being alive and being dead gradually lose all meaning as we're rocked by the waves?

"Why are the people at the Mercury table always silent?" In that open, easy way of his, Akash asked the very question that had been on my mind.

"They have various reasons," she answered. "For me, the most important one is that literary history has forgotten me. Others have lost the will to speak, sunk in despair when they realized that language cannot prevent war. Some are fundamentally honest, but because they're afflicted with an illness that compels them to lie, they've stopped talking altogether. As I said, each of us has a different reason."

At this point, Hella stopped talking and returned to the Mercury table. She came back gently leading a shy, white-haired woman with her eyes cast down.

"This is Okichi. There was a time when she was hailed as a heroine who saved her country. But people are so unkind. In time, everyone forgot her. No one told the children her story, so succeeding generations know nothing about her. She's from your country," she concluded, looking accusingly at Hiruko and Susanoo.

When the woman called Okichi looked up, I was hit by what smelled like a mixture of makeup and camellias, and felt a little dizzy. She'd obviously lived a long time, and her skin was in the process of drying out, yet there seemed to be a residue of alcohol fermenting somewhere underneath it that sent the core of my brain reeling as if I was drunk.

"misty memory," Hiruko whispered in Panska. "of a movie about her, or a play, or maybe manga." For some reason, she didn't speak directly to Okichi. Susanoo, having finished his appetizer, set his fork down with a flourish.

"You're a woman everyone has forgotten?" he asked, expressionless. "Well, I'm a forgotten man. Of the two of us, I might be better off. I appear in a famous book called the Record of Ancient Matters—and as a hero, so I don't think they'll ever forget me completely. But all books are liars, and I have to fight those lies. I'm sure you do, too. In that sense, people who don't appear in books are freer than we are." He said all this in English, probably because he wanted everyone to understand him. What he said was always so provocative and full of innuendo it made my blood pressure go up. Fortunately, Akash stepped in.

"Would the two of you like to join us for dinner?" he asked, and went to get their chairs. Susanoo had nothing more to say. There were now eight people sitting at our table for six, yet it still didn't feel cramped. While the headwaiter's brow furrowed as he watched this disruption of his orderly dining room, he helped us bring the women's plates and cutlery over without a word of complaint. Hiruko and I slid our chairs aside to make room for Hella and Okichi.

I'd probably speak English if I moved to the English table. Would these two from the silent table break their silence now that they'd left it?

"Didn't you help Brecht write some of his plays?" asked Nora, her cheeks flushed pink. "I hear you actually wrote one that was published under his name."

"Collaboration," Hella replied with a confident smile, "is such a passionate process that sometimes you can no longer tell who's doing the writing."

"You claim that literary history has forgotten you," I said, wanting to join the conversation, "but judging from what Nora just said, it seems that may not be entirely true."

"I'm only remembered as the woman who helped Brecht," she said dryly.

"Do you think Brecht was a narcissist?" asked Nora. A fast ball—the kind Nora liked to throw, but Hella caught it neatly.

"Well, he always had a pipe in his mouth, with clouds of smoke billowing out of it. I suppose it's natural for women of younger generations to see him as a wily fox who couldn't be trusted." She sounded like a world-weary diplomat who's spent too long in the field, though I may have gotten that impression because I had so little experience myself.

"He's always seemed like a narcissist to me," Nora said, launching a fresh attack on the long-dead dramatist. "I don't know much about him, but I hear he was full of himself, writing successful musicals and driving around in a big car. I'm sure he loved being surrounded by adoring actresses and singers."

"That was after he went into exile in Hollywood," Hella said in defense of her former lover. "But he was a man who made you feel happy to be working with him." She then put a hand on Okichi's bony shoulder and went on. "I was the one who showed Brecht that play by a man called Yūzo Yamamoto, about Okichi's life."

So it wasn't Kenzo, but Yūzo? I'd heard of a designer named

Yamamoto, but wasn't sure about his first name, so I leaned over and whispered to Hiruko, "Yamamoto the designer?"

"that yamamoto not," she whispered back. "famous writer yamamoto." Her hot breath tickled my ear. Hella smiled at us, then proceeded to tell us about that famous writer as if she were talking about an old high school classmate.

"Yūzo Yamamoto studied German literature, but liked Scandinavian writers as well, and did research on Ibsen and Strindberg. He wrote plays as well as novels. One of them is entitled *Nyonin-aishi*."

"Did you read it in the original?" asked Nanook, ready to let out a sigh of admiration if the answer was yes.

"No, I read it in the English translation. I can't read the language of the original. I'm afraid it wasn't a very good translation, although it may be presumptuous of me to criticize the translator when I can't read the original." While Nanook looked disappointed, Hella grew more and more enthusiastic. "But even in that inferior translation," she went on, "Brecht immediately sensed dramatic possibilities, which shows how important translation is, no?"

"Was Brecht fluent in English?" asked Nora suspiciously.

"No, not at all. Yet even so, he somehow managed to read this rather poor translation, and immediately knew he wanted to write his own version, so the very existence of that translation seems wonderful to me."

She seemed obsessed with translation. Later, when we stopped at Tallinn, I was to find out why.

"Which is wonderful," asked Nora, unable to let go, as if Brecht were an old lover she still resented, "the translation or that guy with the pipe?" Hella, who'd actually loved and parted from Brecht, didn't seem to resent him nearly as much, although she wasn't about to put him on a pedestal, either.

"I think of Brecht as not so much as a man as a phenomenon," she said. "But let's talk more about that later." With that, she put an end to the discussion.

As the main dish was roast pork, Akash, who was a vegetarian, loaded his plate with potatoes while the waiter explained, in a not particularly apologetic tone, that they were out of soybeans, so the chef hadn't prepared a soy burger for him.

"Okichi," asked Hella in English, "can you eat pork?"

"No pork," she answered in a surprisingly forceful voice, "no beef, no milk."

"You don't drink milk," Nora asked. "So, are you a vegan?"

"Milk forbidden," she said, looking determined, then nodded, satisfied with her own reply.

I wondered—probably along with Nora and Akash—when a prohibition like that would have been put in place, but wasn't sure how to ask about it. Fortunately, Nanook, who knows about all sorts of things, cleared it up for us.

"Until Okichi's country started to modernize in the nineteenth century," he said, "they weren't allowed to eat beef or drink milk, either."

"So, did they drink sheep's milk instead," asked Akash, "like the ethnic minorities in Central Asia?"

"No, not that, either. The only milk they drank was from their mother's breast, when they were babies. Isn't that right?" Though the question was intended for Okichi, she just sat there grinning, so Hella answered instead.

"Yes, cow's milk was absolutely forbidden, and that's why Okichi was arrested. After the port of Shimoda was opened to foreign ships, America was the first country to set up a consulate there, but Townsend Harris, the man they sent to be Consul General, got sick, and it seemed nothing would cure him. He himself believed that milk was what he needed, and he begged Okichi to find him some. Had she refused, he might have started a war."

"A war?" cried Nanook, "Over a glass of milk?"

"Wars," Hella said seriously, "start much more easily than you'd think."

"So, was Okichi a diplomat?" I asked, and got an answer I wasn't expecting.

"No, she was a geisha. But she made a greater contribution than the diplomats. When the Americans asked for a woman who could see to Harris's needs, the Japanese officials assumed they meant a geisha, so they forced Okichi to go to him against her will, when what the Americans had actually wanted was a nurse. Okichi felt sorry for Harris, seeing him so desperate for milk, so she got him some cow's milk from a local farm. He recovered, as did Japanese-American relations—at least for the time being—but Okichi was accused of breaking the law."

"Why was drinking milk against the law?" I asked.

"Because of Buddhism," Nora shot back.

"But milking a cow doesn't kill it. I know Buddhism prohibits the killing of animals, but what's the problem with milking cows?"

"Milk gave lots of people diarrhea—that might have something to do with it."

"Surely diarrhea is a problem outside government jurisdiction."

My conversation with Nora made Nanook and Akash laugh, but Hiruko looked more serious than I'd ever seen her.

"People who raised cows," she said, "did what they wanted with meat and hides after the cows died. But they didn't kill them because they wanted to eat meat. While the cows were alive, I think they sometimes milked them. And milk was medicine, so their neighbors probably came to buy it in secret. Drinking it could prevent certain illnesses. So, if milk was actually against the law, the policy was wrong."

Why "if... actually," I wondered at first, but after all, the play this fellow named Yamamoto wrote was fiction, and might not be historically accurate. But then wasn't it possible that Okichi, who was sitting right here with us, wasn't a real person?

"Countries," said Hiruko, breaking the silence, "do not have the right to forbid certain kinds of food and drink."

"That's right," Akash agreed. "If there's freedom of speech, there ought to be freedom of diet as well."

"The samurai, who'd turned into government bureaucrats by that time," said Nanook, "had a subconscious fear of people like priests, traveling players, hermits and the like, who wandered freely through realms that were beyond their understanding. Being in touch with the bodies and souls of animals meant touching the gods as well. So, to the samurai, people who could easily cross borders and move freely between the worlds of human beings and the gods—or people and cows, or life and death—could only exist outside the framework of society. Of course, no one is really 'outside' of society. But the samurai had to tell themselves that, or they'd have been so anxious they couldn't see straight."

"Okichi flowed across the border between inside and out," said Hiruko, "like milk."

"Here's a toast," said Akash, sounding very excited, "to a geisha who succeeded where no diplomat could have!" He raised his glass of water high. Perhaps because they'd overheard the words *samurai* and *geisha*, everyone at the English table turned to look at us.

"When the ship docks at Tallinn," Hella said, "Okichi and I are going to a friend's garden house for tea, so why don't you all come with us? We still have lots to talk about, and it's the perfect place for a leisurely conversation."

Like Riga and Kaliningrad, Tallinn was a beautiful city, where cobblestones held the past in place while brick walls invited you to taste its sadness, and church spires always pointed toward the sky. But, as Hella explained, residents rarely spent their Sundays strolling through its streets, preferring to retreat to the suburbs, where they worked in their vegetable gardens, sometimes stopping for tea. Both merchants and scholars needed to work in the earth—if they bought everything from the supermarket, their faces would soon grow pale, their voices feeble.

This garden had zucchini, kohlrabi, rhubarb, and lamb's lettuce, beautifully arranged and carefully tended, as I could tell by their leaves, all shiny and green, with none of those tiny holes insects make. The simple wooden house was painted the soft blue of a well-worn pair of jeans, and in front of it, surrounded by gooseberry bushes, were a table, a bench, and several chairs. Hella told us to sit down, and as soon as Hiruko, Nora, Okichi, and Akash were comfortably seated we heard birdsong floating in the air around us, shining like an audible crown. I felt like an extra in a movie.

"I blended this tea myself," said Hella, picking up the big teapot, "from herbs grown in this garden." Nora got up to help her pour. Though she looked sturdy enough, Hella seemed off balance somehow, and walked unsteadily.

"In my homeland," Okichi said suddenly, "I am homeless, but in a foreign land, I'm a special guest." Then she burst out laughing. Shocked, Hella held the teapot in midair. While that kind of raucous laughter wasn't exactly taboo, I had the feeling most European adults would try to suppress it in public. Exactly what was wrong with it, I couldn't say. I heard all sorts of things in it—recklessness, smoldering anger, and her determination never to give up, to face the dead end ahead, and brazenly go on anyway, laughing all the while.

"She's really had a terrible time," said Hella, sticking up for her friend. "I've already told you before about how she was arrested even after saving her country from a diplomatic crisis. But there's more. In time, people began to regard her as a heroine, and that's how she was depicted in the film about her, but when it was being shown in theaters, she was poverty-stricken, and no one offered to help her financially. Curious to see how the film portrayed her, she decided to go, but when she appeared at the theater dressed in rags, she was driven away like a stray dog. That last bit is fiction, but it tells us a lot about what her last years were like."

"That film was what Brecht based his play on," said Nora, making the connection. "Or were you the one who really wrote it?"

Hella responded with a vague laugh, but said nothing.

"Of course," Nora added, "if you don't want to talk about it, you don't have to."

Sensing that Nora was finally going to back off, Hella spoke at last. "I got all the materials he needed to write the play, and lined them up on his desk. I explained everything. While he was writing, he asked for my opinion, so I gave him my advice. When we disagreed, there were quarrels. The finished manuscript, of course, was in German, and I translated it into Finnish."

"What's the title?"

"*The Judith of Shimoda.*"

"I've never read it."

"Most of Brecht's manuscripts were lost. There were only fragments, so the play wasn't performed. But then, thanks to a truly excellent German scholar, who translated my Finnish version back into German, it was finally published."

"Did you show your translation to a publisher in hopes that more people would be able to read it?"

"No, I departed quietly, leaving the translation in a drawer. It was later discovered, purely by chance."

Hearing something ghostly in the word "departed," I felt chills run down my spine. Nora, on the other hand, was excited.

"So, the original was lost," she said brightly, "but then restored, thanks to your translation."

"And even if Lomonosov Moscow State University melts away in a nuclear war," Hiruko suddenly added in English, "they can rebuild it, using the Latvian Academy of Sciences in Riga as a model."

Everyone looked puzzled, as if they'd been handed a riddle. I started to explain, but ended up saying more than I'd meant to.

"We saw the Academy of Sciences in Riga, but it's actually a copy of that university in Moscow. The Latvians didn't want it, but there was this dictator who started giving everybody copies of buildings, as presents. Anyway, something just occurred to me as I was listening to all this talk about copies and originals. Maybe people want to leave copies because they're afraid that they themselves will disappear someday. Okichi, on the other hand, seems absolutely fearless, and her fate—her journey through life—is so dynamic. From geisha to diplomat, from criminal to hero, from hero to homeless. And her story didn't stay in her native language, either—it went from English to German, from German to Finnish, then back to German, forward, then back again, looping around, so I have a feeling she'll never stop. Okichi's going to keep on traveling."

CHAPTER 9   *Susanoo Speaks*

Harsh sunlight poured down, dying the deck silver. I saw a young woman with her man, both short, both blond, walking toward me, holding hands. They took a few steps into the strong wind, then staggered back a bit, their whole bodies collapsing into laughter. They were playing with the wind, knowing they were going to lose but enjoying it anyway. Chattering all the while, they came pretty close but didn't notice me. Sounded like they were speaking French mixed with Russian, but I couldn't pick out a single word. But why was I even interested—was hanging around with Knut and Hiruko turning me into some kind of language freak? Nah, couldn't be. I can't care less about people, or about languages either. The wind moaning past my ears had a lot more to say to me.

My hair's a nuisance, falling in my eyes. When did it get so long? I haven't had a good look at myself in the mirror for a while now. Just a glance now and then when I'm in the bathroom, to make sure I'm still here.

The two shrimps were gone—what a relief—but then I saw another couple, tall this time, coming my way. Just before our eyes met, I turned away. Their arms were around each other's waists. The wind was whipping at the man's jacket, but the woman held it down. It was bright blue—a nice color. But what's wrong with me? I never notice things like that. I don't give a damn what other guys are wearing, so why now all of a sudden?

A seagull was circling overhead, watching me. "That blue

matches the sea, the sky, and me—are you so dumb you didn't notice?" the bird asked. I see—I get it now. People pick their clothes to blend in with the scenery. I didn't know, and I must really stand out, like a picture of a man from ages ago, cut out of an old book and pasted on a flashy poster in a travel agent's window.

My own jacket was threadbare, faded, stiff with dried grease. I'd been wearing it so long I couldn't even remember what kind of fabric it is.

Sick of being buffeted by the wind at the prow, I headed for the stern. Two young sailors in freshly ironed uniforms passed by, fooling around, tickling each other's arm pits and stroking each other's cheeks. White cotton covered their muscular arms and the clean line from their backs down to their hips, but didn't hide their beauty.

I, on the other hand, looked like I'd just crawled out from ancient times. Dressed in rags, with a rounded back, my eyes cast down, dragging my feet as I walked.

A man in his seventies slowly climbed up the gangway onto the deck. From his collar all the way down dull gold buttons drew a neat line. Skinny legs but broad shoulders, his chest still ample. In his polished shoes he stood firmly on the deck, reaching down to take his wife's hand and pull her up. She had a scarf on her head, and a shiny silk jacket over her suit. These two fit as neatly into "old age" as two bottles of fine wine side by side in a wooden box. They had undoubtedly lived through all the established stages: childhood, courtship, child-rearing, retirement. My own life had had no such stages. I'd spent my youth as a real terror, and still had no idea how to change, and though I still had the scars from a red-hot love affair, it hadn't led to a family.

There was a wooden deck chair near the stern. Sitting down in it I'd get pretty cold, but I wanted to try it anyway, to see just *how* cold. Before I had the chance, a little man came over to me. Skinny, with big eyes that seemed to shine with a blue flame. But why was he so thin? Like a strand of black thread that had fallen off the needle in a tailor's workshop. That was a metaphor I'd read somewhere. In something by Gogol? We were close to the port where he'd lived, so maybe that's why I thought of it.

What did this guy want to say to me? While I was getting more worried by the second, he just stood there grinning with his hands in his pockets. After a while he dramatically pulled a spyglass out of his right pocket and stared out at the horizon, then put it back, and when a small bottle of vodka appeared from his left pocket, he took a swig, put it back, and producing a tape measure from his right pocket, made like he was measuring me from my shoulder to my wrist, and then finally brought a sort of catalogue out of that left pocket. The way his jacket hugged his thin frame, how could there be room for all those things in the pockets? I was wondering if it was a magic trick when he suddenly poked me in the chest with the catalogue.

"I'm sure you'll find a coat you like in here," he said in English. His vowels sounded kind of sticky. I cautiously took the catalogue and, on the first page I opened it to, found a picture of a sky-blue coat that grabbed my heart.

"I want this one," I said, then immediately regretted being so honest—like a little kid—and quickly added, "But I'm not buying a coat."

"Whyever not?"

"Because I don't have any money." I replied, not the least bit embarrassed about being poor.

"You don't need any."

"So, what am I going to pay with? You're not planning to exchange a coat for my soul, are you?" This was a joke, to show him how little I cared, but he looked terribly insulted.

"We are not in a fairy tale," he said, staring into my eyes.

"Oh, so you don't want my soul? Then what can I give you?"

"Your passport."

That really threw me off balance, like a blow to a soft spot I'd forgotten I had. He took a step forward.

"You don't really need citizenship in any country, do you? For starters," he said quietly, "you were born long before the word 'nation' even existed."

What did he mean by that? Sure, I may have once said that my passport didn't mean any more to me than a supermarket discount card, but that was just talk—actually, it was my talisman. I'd feel awfully lonely without it. I didn't want him to know that, though.

"I wouldn't mind feeding my passport to a dog," I told him, "but I have to show it when I cross borders," which sounded like a reasonable explanation.

"When you reach a country where you want to stay permanently," he replied, "you won't need it anymore, so you can mail it to me from there."

I took a good look at him. Fine gray hair stuck out around his head, but when the wind blew, it didn't move at all. It was quieter here at the stern, but gusts still hit the boat now and then from either side, so hard they seemed to be mad at it for blocking their way. Every time that happened my hair swept across my face— such a nuisance. So, what was with this guy? I almost asked him if he was the Devil, as a joke, of course, but jokes sometimes light the fuse of a hidden bomb, so I decided to try mundane questions, to find out more about him.

"Are you a tailor?"

"That's right. An old-fashioned sort of profession, perhaps, but robots can't sew very well. You think that if we can build robots there's no need for craftsmen, don't you? Your father's influence?"

I caught my breath. How did he know that Dad made robots? It was scary, the way he dug that up from so far back in the past I'd almost forgotten it myself.

"My father? Nah, I didn't get anything from him."

"Parental influence is healthy, both for society and the individual. I myself am in the profession my family has practiced for generations. I never even thought of going into another line of work. Didn't you ever consider following in your father's footsteps?"

"Never. Robotics advance so quickly—new innovations come by the month, not the year. So, there's nothing to learn from previous generations. But anyway, what's your name?"

"Petrovich."

"Are you on vacation?"

"I was visiting my brother's family in Tallinn, and now I'm on my way home to Saint Petersburg. I wanted to stay a little longer, but my wife's been nagging me."

So, he was from Saint Petersburg. I heard that name for the first time back when I was studying in Kiel. So that's what the Germans call it, "the Fortress of Saint Peter," I remember thinking. A student named Peter had told me, joking, about how, as a saint, he was in the name of the city, and he'd asked me if I was in the name of any place, and I hadn't known what to say.

"If I don't get home soon," Petrovich added, "I'll have another fight with my wife."

"She doesn't like you going abroad?"

"She thinks I'm goofing around when I should be hard at work."

"Right now, though, you're trying to sell me a coat. In other words, you're working."

"But what, exactly, is work? My wife and I have very different ideas about that. She thinks it's important to sell the clothes we make for as much money as possible, whereas I don't care that much about rubles, or dollars, either. The true value of a coat can't be bought—a coat is more than just a product."

"More than a product? Aren't you exaggerating."

"Not at all. Put it on and you're invisible, or your sex changes, or you go flying through the sky—that's what coats are meant for, isn't it? Civil servants, students, teachers—each becomes a god while wearing a coat I've made."

"I can see how a good coat could make you feel more human, but like a god? Aren't you claiming way too much for your coats?"

"Actually, feeling human is harder than you'd think. Everyone's always surrounded by things they can't buy. They're drowning in debt, and still can't get what they want. By seeing yourself as a god, you can live like a human being for the very first time. After all, the gods never go shopping."

"Not only gods—ghosts and devils don't spend much time in the stores, either."

"Do you believe in ghosts?"

"I hear the city where you live is full of them."

"Yes, seeing ghosts isn't unusual in Saint Petersburg."

"Why do you use the German name?"

"Why shouldn't I? After war broke out with Germany, people started using the Russian name, Petrograd, but as my wife has roots in Germany, we still call it Saint Petersburg."

"War with Germany? In the twentieth century, or the twenty-first? Which war are you talking about?"

"When I was born, the city was called Leningrad. But it doesn't really matter now. Thinking of myself as a being who's existed since ancient times makes it easier to understand why I'm pouring myself into my work now."

"You definitely seem like somebody with supernatural powers."

"Of course I do. I take the skins animals once wore and transform them into coats for human beings. Through that process, I also borrow the animals' strength. Tailors and shoemakers all have magic. Oh—and so do blacksmiths."

"Blacksmiths?"

"Blacksmiths are descendants of the gods. Your father must have known Wayland the Smith."

Maybe Dad did use magic while he was patiently melting metal, then cutting, bending, and welding it to make robots that looked like human beings. Sadly, he couldn't keep his robots from being used as tools to deceive people. When I was a kid, I wanted to make things, too, but much bigger things than robots, machines so gigantic you'd have to look up at them. Ships! I remember now—I came to study shipbuilding in Kiel. And now here I was on a mail boat, rocking on the water without ever having built a single ship. What in the world was I doing? Had I gotten off the path I was supposed to follow? No, that wasn't it. I was a navigator. The descendant of Charon, in Greek myth. It was my job to guide people to faraway places. Wasn't that as respectable as shipbuilding?

Knut. Nanook. Akash. Nora. They saw reaching one destination as the start of a new journey, but I was going home. Dad and Mom would be happy to see me again. When the excitement had died down, they might ask me: What have you brought back with you from across the sea? What did you learn in that faraway place, what sort of man have you become?

When I was a boy, Dad showed me a photo of one of our relatives, taken when the young man had returned from studying abroad—he sported a British-style cape and shiny leather shoes, and he was about to climb into a rickshaw. The cape was what the people from our village had gathered to see. In the corner of the picture was a woman in kimono who looked like she ran one of those fancy restaurants you see in the movies. Nowadays, that kimono would probably be worth ten times as much as the cape, but back then people assumed that whatever guys like that had brought back with them was extremely valuable, and that's what they saw in that brilliant new cape. My mother and father would be sad to see this threadbare jacket I was wearing.

That's what I was thinking about when Nanook came strolling over.

"What're you thinking about?" he asked in my native language.

"Coats," I answered honestly. "When you go home, do you want to have a good coat on?"

"What do coats have to do with home?" he asked, understanding the words but clueless as to the meaning of my question. And since it was a strange thing to ask out of the blue, I explained it to him in English.

"You went to study in Denmark. Your parents want you to be a success. They may be hoping, for instance, that you'll be a doctor at Copenhagen's Central Hospital after you graduate. Let's say you go home to see your parents for winter break. Would you buy an expensive new coat, or wear the same jacket you had on when you left?"

"You're way behind the times," he said, struggling not to laugh. "Nobody thinks you can get rich being a doctor these days. It's tough just getting through your internship, and the cost of living in Copenhagen is sky-high. Guys who stay home in Greenland doing business online, browsing online stores for clothes in their spare time, are probably much better dressed than any Danish doctor." I said nothing, so he went on. "I've never studied medicine, and I'm not even going to university anymore. I once thought I'd like to study biology, but I've already strayed from that path. My future is clouded in mist, and I don't know what's going to happen next. It's an anxious time for me, yet here I am, on a journey with no fixed destination."

"Do you regret leaving home?"

"Not really. How about you?"

"Me neither. But today for some reason I feel like going back to the place where I grew up. Maybe it's the weather. Don't you want to go home?"

"Not now," replied Nanook. "There are still so many cities and sights I haven't seen yet. My homeland isn't made of ice, so it's not like it's going to melt away and disappear. I can go back there anytime."

"But everyone's getting older."

"I'm not old enough to have to worry about that yet."

"Are you sure? You're getting older—you just don't notice it because you're so far away. When you're at home, everyone tells you to hurry up and graduate, then get a job, get your own place, get married, and then before you know it, they're telling you you're getting gray—time never stands still, and you can't help feeling your age. But when you're away from all that, time keeps passing—and yet you're the same young guy you were the day you left home. Do you know the story of Urashima Taro?"

"Sure. A bunch of nasty brats torment this sea turtle they find on the shore. Then Urashima the fisherman comes by and saves the turtle. And the turtle invites Urashima to the Dragon Palace."

I was impressed at how many words Nanook knew in my native language, but he didn't seem to know what we call "the Dragon Palace."

"The real name of what you call the Dragon Palace," I said, "is Ryūgūjō."

"Ryūgūjō? Is that a proper noun? And where is it?"

"Under the sea."

"Where's the sea it's under?"

"I'm not sure. Somewhere south of China, maybe. Anyway, they fed him gourmet dishes there, and girls danced for him to beautiful, exotic music. But while he was enjoying himself, time was slipping through his fingers like sand, and he didn't notice that he was aging."

"So, was this Ryūgūjō a sort of spa hotel?"

"Much better than that. Hotel Utopia would be a better name for it. But then one day Urashima Taro got homesick, and went back to his fishing village. None of the people he knew lived there anymore. And when he opened the little box the princess at Ryūgūjō had given him as a souvenir, clouds of smoke came billowing up, and he turned into a white-haired old man. Well, actually, he'd been old for a long time—just hadn't noticed it."

"Sounds like *The Picture of Dorian Gray*," he said in English. "All those years were stored up in that little box."

"Are you talking about Dorian Gray?" asked Nora, who'd come over while we were talking.

"Nein," he said in German, as if explaining it to her was too much trouble, "we're talking about the Dragon Palace. As long as you're there, you never get any older. You don't have to work, either. They serve gourmet meals, and there's beautiful music and dancing, too."

"But if it's a Dragon Palace, there must be a dragon there. Scary, no? I'd never go to a place like that." An odd thing to be worried about, I thought.

"There's nothing evil about this dragon, though. He's rich, generous, and knows how to keep his customers happy."

"So, is his palace like a night club?"

"No—everything's free of charge."

"But surely he plans to eat everyone in the end."

"As I told you before, he's not a bad dragon," I said. "He was a little snake who practiced ascetic discipline until he grew into a fine, mature dragon. Strong, but never abusive. He wants to protect, not harm. His spirit is elegant, so he never resorts to violence." For some reason, I'd suddenly become the dragon's staunchest defender, but Nora wasn't having it.

"This dragon may want to make everyone happy, but he still has absolute power. Not very democratic, if you ask me," she said.

"We weren't talking about democracy," said Nanook, glaring at her.

"Is that all you can think about?" Nora glowered back.

Whether due to love or hostility I couldn't tell, but the tension was rising, and since this was all getting to be a nuisance, I walked away and left them there.

I had my hands on the cold railing, watching the patterns the white foam made on the water when a young woman with a bright red scarf on her head came up from behind me, off to the side. When she took what looked like a piece of bread out of a paper bag and threw it toward the sky, several seagulls seemed to appear out of nowhere. One suddenly changed direction, then swooped down to catch the bread just as it was about to drop into the sea. Another veered in from the side to catch the next piece she threw. When she lifted her arm to throw, the loose sleeve of her thin coat slipped down, revealing a plump, shiny arm.

"Do they sell bread for the gulls on board?" I asked when she turned to look at me.

"These are leftovers from yesterday."

"Do you feed them every day?"

"Only when I'm bored. No one will play with me, so I'm playing with the birds."

"That's a light coat you're wearing. Aren't you cold? The wind's awfully strong today."

"I'm not afraid of the wind," she said. "What I worry about is a wave washing over me and getting me pregnant."

I stared at her, thinking I must have misheard, but she calmly added, "I wonder where the gulls lay their eggs."

"Huh?"

"They're always flying, so they must lay them in midair. But what if they break when they fall?"

When she slipped her scarf off, her reddish-brown hair, twisting like snakes, danced wildly in the wind. She then calmly reached into her pocket and brought out combs, one after another, which she stuck into her hair. Held in place, the hair calmed down, and by the time she'd finished, she had a hairdo that wouldn't have been out of place at an Embassy reception.

"Now I'm ready," she said.

"You're a Meister of Combs," I said. "I thought you were a bird trainer at first, but I see now that you've tamed a much wilder creature—your hair."

"I've smoothed my hair down so that I can get married. Why don't you try it, too?"

"Are you on your honeymoon?" I asked in surprise.

"No, my bridegroom isn't on this boat. He's waiting for me at the next port of call."

"Saint Petersburg?"

"That's right," she said, blushing. Those pink cheeks embarrassed me, as if I were seeing her naked, so I turned away and looked down at the water.

"Saints don't marry," she suddenly murmured, "or have possessions, either."

"Saint Peter's Burg," I said. "Is the man you're going to marry named Peter? Or Pyotr? Or Pierre, maybe?"

"I'm going to marry Saint Petersburg."

"You're marrying a whole city?"

"In ancient times, people used to marry islands, and mountains."

What we now think of as scenery used to be our objects of desire. Suddenly, I felt hungry. And it occurred to me that all the things I wanted to eat actually came from scenery. Roots dug out of the earth, fruit yanked off branches, leaves torn off plants. You can't eat scenery, but if you stick your hand in it, you can cook whatever you pull out.

"It's getting close to dinnertime," I said. "Are you at the table where they speak Russian?"

Without answering my question, the woman moved away, gliding down the deck. It wasn't my fault she was gone, but the seagulls kept giving me dirty looks, and that made me mad.

When I went into the dining hall, Knut and Hiruko were already at the table. Hiruko had her hand on top of Knut's—I don't know why, but that irritated the hell out of me.

"Hiruko," I said in our native language, "aren't you ashamed?

Going home like that—dressed like a boy, with gym shoes on your feet, and no makeup? With a guy who's never had a job? What will your parents say?"

"You're too old-fashioned," she replied, not the least bit rattled. "Are you in a bad mood because you're hungry?" She didn't seem to take me seriously. Nanook walked in, then Nora, as if she were chasing him, sat down next to him. Akash followed.

"Susanoo," Nanook asked, "did you find a good coat to wear home?"

"Is there a boutique somewhere, like the ones on luxury passenger ships?" asked Akash innocently. He hadn't been in on our conversation about coats.

"I'm certainly not going to buy one off the rack," I said arrogantly. "I've found a good tailor."

"Susanoo's going to go home," Nanook explained to the others, "wearing a really fine coat. That'll show his parents the true value of studying abroad." Then, he added, "As long as you're traveling, you can stay young. Going home means getting older."

"Don't you mean maturing," Nora said with a pregnant look, "rather than just getting older?" but he completely ignored her.

"Some people may be satisfied to stay in the Dragon Palace," he went on, "surrounded by beautiful things, never having to work. And that's okay, too."

"Do you mean me?" asked Knut, not the least bit offended.

"Nah, that's not you at all," I teased, "You're going to the palace to meet the princess's parents and beg for her hand in marriage, aren't you? Like in a soap opera."

"And what about you?" Hiruko asked me in English. "Are you going to fight the dragon and save the princess?" She was getting cheeky again.

"Sure—what's wrong with that?" I retorted.

"What's the princess's name? Nine Four?"

"What do you mean?"

"Nine and four are the unluckiest numbers in our language. Nine is *ku*, for *ku*rushii (painful) and four is *shi*, for *shi*nu (to die)."

"Is there a princess by that name?"

"*Ku-shi*. Kushi-nada-hime. She's the mythical princess Susanoo saves."

"The age when men used to slay dragons is over," Knut drawled, as if sunning himself on a lazy afternoon. "Look at the women around you. If a dragon was about to attack, Nora would probably negotiate with it, and make it give up the fight like a diplomat."

"Dragons never negotiate," I said, getting irritated. "They eat whoever they want—princesses, children, anybody. You're a man, aren't you? Wouldn't you protect Hiruko?" I hoped that would get to him, but it didn't—not at all.

"Don't think I'd need to," he said calmly. "She'd start a conversation with the dragon before it had the chance to eat her, then record their talk, and write a book on the grammar of dragon language. I guess I'd be her coauthor."

"Yamata-no-Orochi," said Hiruko.

"Huh?"

"八岐大蛇—Yamata-no-Orochi."

"Is that Yama-noro whatchamacallit the dragon's name?"

"Yamata-no-Orochi is not a dragon. He's the god in charge of water. Water is the purest, most valuable underground resource. Human beings can live without coal or oil as long as they have water."

"But what about heating? The long, cold winter is coming. With only water, we'll freeze."

"The sun will keep us warm."

That night's dinner started and ended with red. First, we had borscht. A spoonful of white sour cream was floating on top of the red soup.

"We're about to dock in Russia, so tonight's menu is Russian?" Nanook asked.

"This is Ukrainian," Nora said, correcting him from the side. Nanook looked disgusted but said nothing. I don't know where borscht comes from, so I wasn't about to join in, but the deep red of the beets reminded me of the blood soup I had once near Keil when I was a student. I was riding through the countryside on my bicycle, and when I asked to use the bathroom at a farmhouse, the family invited me to have dinner with them. I remember a slightly sour soup, with pork and pig's blood in it. Guts, too, maybe. After dinner, the son showed me the field where they grew tomatoes, pumpkins, and beans. That was the first time I'd seen beets growing. Their tops were peeking out of the ground, with big, floppy green leaves sprouting from them. The son pulled one up, brushed off the dirt, and cut the beet in two with a knife. It was deep scarlet inside, with nerves and blood vessels running through it like a cross-section model of the human body, but unlike raw flesh, it gave off a clear light, like a jewel. I couldn't imagine a shade of red this vivid existing anywhere else. "It's not blood," I repeated to myself, over and over again. That was the only way I could keep my cool.

That's what I was thinking of as I stared down at my bowl of borscht. This is not blood, I told myself. It's a root. I raised my eyes to see that Hiruko's lips, now dyed red, looked swollen and slovenly. Knut looked sexy, like he'd put on lipstick. Akash gazed at him, not touching his soup.

"Are you going sightseeing at our next port of call?" he asked in a squeaky voice.

"Of course," Knut said cheerfully. "Saint Petersburg—my uncle told me it's the most European city in Europe. I've always wanted to see it."

"We don't have time for sightseeing," Hiruko broke in, her eyebrows slanted downward like an Ashura—I'd never seen her look so angry. "We have to go straight to the station, look for a train to Moscow, and buy our tickets for the Siberian Railway."

"Was that what we were planning?" Akash asked, shocked.

"If we stay on this boat," Hiruko said, nodding gravely, "we'll go back toward the west. Think of the shape of the Baltic Sea. After Saint Petersburg comes Finland. Back to the western world. To keep going eastward, we must now say goodbye to the sea." She sounded so grim, as if her life depended on it, that I just had to take her down a notch.

"Hey little girl, you can't do that."

"Why not?" she shot back. There was fear in her eyes.

"Because without a visa you can't get off in Russia."

The color drained from her face.

"Sometimes," Nora said to comfort her, "you can get a visa on board."

"Do you want to enter Russia?" asked a man's voice, clear and strong. It was the captain, now standing behind me. Doeff, his name was—a Dutchman.

"Yes," said Hiruko, nodding vigorously. "We have to go to Russia."

"Do you have visas?"

"No."

"Then I'm afraid you can't. You'll have to go back to the last country where you went through immigration and apply for a visa there."

"But we're not asking for asylum in Russia," Hiruko protested, blinking furiously. "It's just for transit." Nobody was going to take seriously such ridiculous hairsplitting.

"I'm afraid," the captain said with a sad smile, "you still need a visa. We spend our whole lives in transit, so if your point is valid, then visas wouldn't exist, would they?"

"Isn't there anything we can do?"

"Personally, I'd like to help you. But as a captain, all I can do is transport people from one place to another. I can't stick my hand in my pocket and magically pull out a visa."

"But we got off in Kaliningrad. That was Russia, wasn't it?"

"That was a special case. An exclave."

Finally realizing we'd have to work out a solution by ourselves, Knut thanked the captain.

"Time for a strategy session," he said, looking around at each of us.

Suddenly, *he* was acting like the leader, which got on my nerves. But since no one was going to come up with a brilliant plan, it was like taking charge of a sinking ship—no reason to envy that.

"Wasn't entering the Baltic our first mistake?" said Akash. "We should have set sail, no matter the difficulty, on the Indian Ocean."

"How were we supposed to get to India?" I asked, even though I'd planned to keep my own counsel. "Through the Middle East?"

"We should have crossed the Mediterranean to Marseille, then taken a French ship down the coast of Africa. Once we got to the Cape of Good Hope, nothing would have stood in our way."

Akash wasn't about to give up, so I let him have it: "You can't sail along the African coast. Besides, there are no French ships in service now. What century are you living in?"

"*Happofusagari*," said Hiruko.

"What does that mean?" asked Knut and Nanook in unison. They seemed to pin all their hopes on that one word, as if understanding it was the key to finding a route we could take. Hiruko was too depressed to say more, so I explained in her place.

"It means that all eight directions are shut off. Eight, as in the number of heads people say Yamata-no-Orochi had."

"There are dragons," said Nanook, "with nine heads, too." Then, as if suddenly remembering something, he added, "There's another option—have you forgotten Greenland?"

"You mean go north, then over to the other side of the globe?"

"That's right. Let's go north. It might be closer that way."

"If the nine-headed dragon you mentioned was Nāga, that would be India."

"No, India's out. Wouldn't it be better cross Africa, then go down to the South Pole and come out at Australia?"

The threads were getting so tangled that we were about to

lose all sense of direction, and Hiruko was looking more and more depressed.

"If you want to go East," Nora said to her encouragingly, "first you have to go West." She was talking like some kind of fortune teller, but looking at the map, there was a certain logic to what she said. If we couldn't enter Russia, we'd have to head for Finland. It was a relief, knowing I wouldn't have to get off the boat yet. I couldn't stand being boxed up in a compartment for days on end while we crossed Siberia by train. I liked the sea. Ever since boarding this boat, I'd felt relaxed, as if I were meant to be here—I hadn't realized that until now. We had yogurt with bright red gooseberry jam for dessert.

I left the dining hall and was walking down the narrow corridor on my way back to my cabin when I came upon the captain, feet planted wide apart, hands clasped behind his back, gazing at a nautical map on the wall.

"Odd, don't you think?" he said. "The way all these countries are lined up along the shore with their heads sticking out, like animals around a watering hole."

Taking another look at the map, I saw what he meant. Each country had only a fairly limited shoreline.

"Why do they all want to face the sea, even if it means being so scrunched up together?"

"They probably believe," said the captain, "that having an exit to the sea is an entrance to happiness. But a country like Switzerland that never even thought of having a seaport may be more peaceful than any of them." His voice was full of emotion.

"Islanders are surrounded by water, so we don't really get the concept of 'an exit to the sea.'"

"That may seem lucky—being able to get to the sea from any direction. It's dangerous, too, though. Do you ever have dreams about the sea level rising until your island is swallowed up?"

"I never dream," I said. "I'm not a modern guy who has dreams and then tells his friends about them." What made me lie about something like that? It seemed strange, even to me.

"I see," said the captain, looking a little friendlier than before. "You're a man from an earlier time. Mine is an ancient profession—ship's captains appear even in myth."

Hiruko came by, still looking rather gloomy. Captain Doeff looked down at her, concerned.

"Are you feeling better?" he asked gently. Expressionless, she nodded. "Don't worry," he said, "I'm sure things will work out for the best in the end." Then bringing his bulky wrist watch up to his nose, he said, "Oh, my, I've got work to do. Sorry."

Suddenly Hiruko and I were alone. Awkward.

"Why do you look so angry?" she asked.

"Because I am, a little ..."

"Why?"

"You're so lucky—you've got everyone on your side."

"Lucky?" She looked shocked. "I'm homeless, abandoned by my parents. You're the son, your family's heir."

She had a point. Hiruko wasn't the model daughter, the one her parents were proud of. That was the next child—Hiruko, born with a soft, shapeless body, was thrown away. Cast out to sea in a reed boat. That's the role she plays in myth, anyway.

"I was sent away," she went on, "out of the country. They call it *ryū-gaku* (studying abroad), but to me it sounds more like *ryū-kei* (being sent into exile)."

"Yeah, but everybody likes you. They all hate me."

"Since you know you're going home to take over the family business, you've decided it doesn't matter whether people like you or not."

"Who said I am coming into an inheritance?"

"Men can be troublemakers because they have a home to go back to. If they didn't, and had to spend their lives in foreign countries, they'd practice reading strangers' feelings, and really work at connecting with them. But you don't do any of that, because you know you'll be handed a fortune someday."

Slowly, we were getting nearer to the port. I was standing on deck, squinting in the bright sunlight, trying to see what was off in the distance. There were tours of other historical ports along the Baltic, but none of them interested me. Yet just hearing "Saint Petersburg" was exciting. Feeling a tap on my shoulder, I turned around to see that skinny tailor, Petrovich. Putting his big leather suitcase down, he took a crumpled piece of paper out of his pocket and poked me in the chest with it.

"This is my address. Mail me your passport," he said arrogantly.

"I forgot to ask—what, exactly, are you going to do with a foreign passport?"

"I'm going into exile in your country."

"You must be joking," I laughed. "There's nothing for you in my country."

"Yes, there is. You just haven't noticed it."

"And where's the coat you were going to give me in return?"

"In your cabin," the tailor said, then walked away. Must be kidding, I thought—his way of saying goodbye. He couldn't have made me a coat. There wasn't time, and he didn't have the materials. He probably gave me his address because he wanted me to write to him, but was too embarrassed to ask me to be his pen pal, like some high school girl. Email was often blocked by gag orders these days, but letters were apparently still okay. And after all, this was a mail boat. The tailor must have wanted to make sure he kept in contact with someone in the outside world.

I walked around the deck to where I could see the gangway. A woman in a fur hat carrying a heavy suitcase in both hands was edging her way down, teetering back and forth on her high heels like a child's balancing toy. The tailor followed her. Men in what looked like military uniforms were waiting on the pier for the passengers, examining their documents one by one.

I imagined myself on shore, walking around Saint Petersburg. A strong wind would be whipping through an alley, angry at the tall buildings for blocking its path, and then, taking on human form, attacking a lonely woman. "She's got nothing to do with it," I'd say, "the thief who robbed you—that's the one you want to hurt," but the message wouldn't get through.

"What're you doing?" asked Nora from behind.

"I was imagining walking through the old part of Saint Petersburg."

"You'd get awfully cold. Too bad this isn't the Black Sea, or the Caspian."

"That's just wishful thinking—these days almost all the oceans are off limits."

"You mean we should thank the Baltic, just for letting us in?"

"No, I'm not particularly grateful, but I'm glad I came anyway. I wanted to see Saint Petersburg."

"But we can't get off the boat."

"No matter. I have a good enough view from here. Besides, what I want to see is invisible."

"What, for instance?"

"Envy and resentment."

"What good will that do you?"

"Envy and resentment are everywhere, in the air. But in this city, they appear in the form of ghosts. What would you do if a gang of thieves stole the warm winter coat you'd saved up for years to buy? Or if you were a poor student with high ideals, watching loan sharks enrich themselves by preying on other people's weaknesses while you starved? Or what would you feel if your older sister stole your inheritance? Envy and resentment."

Nanook came walking over.

"This is unusual," he said. "I don't remember the two of you ever holding a meeting."

"Susanoo wants to know," said Nora, with a pleading look at Nanook, "how I'd feel if my older sister stole my inheritance."

"That's an old story," he laughed, "from myth. Amaterasu, the older sister, was put in charge of the sky, while her younger brother Susanoo was supposed to oversee things like the night, and the sea. Whether that's exactly how the world was divided up between them, nobody knows—there're lots of different interpretations, and besides, it's a myth." Nora listened intently to his explanation.

"Ruling over the night," she said, "would be wonderful. That's the time for dreams, and love. The oceans would be just as good."

"The sea doesn't count as territory."

"But if someone picked you to govern the seas," Nora went on, "it would show how highly they thought of your skills as a politician."

"Why do you say that?"

"Well, you'd have to act as Minister of Foreign Affairs *and* of the Environment combined. There's enough industrial waste piled up on the ocean floor now to make a new Dragon Palace. The beauties who dance there are actually dolphins with bellies full of plastic. There are tiny pieces of plastic in the gourmet fish served on all those gorgeous platters, too. On top of that, an oil tanker or warship sinks now and then, leaving a huge oil spill. The whole world will be destroyed if we don't clean up the oceans. And you'd be responsible for figuring out how."

I felt like somebody'd woken me up with a slap on the cheek. Until now I'd spent my life whining, pouting, and acting the tough guy, but now I realized that when my parents put me in charge of the seas, it wasn't because they didn't love me—in fact, just the opposite. If the oceans were destroyed, the whole world would die along with them. The sun could be shining, but its heat would burn the earth up, and desiccate it. I had to stop that.

When I looked out over the sea again, the light glinting on the waves looked cold.

CHAPTER 10   *Hiruko Speaks (4)*

A thin strip of pale orange running parallel to the horizon was sandwiched between heavy gray clouds tinged with purple and the sea, now almost black: In its center was the perfectly round evening sun, a deeper shade of orange. We call it "the evening sun" even though the sun knows no evening or night, morning or afternoon. We're so self-centered, using words like *risen* when it shines on us in the morning, and *set* after it's left us in darkness.

On the dock, a tall set of cranes drifted slowly away like a family of giraffes. A row of square buildings about the same height grew smaller by the minute. I closed my eyes, and the scene changed. The roof of a Byzantine-style cathedral, the onion dome of a Russian Orthodox church, the shining gold and soft, sweet white of the Romanov Winter Palace. I opened them, and it all disappeared. Apparently, there are things you can only see with your eyes closed. We'd come as far as the port of Saint Petersburg, and now we're leaving without seeing the city.

"What're you thinking about?" Knut's voice, from behind. The wind was so noisy I hadn't heard his footsteps.

"saint petersburg smaller grows."

"Sorry we couldn't see it."

"heartbroken."

"Heartbroken's an awfully strong word—is that really how you feel?"

"tears."

"We'll come back again someday. Maybe by then the word

visa won't exist anymore."

"if russia cross not, to childhood house return cannot."

"What makes you think that? Surely there are other routes you could take."

"as a child, niigata port i always saw. opposite bank equals russia. russia equals bridge to europe."

Knut had no answer to that. Wrapped in an evening that seemed as if it would go on forever, I was silent, too. Had I really been planning from the start to go east on the Trans-Siberian Railway? If I'd been serious about it, I would have ordered tickets and applied for a visa ahead of time. Or could I have boarded this boat assuming that things would somehow work out? I only acted that recklessly in my dreams. So, was this a dream? Was I sound asleep, about to be awakened by a voice announcing, "We will soon be landing at Narita International Airport"? Whereupon I'd realize I'd been dreaming and hurry to fasten my seatbelt? That would mean I had boarded the plane in Helsinki, I said to myself as I watched a red fireboat pass by, sending out white spray like the fins of a flying fish. This was the sea, and I was standing on the deck of a boat. I was not on a plane. But why was I on the Baltic in the first place? What sort of travel plan had we worked out before we boarded in Copenhagen? I couldn't remember a thing about it. As if time were a mop that had been following behind me, wiping away any trace of my memories.

"Did we really plan to take the Trans-Siberian Railway?" asked Knut, who'd apparently been thinking along the same lines. "Or did we know that would be impossible from the start, and were just pretending it wasn't?"

"reason for pretending?"

"If we hadn't, we wouldn't have been able to start out on this trip."

"baltic sea blindfold?"

"The feeling that we had to go east was real. It didn't matter which sea we crossed. When people are closed in, the ocean looks like an exit, so we headed for a port."

"desire to understand the heart of the sea. small sea, big sea, many problems have, work hard to deal with."

"Problems?"

"mediterranean, for instance. by poverty driven, in rubber boats many people ride. on opposite shore, a better life to them appears. but waves come, wind blows, boat capsizes, people drown. also black sea, vietnam."

"What does the Black Sea have to do with Vietnam?"

"beneath feet bombs are buried. even now. though war long ago ended."

"You mean mines?"

"in black sea mines are floating."

"I see—torpedoes. If a boat accidentally touches one, it'll be blown up along with all the people on it. Why is the sea so full of suffering?"

"the sea problems create not. human beings problems always manufacture."

"Of course—the sea's much wiser than we are."

"the sea human-made problems could solve, i wish."

"The sea shows us our problems, as if reflected in a mirror, but it won't solve them for us."

"eastward we go cannot."

"The Germans call the Baltic the East Sea, but it's not a taxi that will take us to the East."

"in high school, softball practiced."

"Huh?"

"pitcher arm around swings," I said, "baltic sea we halfway around go." I swung my arm to demonstrate how when the ball is in just the right position, the pitcher lets it fly, straight to the batter. I wanted to explain about momentum—about how you had to know just when to let the ball go, but sometimes you can't find that perfect moment. I couldn't find the right words, though, so I tried acting it out.

"You've got to find just the right time to throw," he laughed. "I'm sure you were a great pitcher."

"to pitch i was allowed not. future equals frightening. so ball let go cannot. future equals answer. final answer want to see not."

"The future may not even exist, you know. The next 'present' will come, followed by another and another—a long series of presents that keeps the future from ever reaching us. Which means you don't have to worry about it."

"no next."

"Sure there is. There'll always be a next port of call. In our case, Helsinki."

"we to the East want to go. helsinki equals west."

"That's true, but isn't Finland connected to the east in a different way from Russia?"

"how?"

"You told me that for people coming from Asia, Helsinki is the gate to Europe. Don't you remember? You said you'd gone through it yourself. So, all we have to do is retrace your steps in the opposite direction."

I had told Knut about the gate of Helsinki once. I was objecting to what he'd said about airports, that they're boring because they're all the same. The Helsinki airport I remembered was unlike any other. The floors, walls, and ceiling were all made of ice, with a blue light that made them sparkle. The chill, clear air bathed my throat, and felt bracing on my skin. In a souvenir shop, I'd stopped in front of a shelf lined with little glass Moomins, Snufkins, and Sniffs, gleaming like morning dew. But since I wouldn't be going home any time soon, I didn't need to buy presents, I'd thought, and suddenly felt terribly lonely, as if needles were piercing my heart. If only I could give my family souvenirs, show them my photos, and tell them about my travels—I'd enjoy that.

As I'd walked along the corridor toward the transfer gate, I caught sight of the English words, "Gateway to Asia." It was also written in Finnish and Swedish, with Chinese characters and hangul below. Gateway to Asia. Not a poem or a song, just a slogan cooked up by the airlines, but knowing I'd finally come to the unknown world beyond that gate turned my joy into a tiny, round drop that entered my bloodstream and started coursing through my body. The people passing by glided gracefully down the icy corridors on skates. The airport staff, too, skated by pushing sleds piled with cases of green gooseberry juice in jars.

"That time when you told me about coming to Europe you looked really happy."

Knut's voice pulled me out of my daydream.

"truly happy i was. that feeling i had forgotten."

If I went to Helsinki now, I probably wouldn't be able to see that beautiful ice airport, because Europe had stopped being a dream to me, and was now simply the place where I lived.

Yet even so, that didn't mean I could settle down in one place and live there forever. The term "permanent resident" was now obsolete, and immigrants were forced to cross border after border, as if they were jumping rope. And only the ones who pretended to enjoy it—claiming with a smile, "I LIKE skipping rope, and besides, it's good for my health"—survived. They could be sleeping in their own room one night, then have to pack up and move to another country before noon the next day. While applying for a residence permit at immigration, they would sometimes feel like orphans being passed from one relative to the next.

Suddenly, I had a good idea. What if I thought of myself as a house? That way, I wouldn't be so anxious all the time. No matter where I went, if I myself were my home, I'd never lose it. And if Knut lived there with me, the morning when we had to part would never come.

"What're you thinking about?"

"i equal house. possible?"

"You—a house?"

"yes."

Taking a step back, Knut looked me up and down.

"You seem kind of small for a house, from the outside anyway. Makes me wonder if a bear like me would even fit in, but you must be roomy inside."

"until you fit, will keep expanding."

"I've always considered myself a big guy, but I'm not, really. Like some countries I can think of."

"large but flexible. because mythical hero you try to be not."

"You're right about that. I can guarantee you—I'm definitely not one of those giants from Scandinavian myth."

"I'm nothing like a mythical hero either," said Akash, who had come up behind us. "So can I join you?" While I was searching for an answer, he grew impatient, and rephrased his question. "I mean, is there room in that house for me, too?"

"welcome!" I said, and he jumped straight up into the air, his scarlet sari dancing wildly around his slender body like a flame.

"I've been looking for a home that would accept me for a long time, but I'd just about given up."

"Why?"

"I'll never be a father. Or a mother, either. And I can't go on living as a child."

"I don't see why not. It seems to me that you can be a father *and* a mother. Staying a child is fine, too. But what do you want to be?"

"A bird."

My mouth was still hanging open in surprise when I saw Nora walking toward us, gawking around.

"Have you seen Nanook?" she asked.

"No Nanook, no risk," said Akash, flapping his hands up and down like a bird's wings. A strange thing to say—not quite a joke, or even a pun—but Nora burst out laughing.

"You look so happy," she said. "Did you win the lottery?" Akash was the only one who could get her to relax, and make her laugh.

"Hiruko says she's going to be a house, and Knut will be living inside her. I asked if I could join them, and she said I'd be welcome."

"Aren't you afraid of making a nuisance of yourself?" she asked with a worried look. "They won't treat you badly, but you'll still be the third wheel, an 'extra,' because Hiruko and Knut are a couple."

Akash's head sank, and he got very quiet. I wanted to cheer him up.

"The word 'couple,'" I said to Nora, "is like the bathtub—only one part of the house. No one soaks in the tub every day from morning to night. I want to be a house, not a bathtub. A houseboat. A bohemian on the sea. A houseboat has a better chance of staying afloat with Akash on board."

"You're really talking about this journey we're on," said Nora, "comparing it to a house, aren't you? In a sense, you're the houseboat we're all riding on. But this trip is about to end. We can't spend the rest of our lives traveling together."

"Are you sure we're near the end?" Knut asked quietly. "I can't believe we'll find the answer we're looking for so easily."

Nora ignored him and turned to Akash. "You want to be loved by one person—to mean everything to that person, don't you?" We heard someone clearing his throat, and turned around to see Nanook standing there, a sullen look on his face.

"Say Hiruko and Knut get married," he said. "Right after the wedding, Knut sets out on a long journey. Hiruko stays at home, spinning for years as she waits for him to return. She doesn't want to be trapped in that kind of story, which is why she's talking about being a houseboat. And why it's good to have Akash on board, but nobody needs a fourth person, making comments from the side."

Knowing he was referring to her, Nora fell silent.

"Nora," Nanook went on, "thinks Hiruko and Knut are like Izanami and Izanagi, in a world where there's only one woman and one man. That would definitely make Akash the third wheel. But we've left that world behind."

"Iza—what? Who are they?" asked Nora eagerly, her curiosity getting the better of her.

"A goddess," Nanook explained, happy to be the expert, "and a god. They stand facing each other, naked. They examine each other's bodies, noting what sticks out, and what doesn't, all the while seriously considering how to have sex, anatomically. They don't know modern phrases like 'romantic love' or 'carnal desire,' but they're sure they have to produce some descendants. So, they discover how to have children, all by themselves. No one gives them any hints."

"No one at all?"

"Well, there were no biology teachers back then, no snake in the garden, no instruction manuals or videos."

"When is 'back then'?"

"Before history began. Seems they already had language, though prehistoric language does seem like a contradiction." He was trying not to laugh as he rattled on, saying whatever popped into his head, but listening to him, I felt more like crying.

"I don't want to stand facing someone, examining each other's bodies as we grow older. I am not Izanami. Not a female sample. I'm Hiruko. There are many different kinds of bodies living on the earth. We forget that when we see only human beings. I want to keep all sorts of other bodies in mind—lions, eagles, snow grouse, deer, spiders, fish, starfish, amoeba." A seagull overhead squawked as if warning me not to leave it out.

"Men are all shot down by women." Nanook was now talking like an actor on a stage. "They lie on deck like wounded seagulls. For Knut, the shooter's his mother, for me, my future wife, for

Susanoo, his older sister." Nora, her eyes filled with tears, looked up at the gray sky to keep them from rolling down her cheeks. I remembered the time my high school drama club put on Chekhov's *The Seagull*. I worked on the scenery, but went to all the rehearsals.

"Did Chekhov live in Saint Petersburg?" I asked, suddenly changing the subject.

"No, he didn't," Nanook replied, unfazed.

"I thought all the great masters of Russian literature lived in Saint Petersburg."

"Gogol and Dostoevsky did, but Chekhov lived in a port on the Sea of Azov." He answered so smoothly he must have had Chekhov in mind, too.

"How do you know that?"

"I've been reading every day. Have you guys been to the library? It's full of Eastern European and Scandinavian literature."

"So, you've been studying all this time," said Knut with an envious smile, "just like you would have at university. My store of knowledge hasn't grown at all since we started out."

"In the world of books you can enter any country without a visa. You can even go to places that don't exist anymore, like the Roman Empire, or the Soviet Union."

Nanook was starting to sound full of himself.

"If you can learn about everything just by reading," snapped Knut, "then you didn't really need to come on this boat trip, did you?" I'd never seen him so irritated, but Nanook, his nose lifting slightly, seemed to have an even greater sense of his own superiority.

"The relationship between books and boats," he went on confidently, "isn't as simple as you think. People who write books sense that a crisis is coming. They know that any civilization could sink into the sea. So," he concluded dramatically, "all libraries are boats."

Nora, whose eyes had looked so sad before, were now filled with warmth and admiration for Nanook. After switching personalities with that arrogant, ill-tempered doctor, Nanook was sounding more intelligent, more articulate by the day. As this made him all the more attractive to Nora, it didn't seem likely that she'd be able to reign in his arrogance.

"Can't the passengers do something to keep the boat from sinking?" she asked.

"All boats sink," declared Nanook, ignoring her question. "All seagulls will be shot down. All countries will eventually disappear."

"So you're saying the houseboat called Hiruko will go under, too?" asked Knut, his nostrils flared with anger, his voice deeper than usual.

Nanook's reply surprised us: "No, Hiruko will stay afloat. She was thrown into the water right after she was born, so there's no reason for her to sink now." After saying this much in English, he turned to me and added, in my native language, "Remember—*ie* (house) and *iie* (no) are pronounced the same." *Ie* and *iie*. Not exactly the same, but definitely similar. A whirlwind formed in the tiny space between the two words, sweeping into the room of my memories, whipping through the pages of an old notebook, covered with dust.

"Since childhood, my *house* kept on saying *no* to me. The house wanted a perfect daughter, or a princess, and I didn't feel I was either. So I decided to say *no* to the *house*, and went far away. But now here I am, moving away from *no* back toward *house*. And not just moving—I want to *be* a house that everyone can live in. Which is a contradiction. Maybe I'm an imp—an imp of the perverse."

Though he seemed not to know the word "imp," Nanook nodded along as he listened, showing that he'd understood everything else. As I felt myself grow closer to Nanook, who truly loved my native language, Knut receded into the distance, so I quickly took his arm in mine and said in Panska, "vanished home i search for not. myself equals home."

Things I needed lots of words to say in my native language were much shorter in Panska—like a haiku. Tiny wrinkles formed at the corners of Knut's eyes as he smiled, seeking out the fingers at the end of my arm linked with his, squeezing them so hard it hurt.

"I will be a house," I chanted softly in my native language, "I myself will be a house," but since that sounded too much like some kind of slogan, I tried for something a little more poetic. Still in my native language, I whispered, "in a small house, floating on the sea, spacious rooms," but got no reaction from Nanook. He did seem to like the general idea, though.

"Not having a house, but becoming one yourself—splendid!"

"You mean women should guard the home," said Nora, glowering at him, "while men work outside?" Now it was my turn to explain.

"No," I said, "I myself am going to be a houseboat—tied to the pier, but then the rope broke. Knut will be on aboard, and Akash, too."

"Do you really not want to be alone with Knut—just the two of you?"

"A boat with only two passengers will sink."

"So you need three?"

"I'd like to be a fourth," said Nanook.

"I'm in, too, then"—a Pavlovian response from Nora.

"Oh, no you don't," protested Nanook, suddenly changing from an arrogant doctor to a little boy.

"Why not?"

"Women are boats. You should be a houseboat, too, and find your own passengers."

"That sort of division of labor by sex is obsolete."

"You're not the kind to tag along on another woman's journey. Akash and Knut are both parasitic types—like mistletoe in the plant world. I'm a little like that myself. That's why we're traveling with Hiruko. But you're different—you and Susanoo both. Why did you come on this trip in the first place?"

"I wanted to see the Pacific Ocean."

"What good's that going to do you?" asked Nanook, flabbergasted, but to tell the truth, I was just as surprised as he was, and wanted to hear Nora's reply.

"I heard about some strange new islands that have appeared in the Pacific, and I'm dying to see them."

"I read something," said Nanook, his eyebrows twitching nervously, "about an active volcano deep beneath the sea, called Nishinoshima. You can see its crater on the surface. Every time there's a new eruption, lava pours out and then hardens, making the island bigger. Some scientists think that if the eruptions keep coming, the island could get so big we'll have another continent in the Pacific."

"No, that's not it. The islands I'm talking about are made of garbage. There are several in the Pacific—huge piles of trash floating in the ocean that came together to form islands. Apparently there's an archipelago of them that looks just like Hiruko's country—that's what I want to see."

My heart started clanging like a fire bell. Maybe the people who'd lived on Honshu took refuge on garbage islands just before their homes disappeared. Once they were there, they might have decided to create a new history for themselves, forgetting everything that came before. Was that why I couldn't get in touch with anyone? There might not be a single person left who remembered me. While Nora and Nanook were talking about the birth of new islands, I was obsessed with thoughts of the old one, the island I'd known, that might have sunk beneath the sea.

The position of the evening sun had barely changed, but storm clouds were forming overhead like a cape that covered the sky, turning everything dark.

"Honshu has sunk," I said, no longer able to bear the weight of the darkness within me, "and the people have moved to an island made of garbage. What if that turns out to be true?"

"A really big island wouldn't sink so easily," said Knut, placing his hand on my shoulder. "And if there was a mass migration, we'd have heard about it on the news."

"Evaporation."

"Huh?"

"In my country, people sometimes evaporate into thin air, like water boiling in a kettle. They suddenly move to a different place without telling their family, friends, or coworkers, and using an alias, start a new life there. That kind of thing really happens. So, what if the whole country—everyone—suddenly disappeared like that, all at the same time? Without a word to their friends or family abroad?"

"I can see why you're upset," said Nanook, "but if you look at it in a different way, it might not be so terrible. They will have moved elsewhere—that's all. Which means nobody died. And psychologically, relocating to a garbage island might be easier than going into exile in a neighboring country. At least there wouldn't be any anti-immigrant mobs waiting to attack you." I think he was trying to comfort me, but the clouds were now as black as India ink. Nora was encouraging in her own way.

"A garbage island might be like heaven on earth," she said cheerfully. "You could get your energy from the garbage, so you wouldn't need nuclear power or coal. There'd be things in the trash you could use to make cars, or refrigerators. You wouldn't need to import natural resources, so you wouldn't be dependent on other countries. Maybe they figured that since foreign relations always seem to lead to wars, it's better not to have any, and cut themselves off. Couldn't that be possible?"

"You mean countries only deal with each other to get fossil fuels?" said Knut angrily. "Or so they can force what they dig out of their own mines on somebody else? That's the only reason?" Watching Knut fume, Akash nodded in agreement.

Across the dark sea, I saw winking lights like fireflies—were they fishing boats, or warships? I imagined a mountain of broken TVs and old tires growing hotter and hotter until sad, transparent flames like the tails of goldfish rose from it, wavering in the air.

"Hey, do you have a fever?" Knut asked. I put a hand on my forehead—definitely hot. Flammable, ignitable, combustible— burning with resentment at all these silly human labels—fire twisted its way through a rumbling, chaotic mass of garbage, setting off ominous heat rays in my brain.

Then, something hit my forehead, sending me staggering backward. A violent gust of wind. Everyone was bent over as if they had stomach cramps, so I leaned forward, too. A thunderous roar passed overhead. I took several deep breaths, then timidly raised my eyes just as the boat careered to one side, causing me to lose my balance and lurch forward, my hands hitting the deck. When I stood up, the sea seemed to be bearing down on us, deep green waves rising from it to crash together and break. Two walls of water then collided head-on, sending a pillar of white spray straight up into the air, which splashed coldly over my head a moment later.

"Come below, now!" shouted two sailors in rubber boots as they ran toward us. My feet were stuck to the wet deck, so I couldn't walk. While I struggled to lift one leg, the wind almost blew me over. One of the sailors put his arm around me and we slowly started to walk. I saw the other helping Akash, diagonally behind me. We came to the door, and just before we started downstairs, I looked back and saw Akash, smiling weakly. Knut and Nanook were staggering along behind him. But I didn't see Nora.

"Where's Nora?" I yelled as loud as I could, but could hardly hear myself above the wind. I was soon safely below deck, followed by Akash, Knut, and Nanook. But I still had to look for Nora.

"Where're you going?" asked Knut, grabbing hold of my wrist as I turned to go back.

"Nora's not here. I have to look for her." Since he wouldn't let go, I dragged him along with me up the stairs. I opened the metal door with its round porthole, and was met with a strong gust of wind. Sticking my neck out to look around the deck, I saw Nora walking through a curtain of rain. Shielding her face with her left arm, clutching the railing with her right hand, she took one firm step at a time, coming slowly toward us.

I remembered the first time I saw her. We were in Trier, in one of the tunnellike passageways in the Kaisertherman, the ancient Roman baths, and Nora appeared at the exit with the sun at her back, straight and tall as a goddess of war, the light making her blonde hair look like a golden halo around her head. She trod firmly over those ancient Roman stones, never stumbling, never hesitating. Even if paving stones were exchanged for a turbulent sea beneath her feet, she wouldn't lose her balance. She walked through the storm by herself, with no need for support.

Compared to Nora, I was like a reed on the water, with no special skills aside from my ability to stay afloat. Wasn't there something ridiculous about me claiming to be a big houseboat?

"What were you doing on deck in the middle of a storm?" barked Susanoo like a high school coach bawling out his team.

"We were talking about what we're going to do from now on," I retorted angrily in our native language, "when the storm came up. I gather no one asked you to the meeting." I hoped the sarcasm would get to him.

"I couldn't care less about your meetings," he said with a chuckle. "Are you the chairperson? Sounds like fun. But you can't just say 'Dismissed!' when things get out of hand. Ha, ha, ha. Dismissed—takes you back, doesn't it? I had this lazy teacher in grade school who'd leave us at the train station after a field trip. 'Dismissed!' he'd say, 'You can all go home on your own.'

Probably wanted to go off drinking with his cronies. Some kids had parents who'd come pick them up, but the rest didn't even have money for the train, and they'd all start whimpering." He rattled off this story without taking a breath. Memories of how sad I'd felt when school field trips ended came floating up from the past. I didn't want this trip to end that way.

"What did you just say?" Knut asked him nervously. As Susanoo wasn't about to translate it into English for him, I gave him the gist of it in Panska.

"if chairperson equals me, to everyone 'dismissed!' say cannot."

"So you can't tell us when our journey's over? Is that what he said?" Knut then turned to Susanoo. "What a nice thing to say," he teased, putting a friendly arm around his shoulders.

Shuddering as if he couldn't bear to be touched, Susanoo roughly broke free and said, "Hiruko's ideas are fundamentally sound. All we have to do is follow her. Not that that's always the best thing to do, but basically, it is."

So now he seemed to be praising me—just the opposite of his attitude before. That made the burden of responsibility I carried on my back like a rucksack all the heavier.

"Why don't we go to the salon," Akash suggested, so we all headed that way. Salon didn't seem like the right word for such a dimly lit, low-ceilinged room. Portholes lined the walls, and outside, the dark sky and high waves battled to steal each other's territory. Though smoking was supposedly prohibited, the salon reeked of stale cigarette smoke. The bar at the front was lined with bottles—whiskey labeled in the alphabet, vodka in Cyrillic—but no bartender. The salon might have had an atmosphere if only the counter and individual tables had been lit up, surrounded by darkness, but this dull lighting made the whole room seem dreary.

Since we were the only ones there, we could sit wherever we wanted. I noticed something on one of the tables and went over to see what it was. A ballpoint pen, dice, and a sheet of plain white paper. Someone seemed to have handwritten a *sugoroku* board game, with the names of the ports where we'd stopped until now written in the blocks: Rügen, Szczecin, Gdansk, Kaliningrad, Riga, Tallin, Saint Petersburg. Two spaces had been left blank.

"Sugoroku," I said. When I was little, sugoroku games with retro pictures from the Edo period were popular, and I remember playing one at a friend's house. Old-fashioned sailboats floating on indigo seas, a river bank lined with cherry blossoms in full bloom, pine trees with gnarled, twisty trunks—we'd roll the dice, and move from one famous Edo scene to another. Now that I think of it, those illustrations must have been ripped off from Hokusai's ukiyo-e, pictures of the floating world. Perhaps Hokusai himself had once designed a sugoroku game, and the one I saw was a copy of it. The name Hokusai took me back to my childhood, as if he'd been an eccentric but kindly old man who lived in my neighborhood. Sugoroku, too, felt warm and homey.

"What's sugoroku?" asked Knut.

"Something like Monopoly," Nanook shot back.

Monopoly is American-style sugoroku. The Märchen Center where I work bought a Monopoly set for the immigrant children—"to teach them the skills to survive in a capitalist society," one of my coworkers said sarcastically.

We sat down at the sugoroku table.

"Handwritten," Nanook said softly, taking the paper in his hand. "I wonder who left it behind." I rolled the dice. Six came up. The number of people in our group—I didn't see how that could be a coincidence.

"So, we six are going to keep traveling together."

"The prophecy of the dice?" asked Nanook. "Did they tell you anything else? Like when we'll reach our goal, of if we should go back to our starting point?" He looked like a child, ready to lose himself in the game, but I suddenly felt much older.

"In sugoroku, it's unlucky to be sent back. But if you get lost while you're traveling, returning to where you started is the right thing to do. My first point of contact with Europe was Helsinki."

"I see—you started from Helsinki," said Akash, looking surprised, as if he'd never taken that in before. "But how would we proceed from there?" He sounded worried. "If we got off the boat at Helsinki, we wouldn't be able to go east without crossing Russian territory, would we?"

"It would be best to go north," replied Nanook, sounding like a know-it-all again. "We could travel up through Finland by train, then head for the top of the world—the North Pole—from the northern coast of Norway. Once we got there, we'd go south, through the Bering Strait. You guys are too hung up on the East-West axis. Why not broaden your horizons to include North and South?"

"Not just the North Pole," said Akash. "We should also consider the southern hemisphere."

"But we can't go south," said Nanook. "We're locked into the northern hemisphere. You're acting like you represent the south, Akash, but India's actually in the northern hemisphere. We have to stay in the north, and keep on going north. Further and further—to the northernmost place imaginable." Listening to Nanook, you might have thought the word "north" meant "truth" to him, or "god."

"That might be a good idea," I said, picturing the six of us as a team of huskies dashing through the snow. "We could get off the boat and cross the ice, where cars can't go."

"So, we're going on an Arctic expedition?" asked Akash. Somehow, I couldn't see him in a heavy parka.

"There's this guy Knud Rasmussen, an Arctic explorer, I read his biography when I was a kid—*The Dogsled Anthropologist*—and got really excited," said Susanoo, chuckling. "Even I was innocent once. Another Knud—one of your ancestors?" he teased.

"Rasmussen was from Greenland," said Knut, not sounding very interested, "so if he's anybody's ancestor, he'd be Nanook's."

"He was born in Greenland all right," retorted Nanook, not wanting to let Knut get the better of him, "but he was actually Danish, so he'd be from your family, not mine. I sure wasn't expecting Hiruko to think of traveling by dogsled, though. With so many modes of transportation to choose from, very few people would want to go home that way. Where'd you first ride on a dogsled, Hiruko?"

That wasn't what I'd meant at all, I wanted to tell him, but before I had the chance, we heard a voice from the other side of the wall calling, "Someone get a doctor, quick!" Nora and Akash, followed by Knut, jumped up and ran in that direction. Nanook slowly stood up and went after them. For some reason, I just sat there, glued to the chair.

"I see you're not the helpful type," said Susanoo with a wicked grin. "You wander aimlessly around, like a sleepwalker. Never rushing to anyone's aid, yet not self-centered, either. That's because you hardly have any desires of your own. You're like an amoeba."

"I do, too, have a desire."

"Oh? And what's that?"

"I want to be a house that lots of different people can live in."

"You're suddenly talking about being a house only because you've finally realized you have no home to go to."

Knut and the others still weren't back, so I left Susanoo and went to look for them. Walking down the corridor, I saw a crowd gathered up ahead. I couldn't get close enough because of all the people blocking my way, so I waited, and when the onlookers had left, one by one, I finally saw Knut, Akash, and Nora. Knut came over to me.

"what happened?" I asked him.

"A woman put wings on and tried to jump into the ocean, but someone stopped her."

"in storm?"

"Maybe she thought the wind would help her fly."

I heard Susanoo's slow, shuffling footsteps from behind. When the last onlooker had left, I saw a woman sitting on the floor with what looked like white swan wings, about three feet long, attached to her shoulders. A medic crouched beside her, taking her pulse. The wind and rain hadn't died down, and the woman's reddish-brown hair was drenched, plastered to her forehead and cheeks. Susanoo walked straight over to her with no hesitation.

"Are you all right?" he asked, squatting down beside her. He seemed to know her.

While the medic glowered at Susanoo, the woman raised her head at the sound of his voice.

"I was all set to marry Saint Petersburg," she said, seductively narrowing her eyes, "but I couldn't get off the boat." Her lips were fiery red.

"Were you planning to fly there, like a seagull?"

"No," she said in a matter-of-fact tone, "this is the costume I perform in. Since this boat doesn't even have a dinner show, I volunteered to put one on. I may not look like it now, but I was once on the stage, in the Reeperbahn," she added, suggestively blinking her big eyes, set off by eyeshadow, deep gray tinged with blue.

"Why did you try to jump into the sea?"

"Domestic violence. It started before I was married. I was sure it would get worse afterward, so I decided to escape. I wanted to live abroad. But I was doused with sea water, and got pregnant. Look at me—I'm sopping wet."

"You don't need to worry anymore. I'm going home, to be a blacksmith. I'll keep the fire going, so your wings and clothing will be dry in no time. Won't you come with me?"

It sounded like Susanoo was proposing to her—and what's more, he'd said he was going to be a blacksmith. I couldn't believe my ears. I'd been traveling with him all this time, and yet without my knowing it, he had met someone, talked to her, made plans for the future, and even fallen in love.

"You need wood to build a fire," the woman said, looking at Susanoo with eyes like a bird's—hard to read, "which means cutting down trees in the forest. But there has to be one left, for the birds to perch on. You are that one tree, aren't you?"

Nanook came over with another man.

"This guy's a doctor," he said by way of introduction.

After consulting the medic, the doctor told the woman to go to her cabin, remove her clothes, and dry herself off. "I'll be in to examine you," he said. "What's your cabin number?" Accompanied by Nanook and the doctor, the woman left for her cabin.

The rest of us traipsed back to the salon as if returning from the memorial service for a dead relative.

"I didn't know you were such a romantic," Knut teased Susanoo.

"The air is bad in here," Susanoo said quietly, ignoring Knut. "Passengers from a century ago are still smoking." He sounded like a voice from my long-ago past. Exactly like the kid who used to sit next to me in elementary school. Even though I knew he wasn't.

We sat down at the same table, with the hand-drawn sugoroku still on it.

"After Helsinki comes Pohjola," said Susanoo, picking up the paper. "Sounds interesting."

I looked over and, to my surprise, saw that "Helsinki" and "Pohjola" had been written into the blank spaces. Knut was just as shocked as I was.

"It's probably true that Helsinki is our next stop," he said, "but Pohjola? That must be somebody's idea of a joke."

"Helsinki might be a myth, too," said Nanook casually.

"What do you mean?"

"Finland has always struggled to keep its balance between East and West. But how long can they keep it up? Isn't that in itself a myth? It's like walking a tightrope, on and on without a break—they can't stay up there forever, so they're probably about ready to come down to earth, get their feet on the ground and retire."

"Where's Pohjola?" asked Nora.

"It's a mythical place that appears in the Kalevala," said Nanook, looking pleased with himself.

"Weren't the Sami supposed to have lived in Pohjola?" asked Knut, not sounding very sure of himself.

"Real people don't live in mythical places," Nora protested. "And you don't find mythical people in real places, either." The idea of an ethnic minority being turned into myth must have been unbearable to her. If my country had really disappeared, I myself might be regarded as the resident of a legendary place. If that was the case, I wouldn't mind traveling there in the least, because that would be the only place where I could live. We might, in fact, already be on that journey.

When traveling to a legendary place, it's best to use a means of transportation that appears in legends, like boats or dogsleds. Airplanes are out. If you have to fly, ask a bird to give you a ride on its back.

A legendary place? What was I thinking about? Coming back to myself, I realized that the country I was heading for was, in fact, real. And while I still would have liked to ride on a bird, I couldn't let that keep me from landing somewhere real. A perfectly mundane airplane would be best after all. I'd fasten my seatbelt for takeoff, then fly through the air while chatting with Knut in the next seat, eating our in-flight meals with plastic knives and forks, and stretching or flexing our knees from time to time. That would be enough. If that sort of reality came back to me, I wouldn't ask for anything more.

With these thoughts running through my head, I looked down at the place names on the sugoroku paper. Who could have written Helsinki and Pohjola in those two black spaces? We'd only been away from this table for a short time. I hadn't seen anyone, then or now. The salon was the least popular place on board. Yet this is where we'd come to talk as we breathed in the depressing smell of stale cigarette smoke. We were on a journey without knowing where we were going or how we'd get there. Not in search of breathtaking scenery, or gourmet food to stimulate our taste buds, or information we needed for a research project. Nor were we escaping from political persecution, or trying to find utopia.

"The characters for 'bird' and 'island' look an awful lot alike," Nanook said out of the blue. His eyes shining like a boy who's thought of an amusing game, he picked up the ballpoint pen and wrote the characters for bird 鳥 and island 島 side by side in the margin of the sugoroku paper. Knut looked a little envious, while Nora gazed down at them with a dreamy smile.

"So what?" said Susanoo as if he couldn't care less. I liked Nanook best when he was playing with language, so to me, his little game was anything but childish. In fact, I was sure it would take us somewhere far away.

"A bird flies in the sky," I said, hoping this would start us off, "and when its shadow falls on the water, it becomes an island." The bird I had in mind was a seagull, flying above a gray sea with Sado Island floating on it.

"And when migrating birds fly in a straight line," said Akash, smiling with his eyes closed, "their shadows make an archipelago. I like archipelagoes." He looked like Jizo, the little stone Buddha that protects children.

"Each island in an archipelago," I said, "is independent, but not alone. They're held together by invisible movement, like a line someone's drawn with a brush, lifting it occasionally to leave spaces on the way." After I'd said that, an image of the place I was aiming for rose up before me like a whale out of a dark sea.

"But the people who live there," Nora said, looking worriedly out the porthole, "must worry about things like storms, earthquakes, tsunami, or epidemics, because unlike on a continent, no one will come to help them."

"They worry more about helpers from the outside," I said,

"because there's always the chance that they've actually come to take over their island. They know that from history." I couldn't imagine where that train of thought had come from, even though it had just come out of my own mouth.

"Are you saying they choose to be isolated?" Nora sounded miffed. Then, shocked to hear the sound of glass breaking, we all turned toward the porthole. Fortunately, it seemed to be intact. Endless waves battered against it, drinking our time away. Had there at least been a lighthouse somewhere in the distance, we might have been able to make out the hazy outlines of land and sea, but there was no light, only a whirlpool of darkness that had lost all sense of direction.

"We can't even see which way we're going." said Akash, "This is a journey without an answer." I'd never heard him sound so reckless.

"Hiruko, you're the one who needs an answer more than anyone," said Nora, "but to get one, first you need a clear, well-focused question." I tried to think of one, but couldn't come up with anything.

"Maybe we've already found the answer many times along the way," I said, "but we won't realize it until we're looking back—when it's already in the past." This was far from the well-formed question Nora said I needed, but then Knut put a question to Susanoo that was even further off the mark.

"Who was that angel I saw you with?"

"My fiancée, Princess Peigne."

"Peigne?"

"It means 'comb' in French."

That gave me a jolt. "You mean Kushinadahime?" I asked.

"That's right—Kushi Inada Hime. The *ku* of *kushi* means strange, full of wonder. *Inada* is rice paddy, one where rice plants never stop growing. That's what Inada Hime is. Because people can't settle in a place where they can't grow crops. Then again, if they stay in the same place, seeing the same people all the time, they'll eventually go crazy. Each crazy thought becomes a strand of hair, dancing madly around. And it's Kushi-inada-hime—Princess Peigne—who uses her combs to calm that wild hair down, to keep it in place. As long as she's on this boat, we'll be fine. Look—the storm's not so bad now."

We got up to look out the portholes, and saw that he was right—the waves had started to calm down. They now splashed cheerfully against each other before breaking, and didn't look so frightening anymore. And we were like those waves. We pushed against each other, bumped into each other, lost our shapes and found new ones, and gently rocked as we faced in different directions.

"It's dinnertime," Knut said, and we all stood up, each in his or her own way. Even if we didn't know what would happen tomorrow, it seemed we'd keep on traveling together.